I0536685

THE TROUBLE WITH MOLLIE

RAFAELLA ROWELL

Published by Blushing Books
An Imprint of
ABCD Graphics and Design, Inc.
A Virginia Corporation
977 Seminole Trail #233
Charlottesville, VA 22901

©2020
All rights reserved.

No part of the book may be reproduced or transmitted in any form or by any means, electronic or mechanical, including photocopying, recording, or by any information storage and retrieval system, without permission in writing from the publisher. The trademark Blushing Books is pending in the US Patent and Trademark Office.

Rafaella Rowell
The Trouble with Mollie

EBook ISBN: 978-1-64563-372-3
Print ISBN: 978-1-64563-373-0
Audio ISBN: 978-1-64563-374-7
v2

Cover Art by ABCD Graphics & Design
This book contains fantasy themes appropriate for mature readers only.
Nothing in this book should be interpreted as Blushing Books' or
the author's advocating any non-consensual sexual activity.

Chapter 1

Zac was furious. He'd started a hazardous drive in blizzard conditions. Due to meet with his friends in town, he was cold and bothered. Still, not the only reason for his temper.

England was in the grip of a bitter winter. A powdery snow had fallen since the early hours of that morning, burying Oxford under a deep white blanket, causing havoc with the traffic as it settled on the roads.

His perilous journey had been slow, but he'd made it in one piece.

Zac's friends came from modest backgrounds, but they made full use of their Oxford University scholarships where they first met. They worked hard to get where they were, successful and achievers in their own fields.

Even though they led different lives and came from contrasting backgrounds, his friendship with the "boys" as he called them, was based on trust and understanding. They had a strong bond, still formidable twelve years later. They tried to meet as often as their hectic lives permitted.

That night, they had dinner plans, but the snow curtailed the option of going out. So, they were dining in instead.

Zac was now sitting back in a comfy armchair by the fireplace with his friends. At long last, the blazing fire restored life into his frozen limbs. He rubbed his hands together.

The wooden logs, blistering heat from the large open hearth, crackled every so often with a pleasing sound as the mild scent of the wood burning wafted through the room.

He felt more comfortable, human again!

Finley Harman, kneeling by the fireplace, tried to shove a drifting log back into the roaring flames. While Alex West, perched on the matching couch opposite him, was stomping his feet, attempting to get warm blood flowing black into his numb toes.

They glanced at Peter Blake in the kitchenette. He was preparing the much-desired drinks after a biting wintry day.

They were in Peter's chambers at the university, but Zac was sulking, and it was not just the icy weather bothering him.

The gloom of the season had led him to a rude awakening. He found himself at something of a crossroads, and the 'road' called for a change.

The light from the fireplace cast a shadow on his glum face. "The Board is not keen on me becoming the next CEO when my father retires," he stated.

"Oh?" said Alex.

"The Board of Directors voiced their displeasure in no uncertain terms. Dad warned me last night after the meeting," Zac said.

"What's the trouble now?"

"Damn fools! The directors worry that my attitude does not become a head of industry." He paused. "It seems, I have a lot of growing up to do! My personal life is getting them into a huff," he went on, "and these are just some

2

lame and repeatable observations. They are really annoying me!"

They were concerned about his women. The Board thought it would impact the company's reputation, and they didn't mince their words venting their disapproval at the last meeting.

"Hey, I suppose your playboy days are catching up with you, huh?" Alex grinned.

"I am serious, guys. I assume they want me married and settled before they will even consider me as a likely candidate to replace my father when the time comes," Zac snapped.

"Thirty, and still single! What do you expect?"

"I don't see your law firm ordering you to marry," he blurted out to his friend, "or the university asking Peter."

"True. But I am only a simple professor," Peter teased. "For one, I am not wealthy. And two, I don't have your chiselled good looks. So, there are no voluptuous women flocking around me all the time." He chuckled. They all echoed.

"You are all single but not a sodding problem for you, eh?" Zac growled, exasperated with an emotion close to envy.

"No. But we are not taking over your family empire, nor are we heirs to a fortune. Get my point?" Peter replied, distributing crystal tumblers filled with a large measure of whiskey and a dash of soda. His friends looked at the glasses with delight.

"Well, inherit, yes. But not run it, by the sounds of it. Not while the damn Board is against me," Zac huffed, and he took a gulp of the amber liquid. He glanced wistfully at the glass in his hand, and he relished the liquor's blaze going down inside him. It warmed him, took the strain off his shoulders.

Zac Sorensen was used to commanding his way in life. As an only child, his destiny was to inherit the family empire—a multi-billion-pound conglomerate with several corporations, with multi-industry subsidiaries across real estate, and first-class hotels with thousands of employees around the world.

In addition, the fact he had created his own personal and prosperous business on the side had surprised everyone, but it had catapulted him even more into the limelight.

Successful, powerful and wealthy, he was the golden bachelor par excellence, as the press labelled him. His personal organisation was doing well, and eight years down the line worth several millions. His security firm protected the rich and famous, sporting personalities, actors and politicians, including managing security at top music and sporting events. It had over one hundred and fifty employees.

Finley was his number two in the company, his right-hand man.

Zac had built his own organisation from scratch, with hefty bank loans, with no help or money from his family, and proud of it. Loving every minute, it was a great success.

Though his destiny was to inherit his family's business, whether or not he became its CEO. So, he still had this to look forward to in the coming years.

But Zac had ambition! He had always envisioned running the family business too, with him in the driving seat.

As a child, his father Victor used to take him to his office, overlooking the City of London. "See this? From here, you can rule. You can run and control every piece of this business. It is all yours. But you will have to earn it and work hard for it," his father used to say, staring out of the window and pointing at some of his hotels' landmarks across town.

Zac's passion for his family business was unequalled. And so, the care he felt for the thousands of employees working within it. Like his father and his grandfather before him, he felt responsible for them. His grandfather had inculcated that responsibility since he was a child of eight. Thousands of lives depended upon him. So, no one else could have it. No one would care for it like he would. No one would work as hard as he would.

So, he grew up loving it, wanting that coveted spot with a hunger that had no limits, expecting it with a passionate desire!

From a young age through to his early twenties, Zac spent most of his summer holidays working in the periphery of his father's companies, learning the ropes.

He spent every holiday working in a hotel of the company, from the bottom up. And he learned the job fast, getting to know the people by name and about their families. And they all liked him.

With his own business to run in Oxford, he dedicated time to his family business too, with frequent visits to London and other parts of the world to grow the company. He devoted most of his time diligently between his own business and that of his family. A workaholic! No one could deny it, with a great talent for the job.

It is my birth right; he thought. And he wanted the CEO position. He was ready.

On occasions, he even joined his father in Board meetings as an observer, and he craved that top spot. The CEO spot of his family's powerful business! It had to be his when his father retired…

So, he was not about to give it up easily, regardless of the Board's opinions of him. Thousands of people depended upon him, and he would not let them down. He would not relinquish that top position for any reason!

But the Board's objections were strong and worrying him. They were against him. He had to do something about it. The problem was, with his background, he couldn't escape fame. He was a golden bachelor, often in the papers, but for all the wrong reasons. His bachelor's lifestyle was energetic and even outlandish. No doubt he worked hard, but he played hard too.

In the last two years, his choice of less than desirable companions worried his mother and his grandmother, let alone his father and the Board. His father was furious with him for letting it get to this stage.

Victor had tried to warn him several times. Alas, Zac was stubborn, and he didn't enjoy committing to one woman when he had hundreds to choose from.

"I am too young to marry," was his response, but Victor had just rolled his eyes.

"You've got to stop these playboy games of yours. It won't do!" It was his father's usual warning.

So, that evening, Zac took stock of his situation.

He was at a crossroad. He must make up his mind, find a solution that would enable him to turn his image around for the benefit of the Board, thus reaping the reward.

"It seems, you are in a tight spot," Alex said.

"Bloody hell, you don't say!" he cursed. He swiped a hand across his face with a sigh.

"You are a desirable bachelor. Your security firm is making tons of money—I should know; I am your lawyer—with an even bigger family fortune coming your way at some point. But you are a soft target for women," Alex pointed out, ignoring his sarcasm.

"Women flock to you like flies to a candle, but if you're not careful, they will be your downfall," Peter emphasised while refilling Alex's glass.

"Please—" Zac's voice had a hint of warning. He didn't want to hear it.

"Hey, man, don't let what's in your pants rule your head." Finley chuckled, raising his eyebrows. True enough, and to his detriment, Zac had never resisted women. But he must face the problem now.

"Here, have another drink!" Peter tried to cheer him up, refilling his glass. The whiff of alcohol filled his nostrils, and Zac took another gulp of whiskey. He liked the burning sensation in his throat! *Christ, it will be a long night!* he cursed.

"For a start, stop the luscious starlets and models. Why don't you find a woman with a good head on her shoulders?" Finley suggested.

"You have plenty of time before your father retires. So, show a new image, a different Zac," Alex proposed.

"Hell, present a mature, grounded man, with a good lady. That's what you need to do," Finley added.

Zac realised where this was heading, but true, he needed to do that. "It is fundamental until I have what I want!"

"And you always get what you want!" his friend observed, curling his lips.

"I wouldn't be so sure. Not this time! This one may hang in the balance," he retorted.

"Take a bride, man, a clever and a pretty wife, a dependable one! None of those crazy starlets you go for, they don't give the Board any confidence!" Finley urged.

"Did you see the papers last week?" Alex asked with a devilish grin, crossing his left ankle over his right knee, and sprawling back on the sofa.

"Oh, yes! Your latest starlet... drunk as a skunk trying to get into your car." Peter chuckled.

"How could I forget?" His eyes narrowed into a slit, looking into his glass.

"Wham, the photographer snaps her up in all her glory! You could see up to her..." Peter whistled. "...eh, well, you saw a hell of a lot." His friend was clearly amused.

"Up to her ass! Christ!" Zac cursed, rolling his eyes.

"Bloody hell, man, you seem to date an awful lot of women who are too... Well, the Board does not approve!" Finley remarked, raising his eyebrows.

"They are great fun, though!" he said with a wink, taking another sip of his drink.

"If it's fun you want, then carry on. But if you want to succeed your father as the next CEO, then—" Peter chided.

"You should take your personal life as seriously as you take your professional life!" Alex stated, uncrossing his legs, leaning forward with his hands outstretched towards the open fire.

"Yes, yes, I know!" he snapped, massaging the back of his neck.

"Maybe you should treat this like a business proposition. That'll take the pressure from you, while you turn the Board around," Finley ventured with a laugh.

Zac looked at him seriously and stood up. He paced up and down the room, then he stopped. "A business arrangement, rather than one of the heart; a hired wife; this is the answer." He smiled triumphantly.

"Hey, Fin was kidding. A joke! He didn't say you should hire a wife. That's dangerous, in your position. As your lawyer, I would not advise it," Alex warned him.

"No, but I should consider it." Zac cocked his head, thinking.

Chapter 2

That evening, The Haven's Arms pub was packed with students. It was so busy, one could hardly stand. As usual, booming with noise, there was a warmth and a familiar glow to it, with the pungent tang of alcohol and body-heat mingling in the air.

Mollie Belloc stepped inside and paused for a second, closing the door behind her swiftly. She tried to raise her neck to find her companions, but she did not spot them, as the place was jammed.

Searching for the tall student of physics instead, she figured her friend would be somewhere in his proximity, thus, giving her a better chance at spotting her classmates in the crowded pub.

Mollie saw the towering student, a head high above the rest. And, as expected, Kathryn was standing at a table a few steps away from him, waiting for her. Her classmates had gone ahead of her, from the house they all shared. It was early February in Oxford, and the coldest day of the winter.

She rubbed her hands together to warm them up, her feet numb, shedding the snow from outside, but soon the glow of the pub started to envelope her. She sniffed with a slight head cold.

Mollie moved further in, trying to reach her friends in the heaving place. She shed her hat, gloves, and her voluminous, woolly green scarf.

"What took you so long?" a bass voice said in her ear. She turned with a grin when she recognised his sound. "I thought you were right behind us!" George shouted over the hubbub of laughter and loud conversation in the pub.

"I couldn't find a parking spot for my bicycle. Lucky, someone left on my second round, otherwise, I would have frozen to death." She grinned with a bright open smile, and he winked at her.

Her smile was infectious. It started from her baby blue eyes, thus becoming bigger and brighter and illuminating all of her face. It was like a beam of sunshine in the frozen landscape.

It gave her an ethereal expression.

GEORGE RECALLED the first time he set eyes on her, three years ago. She reminded him of the girl in that movie. Mollie's looks bore a passing resemblance to the actress in the Fifth Element. A mass of flaming red hair, cut in a blunt bob of soft curls down to her shoulders, framed her heavenly face. A radiant, almost translucent skin made her stand out.

He thought her to be pretty. Her grace, not apparent, but it was there. One had to observe her to discover her beauty, but it was worth it, in more ways than one. At five feet and six inches tall, her figure was willowy and diminutive, though rather shapely for a slim girl, with a round bosom. She passed for a slip of a girl, even at twenty-two years old, and he liked her a lot. They got on very well and were great friends.

He gripped her upper arm and, stepping further into the crowded room, led her to their table. They were fortunate to have one in such a packed pub.

"What do you want to drink? And no soft drinks, please," he protested, raking a hand through his dark short hair, but he winked in humour.

George was a well-built and muscular young man, a few inches taller than Mollie. A handsome youth, with dark intelligent eyes, girls looked at him a lot! But he only had eyes for her.

They settled at the table.

"Don't force her to drink. You know she doesn't like it much. And when she does, she doesn't hold her alcohol well, either!" Kathryn glared at him.

He laughed.

"The pub is so crowded tonight," Mollie mumbled to move off the conversation.

"It's freezing today, and this is best place to be!" Her friend grinned.

"Oh, come on, just have one proper drink!" he taunted, sensing her indecision.

"Okay, a pale lager then… a Corona, please."

"I'll have one too," Kathryn said.

George moved to the bar to order their drinks.

"DID YOU SEE HIM? He's over there, near the bar. Isn't he handsome? Is he looking this way? At me?" her friend asked.

Kathryn's eyes twinkled with a mischievous glint, and she giggled. Her beautiful eyes, the colour of chestnuts, couldn't hide that expression.

"Kat, I can't tell. He turned away. I saw him staring at you earlier, though, when I came in. I knew you would sit somewhere near him. Mind you, I'm sure, next week, your infatuation will be over someone else. You are so fickle." She chuckled.

"I can't help it. I like people; there are so many." The girl laughed and flicked her long dark hair over her shoulders, staring at the student of physics, directing a sweet smile his way.

"People? Do you mean men?" Mollie snorted.

Kathryn smiled.

MOLLIE BELLOC SHARED a house with Kathryn Ellis and George Wilde. They were students at Oxford university. They attended the same courses. Thus, they had become good friends in the last four years. Sharing a house cemented that friendship even further.

But they were not average students, not in the common sense of the word. They were what people might call gifted students, with high IQs. Not geniuses by any means, as they were often referred to, but smart. Their brains had the ability of enormous, raw processing power.

At twenty-two, Mollie had a First degree in Mathematics and Physics from Oxford, with a Masters in Finance already under her belt. She trained to analyse and manage the monetary practises and transactions that underpin businesses, economics, and wealth management, including banking, taxation, and investment.

She had also taken up more abstract theoretical disciplines, such as Actuarial Science, her current course. This science applied mathematical and statistical methods to assess risk in insurance, finance, and other industries and professions. An actuary was a professional who made high-level decisions, and they were in great demand.

Therefore, at the tender age of twenty-two, Mollie was also studying this discipline and reaching the top fast, besides her degree and Master already in the sack.

"Intellect is a gift. God blessed us," she'd said to George when they first met.

She'd had internships with big industries as part of her university tutorials; the result, half of them wanted to employ her straight away. The other half dreaded her, and were too foolish to admit it.

She loved being clever most of the time, but sometimes it was a curse! This was when it led her into labyrinths of thoughts, and she feared she would never find a way out of it.

But to her detriment, over the years, she had learned, at her own expense, that despite her intelligence, she was naïve. And above all, she lacked prudence and common sense. These flaws in her character got her into trouble more than once, for all her cleverness.

'Often,' her mother would say, 'too often! Oh, God, your downfall!'

Though she was a scholar, she controlled the urge to show off. She was humble. Mollie tried to fit in with her fellow students at university, and she was popular but quirky.

Her quirkiness couldn't be explained, but it was part of her DNA.

Her friends had gotten used to her peculiarities and offbeat humour. And even with all of this, they liked her for her good nature and sweetness. Those who knew her well adored her. She was a kind-hearted girl. She liked to please others, sometimes, to her own disservice.

George worshipped her. Somehow, he harboured light, amorous feelings for her, but his time had passed. He resigned himself to be her friend, and he was a great companion to her.

Mollie dated, but not successfully. In her mind, boyfriends wanted all of her time, and her body, which she was not prepared to give out without love. So, after a few chaste dates, she would part ways to focus on what she excelled at, which was her studies.

She thought she sucked at relationships, until she met him, her new boyfriend.

That night at the pub, she was sipping her drink. Suddenly, she stood up.

"What is it?" Kathryn asked.

"Sorry, I've forgotten to give my paper to professor Blake," Mollie said, and she gulped the rest of her beer down.

"It's late. You can do that tomorrow," her friend pointed out.

"The lights in his chambers were still on earlier, on my way to the pub. I'll check," she said, shrugging her shoulders as she said her goodbyes.

"OH, I am so sorry, Professor Blake. I didn't mean to interrupt you," she said, when after a brief knock at his door, she barged into Peter's rooms.

"Mollie, have you not learnt good manners yet?" he chided.

She blushed and tugged at her sleeve.

I should not have had that beer! she thought in disappointment. Drinking always let her down! She was embarrassed and bit her bottom lip.

"Apologies, Professor," she mumbled again. Her red hair was a good match for the colour on her face.

"All that cleverness, my dear, and no manners. What can I do for you at this late hour, anyway?" Peter urged. His voice had a stern tilt to it.

"Oh, I didn't realise you had company. I'm sorry. I'll come back tomorrow."

"What is it?" he asked, exasperated.

"It's nothing urgent. I saw the lights on in your rooms, and I wanted to leave my paper with you," she replied, and for the first time, she looked at his friends.

She grinned, but the colour returned to her cheeks.

Zac smiled back.

He scanned her over and stopped at her bosom then at the bow-shaped lips she was biting furiously. He stared at her.

Zac's immediate assessment: she was pretty with a beautiful smile, round and pert small breasts but not his type, not the fuller figure he liked so much.

She blushed again when she realised his eyes were scrutinising her.

She had recognised him. She had noticed his pictures in the papers often. The photos didn't do him justice.

No one is this gorgeous, surely, but he is! Well, apart from him, *that is.* Mollie's new boyfriend may not be as good-looking as Zac, but he was wonderful to her.

Even with her boyfriend's praises, Mollie couldn't help but find Zac handsome. She caught his eyes first, sultry and intense, light brown eyes, the colour of vintage cognac. Long, curling eyelashes framed them, to the extreme envy of women. It suggested to her… his eyes were brooding.

The small scar on his left eyebrow and his high sculpted cheekbones gave him a refined and rugged look. He was captivating. He turned heads. His longish, strawberry blond hair had a dishevelled look about it. *Was it for tonight? Or always so?*

Peter noticed she was studying him, so he said, "These are my friends, Zac Sorensen, Finley Harman, and Alex West." He hesitated, then he went on, "Miss Mollie Belloc," closing the introductions.

She shook Alex and Finley's hands and smiled.

These men are handsome, but Zac... he is exquisite, perfect!

She held her breath until it was his turn to shake her hand. She sighed.

"Miss Belloc," Zac said with a grin, knowing too well the effect he had on women. He took her hand in his. She glanced at it. A firm and a brief handshake, but at his touch, her hand warmed despite the blizzard outside.

"So, what are you studying?" he asked.

"I-I... am…" She was not expecting his question. Over fifteen seconds later, she could explain. She had not been tongue-tied since she was two years old. She glanced at Finley and blushed even more.

Then she spun to Peter. "I'll see you tomorrow, Professor." She gave him her paper and was on her way out.

"Nice meeting you," Zac blurted after her.

She paused and turned to him. She raised her hand and waved at him with a tender smile.

And his grin spread from ear to ear.

Jesus! What the hell is wrong with me? she thought, *waving my hand? Idiot! Who does that? A child, that's who.* Mollie silently cursed.

All that cleverness and not a clue. Stupid girl, she thought, chiding herself as she closed the door behind herself on her way out. A foul curse mumbled through her lips.

"GRADUATES, HEY!" Peter said, glancing at his companions when she left.

"Is she one of your geniuses?" Zac asked him.

Peter Blake was a respected professor of Physics at Oxford. At thirty-two, he was one of the youngest to run for the chair, the previous year, winning it from a more senior member of the faculty. He trained gifted students like Mollie.

"Oh, I wouldn't say a genius. No, no, but she is smart. Shy, quirky, and I have heard she swears like a trooper, but fascinating."

"Is she? Uncommonly pretty. Not my type, though, but a pleasant girl if you ignore the frumpy student's clothes," Zac said.

Finley chuckled, and Alex snorted.

"What?" he asked, lifting an eyebrow.

"Nothing," they answered in unison.

"You see? I should marry someone like this girl, bright and cute," Zac teased them.

A line appeared between Finley's brows.

But Zac diverted back to the troubles with the Board.

Chapter 3

Her old, red, battered mini was still doing a good job. So, it didn't take her long to drive to the outskirts of Oxford. The snow had ceased a few days earlier. Despite the bitter weather and the softening snow, the drive had been easy.

She left her car in the visitors' parking and raised her head to stare at the building, a formidable architecture. The warm, honey-coloured Cotswold's limestone and its timber old-style cased windows created a striking old building, in harmony with many in Oxford. She guessed, it dated back over three hundred years, modernised to fit longevity and to simplify modern living. It used to house one of the many colleges of the university, but now it served a well-established security enterprise.

She made her way to the ground floor reception desk. However, the clerk pointed out that without an appointment, she couldn't see him.

She stood resolute. "I must see Mr. Sorensen. It is essential I speak to him," Mollie said.

The receptionist offered her an alternative date, but it would not be for two months at least.

"I can't wait two months. It is important I meet with him today. I can wait for as long as it takes, but it must be today," she pressed again, unshakeable.

It had been a hectic morning, and the pleasant woman at the counter was losing patience. Mollie could see it in her eyes, despite her perfunctory smile.

"It is imperative!" she insisted, her lips in a thin line as she cocked her head to one side. Nothing would discourage her.

The lady looked at her with a frown. But she persisted.

Taught never to send any potential clients away, in particular when the boss was concerned, the receptionist offered her an alternate, but Mollie declined. "I am sorry, but the conversation is confidential. I must speak to Mr. Sorensen in person; no one else will do."

The woman gave her a sceptical glance and thought the persistent girl must be one of his floozies. But the lady changed her mind. Though lovely, Mollie didn't quite make the grade in her opinion. His women were rather voluptuous, and this girl was not...

Though, the receptionist relented and called Zac's secretary.

"SIR, there is a young lady downstairs. She asked for you. No appointment. She says it is important," his PA told him over the intercom.

"Who?"

"Mollie Belloc, sir. No appointment. I can tell reception she must make an appointment, but she seems determined on today," his PA continued.

"Mollie?"

"Yes, sir. She won't take "no" for an answer."

"I don't know any Mol..." He scratched his head. "...
wait, does she have a mass of red curly hair and crystalline
skin?" Zac frowned, remembering that girl.

"I will ask, sir." His secretary went back to reception.

He waited. "Well, does she?" he snapped after a minute,
over the intercom on his desk.

"Yes, sir."

How on earth did he remember her? *She's not even my type.*
His frown deepened.

*Mollie! The student in Peter's chambers, over a week ago, who
blushed when I gave her the once over.* He grinned. *Blushing and
waving,* he thought, recollecting the little hand wave before
she left. Now that was new to him. The women he went
for, didn't blush or wave sweetly. He chuckled at the
thought.

Why is she here?

Zac's week had been a hectic one. He had worked long
hours spread between his own business and that of his family,
with not a minute to spare. He pondered for a moment, his
index finger tapping his chin.

*The cute girl... umm, a welcome respite in between meetings and
phone calls, a nice interlude,* he thought with a smile on his face.

"What does she want?" he asked. Besides, curiosity took
over.

"She didn't say, sir, but she says it's important. She will
only speak to you."

His interest grew even more. *Ah, the clever one! I wonder.*

Her flaming red hair was a sign of feistiness. He
wondered if she was gutsy and feisty. He liked women with
character, but then she was a scholar, so perhaps not! But
here she was, with no appointment, insisting on seeing him.
She must be gutsy... *Let's see.*

"Gladys, when is my next meeting? Do I have time to see her?"

"You have a call in a few moments, Mr. Sorensen, I have scheduled ten minutes for the call. But then nothing in your diary for half an hour."

"Okay, send her in after the call. I'll meet her for five minutes; that's all. I have too many emails to catch up with."

The receptionist was still eyeing Mollie when, to her surprise, Zac's PA told her to send her up.

SHE WAS SITTING in the outer room, her heart thundering in her chest now.

While she had gone up the historic staircase to Zac's office on the third floor, she had rehearsed in her mind what she would say to him, as she had done many times in the preceding week.

But now that she was staring at his PA whispering over the phone, she got nervous. It amazed her that they had allowed her to go up with no appointment. But she was sure he would dismiss her quickly. *Yes, he is just polite,* Mollie thought and relaxed for a second.

"Mr. Sorensen will see you shortly, Miss Belloc. But he doesn't have long before his next meeting," his secretary said in a firm voice, giving her a courteous smile.

She gulped.

"Can I offer you anything? Tea, coffee, water?" Gladys asked.

"No, I'm fine, thank you." Mollie smiled back.

This is it. Her heart was racing, her head spinning. She started to perspire, a rivulet of sweat coming down her eyebrow despite the cold weather. She wiped it off with her hand, trying to look composed.

Zac had given her a few minutes, just a few critical minutes. So, she must go for it, fast! She would have to be brief, but she would do it.

She would do it for him, for her new man!

WHEN SHE'D MENTIONED to her boyfriend about the conversation she had overheard, that's what he wanted! So, Mollie would do it, for him. She even took care on her looks that day. Her lover insisted upon it. She had to be presentable for Zac.

She'd said "no" to her man. She had laughed it off, thinking it was a joke. When she understood that he was serious, she was astonished. She didn't believe her ears.

But her boyfriend smiled. He took her hands in his, "Darling, you understand, don't you?" he asked her in an intimate voice. His mouth close to her ear, she could feel his breath caressing her.

"You want to give me away to another man," she whispered sadly.

"No. I want us to be happy. I assumed that's what you wanted."

"I do, but how can you ask this of me?"

"Think of it as a business arrangement. Zac gets what he wants, and we get what we want."

"No, that's what you want, not what I want. I don't care about money!" she spat.

Her lover ignored her protests. He caressed her face and kissed her, his lips lingering on hers, but he dismayed her.

An absurd request!

Her boyfriend wanted her to work on a plan to become Zac's hired wife. Why? For money!

A preposterous idea!

Mollie told him a hundred times, "It won't work!" But he persisted with the idea. He demolished every one of her arguments, but she counter argued him, coming up with new reasons it would be a disaster.

He was Mollie's first love. The man who'd initiated her into the pleasures of sex. So, she believed herself utterly in love with him. Most of all, she wanted to please him, but his request was ludicrous.

Her lover's plan would never work, and above all, it was abhorrent to her.

How could her boyfriend even think of giving her to another man, no matter how handsome Zac was, she couldn't do it?

She shook her head.

Thus, many hours had passed while her man insisted why she should do it, and how, while she said "no" until they were both worn out.

Then, her lover had caressed and kissed her, with deliberate and ardent kisses, his lips owning hers. Matters went invariably further, and they ended up making love. He kissed her body. He savoured every inch of her skin. He made ardent love to her for hours until they were both drained.

She'd felt good. It had cooled her for a while, but soon her lover came back to the idea. He tried to persuade her that it was the right thing to do!

He demanded that she work on the plan. He persisted; Mollie had to convince Zac to marry her, to use her as his hired wife.

For days, they discussed nothing else, but he didn't convince her. She loathed the idea. But her lover persisted. If they were to be happy, Mollie must do this.

So, foolishly and against her better judgement, after days of relentless insistence from her man, she had surrendered.

She wanted to please him, so she would do it.

"But why are you doing this? Money? Is that all you want?" she asked him.

"Zac won't even notice a few millions. He has so much money; trust me! But the money will rescue us from the daily grind," her lover excused.

"But, darling—"

"Besides, you will do him a favour, a service."

"I wish it was that simple," she quipped.

"But it is if you devote yourself to it," he snapped.

Mollie's liaison with her lover was a secret. Under his insistence, she'd agreed to keep silent. She had told no one about her new boyfriend.

Clarissa, her childhood friend, would not understand. Not even her mother realised.

Kathryn knew about her fascination for this man at the beginning, but once the relationship developed, Mollie pretended her infatuation had fizzled out.

She had not spoken another word to her friend or anyone else, when she'd agreed secrecy with her boyfriend.

He was adamant about her silence.

So that day, he gave her an ultimatum.

"Marry Zac! You must persuade him; no more discussion." It was his last warning.

She must work on a plan to become Zac's wife. A plan for a marriage of convenience, a reliable one!

If she loved him, she would have to do it.

Ultimately, Mollie convinced herself by agreeing to it, she would do a good deed. Zac wanted that coveted CEO spot, and it positioned her well to enhance his image for the Board's purposes. She would not take advantage of his money, other than what they would agree on for the deal. Instead, she would do the best for him, be a devoted wife. She would work hard to help Zac reach his goal.

That desired CEO position.

So, Mollie convinced herself she had a genuine good reason to do it, feeling less guilty about her decision.

She still harboured suspicions, many doubts, but reluctantly, she had agreed.

She would do it for her boyfriend.

"MISS BELLOC, Mr. Sorensen will see you now." Gladys raised her head and motioned to her.

It released her from the sad musings. She gulped.

Mollie followed her but remained a step or two behind. Gladys knocked on the oak double doors and opened them.

"Miss Belloc, sir," his secretary announced and ushered her in.

Mollie stepped in, and her eyes landed on him. He rose from behind his desk and smiled at her.

In her tutorials as an actuary, she had been in the senior executives' offices of several corporations, but it never ceased to amaze her, the splendour and richness of those areas.

This one was more!

There was a magnificence to his office, that suggested, "*I have power.*" A luxury to it, that said, "*I am rich.*" A refinement that revealed, "*I am a man of class.*" *His statements to the world!*

The floor-to-ceiling windows behind his desk, with a panoramic view of Oxford and its surroundings, were mesmerising in the background. She couldn't help but glimpse out. She spotted the familiar shapes of the spire and cloisters of the Christ Church Cathedral and the stunning circular dome of the Radcliffe Camera in the distance. Aside from the dreaming spires of the city on one side, quaint villages and countryside completed the view.

It was amazing! She turned back to the room.

The vivid colour of his antique mahogany desk, inlaid with motifs, gave the office a sophisticated air. A modern caramel leather sofa that looked so inviting and soft stood at one wall, a library of mahogany panels at the other end. Pictures with contemporary art completed the room. It was an elegant, classy mix of old and new.

In a flash, her eyes examined him. She took all of him in. *So handsome. Immaculately dressed.*

He wore a dark grey, double-breasted suit in fine wool,

with white chalk stripes and lapels. It enhanced his masculinity. It fitted him to perfection, down to his pristine open collared white shirt and his silver cufflinks. She assumed it was a designer suit; it was so beautifully cut. It made him even taller and elegant.

Blast, so damn gorgeous! Delicious, as if he had just stepped out of a fashion magazine.

She would have loved to smooth the palm of her hands over his lapels and brush a microscopic piece of fluff from his broad shoulders, get closer to him and take a deeper breath of that tangy and fresh whoosh of scent that reached her.

A classy but modern man, she thought as she appreciated what she saw.

His elegance and ruggedness made him so fashionable and attractive. His dishevelled long, strawberry blond hair went every which way with his hands. It added to his masculine but graceful strength. She wished she could touch his hair and push it back with her palms.

But those eyes… alluring and sultry. She couldn't help a lick of her bottom lip.

His eyes shone with a light which turned him from handsome into a semi-god. She was sure women and men found him irresistible in equal measure.

That day, the expression in his eyes reminded her of that photo of him she liked so much in a gossip magazine. *Sultry, sensual, inviting!* Eyes marked by passionate intensity.

Those eyes mesmerised her, warm and tempting, the colour of vintage cognac, like mellow honey.

A seductive look, yes, alluring!

His lips, now smiling sexily at her, seemed so soft and fleshy, a mouth graced by even white teeth. For a moment, she wondered how those lips would taste on hers, how it would feel if those perfect teeth were to have a nimble on her breasts.

Her breath hitched.

She bit her bottom lip at her unorthodox conclusions about this man. She tugged at her sleeve and blushed at the momentary pinch of lust she had just felt in her belly.

She wondered what her boyfriend would say if he learned of her lascivious thoughts about Zac. She smiled at her misdemeanour.

Would her lover let her go ahead with his crazy plan if he knew?

ZAC WAS EXPECTING the creature in jeans and a big shabby sweater he had seen over a week ago. Instead, he saw an elegant young woman enter his office. For a moment, it confused him. He stared at her.

Oh, yes, her baby blue eyes, those red hues in her hair, that skin... yes, unmistakable.

He surprised himself by recalling those details. He grinned, watching her, and not for the first time.

Mollie was wearing a demure, black, figure-hugging, long-sleeved light wool dress. Above the knee, with a square neckline which enhanced her small round breasts. Although still slim and willowy, she seemed curvier. Red stilettos and a matching red belt completed the look. She didn't dress as a typical student that day but as a sophisticated young woman. Her hair was gathered in a loose bun at the nape of her neck, and light make-up completed the ensemble.

Well, well, well... He enjoyed the view!

A different Mollie from a week ago, a sexy one. He glanced at her legs, and on impulse, he marvelled at how long they were. *Those legs! Climbing under that dress!*

Perhaps one day… His grin widened.

She looked beautiful and comfortable in her own skin. For his benefit, but why? *What is she after?* he speculated.

He didn't realise he was staring at her. *What to make of her?* But he saw that blush across her face which delighted him no end.

She smiled back. And he caught her beaming smile. Her baby blue eyes lighting up with intensity. Her beautiful lips curling up in a beam, in perfect harmony with her soft features, an enchanting smile. Her eyes had a twinkle.

Adorable and foxy, what do you know!

"Mollie. What a surprise. What can I do for you?" he asked, offering his hand to her. She took it, but he held her hand a tad longer than he should have done. And there it was again, that blush.

It was endearing. *Charming!* Had he set her up to it? He enjoyed watching her blush.

He motioned to the chair in front of him. "Can I get you something to drink?"

"No. Thank you, Mr. Sorensen. You have limited time so I will get straight to the point."

"Please do," he said, raising his eyebrows, while his eyes caressed the soft flesh of her lips. He sat, fully comfortable, in his high-back leather chair and placed his hands on the armrests. He was at ease watching her. She seemed nervous instead.

He inspected her, taking her in. Curiosity took hold of him.

"You'll forgive me. The other night, I couldn't help over-hearing the conversation you were having with your friends at Professor Blake's. I am offering my services to be *that woman, your wife.* You can hire me as your wife for a limited period. We can agree on the time you need. I will ensure that we enhance your image for your Board of Directors, and you will, in turn, compensate me for my time." She rushed out in a single breath, looking at him and making sure to emphasize the keywords.

He stared at her. His eyebrows furrowed, and his head pulled forward. He wasn't sure he had heard her correctly.

But he said nothing, so she continued before she lost her nerve. "I have drafted a paper; I suppose you can call it a contract of sorts, with details of our transaction. My aim is to rebuild your image so you can gain the trust of your Board of Directors until they will not doubt you are the best CEO to succeed your father. I also have examples of the work that I have done in businesses like yours. I am training as an actuary, so both your firm and your family's company could enjoy my services. You know, I am not your average student per se, don't you?" But she didn't wait for an answer, glancing up at him from her papers, while shuffling them nervously on his desk. "I have a degree in maths and physics and a Masters to my name in Finance, too." She paused. She looked at him, and their eyes locked.

And there it was, that blush.

"Yes, I am aware of it," he said, nodding once with a smirk, seeing her cheeks colour. But there was no doubt she had impressed him. It captivated him, not to mention baffled him.

"We can both enjoy our partnership, benefit from it," she added.

Zac's amazement grew as she continued deep into the details of her proposal. She was in perfect flow. And no doubt, she had passion in every detail of the proposal she was presenting to him.

"You would do this for money?" At one point, he interrupted her after some minutes.

"Yes and no, Mr. Sorensen. I want to be a full-time academic, a scholar. But to dedicate myself to intellectual pursuit,

I need to be viable financially. Such a... ahem... transaction would allow me to do that." She spat the word transaction but tried to continue, not without a little loss of composure. "The money is a means to an end, to be honest. It is not important to me. I don't seek material things. But don't worry; the world will see us as a devoted husband and wife. I have outlined it all in my papers. Please review them at your leisure, assuming you still like the idea."

Her statement was partly true. She wanted to remain in academia, and she was not interested in money. But the fact was she was reluctantly offering her services to Zac. It was not Mollie's wish to be his hired wife, but that of her lover's. She stopped for a moment to take a breath as that thought crossed her mind, but then she went on, struggling to keep focus. "I am the soul of discretion; no one will ever know of our arrangement."

She had rehearsed these points with her boyfriend many times, but she couldn't help the uncomfortable feeling that was creeping up in her soul.

"I see," he interjected.

He was giving nothing away but fixed his eyes on her, his penetrating and sultry eyes examining her. It made her nervous and anxious. Her palms were sweaty, but she carried on.

"When the time comes, there will be an amicable divorce with a settlement for me. In reality, the settlement will be my pay out," she paused, "a beneficial transaction for both of us."

She tried to sound calm and collected, putting forward all the many benefits of the arrangement. She'd spent the last week, night and day, writing the papers with the outline of her proposition, and she was delving into it now.

She was aware of his deep gaze on her throughout. *Bloody hell stop looking at me like that!* It made her edgy, apprehensive. But above all, it prickled her skin, causing flutters in her stomach. She wrung her hands together.

At one point, Gladys entered the room, interrupting them. As she announced his next meeting, he shook his head and told her to reschedule.

Surprised, his PA widened her eyes, but she retreated without a word.

"Apologies, Miss Belloc, please continue," he said.

She smiled and resumed, trying to be more confident.

"Think of me as any other employee. You will be my boss at all times, with absolutely no emotional attachment. A hired wife, just a plain business transaction, so we both achieve what we want."

He riveted his eyes on her, as if he was seeking to reach into her soul.

She blushed again at the thought.

"I see," he said again, non-committal, but her cheeks flushed. His eyes danced at her blush.

She mesmerised him. He couldn't help having a moment of distraction, thinking how he would like to make those cheeks flush in his bed, but he soon recovered.

She described the plan to rebuild his image, going into the details of how it would all work to make it credible, until it was time for him to comment.

"You seem to have thought of this long and hard, Ms. Belloc," he said, after he had listened for over an hour. He glanced at the papers in front of him and then stared at her.

"Please call me Mollie." She tugged at her sleeve. Again, his reward.

"Well, you have, Miss B... Mollie. I know you overheard us, but my hired wife, really? I realise the money is useful to you, but are you sure about this? It's a long process, and not an easy one," he said with a frown, trying to control his features.

The whole thing was weird. But deep down, she amused him. It beguiled him that this slip of a girl had put together a project plan for restoring his image, with her at the centre of the equation as his hired wife.

"Time is no matter to me, and I am accomplished. You get to succeed your father as CEO, and I get the money, which will allow me to pursue the things that interest me. That's all there is to it. A devoted wife, the best!" She coughed nervously, lowering her eyes, but she added, "Your Board of Directors will adore me. You'll have the finest image the world has ever seen. By the time I am finished, they will idolise you too. I promise!" She cleared her throat again, but then she smiled the sweetest of smiles, and he was hooked for more.

A zealous, intense girl! He knew, *and in bed? Is she as passionate in bed?* But his smile gave nothing away.

The realisation of her detailed plan unfolded in front of him as she continued.

Bloody hell bugger me! Only silent curses in his mind after this young girl planned so meticulously for his success with the Board! It impressed him! But above all, she held him spellbound. Her heavenly face was just lovely. Her smile had captivated him.

THERE WAS one thing she had not said. That this was not her idea! Her lover had pushed her into it, practically bullied her into it. She didn't want to do it. But this was what he wanted. And she wished to make him happy; she wanted to please him.

So, she would do it for her man.

ZAC DIDN'T KNOW there was another person in this equation, who was dictating the rules.

She astonished him.

During the conversation with his friends, over a week ago, although for a moment, Zac had contemplated this very idea, after a few more drinks, they'd dismissed the hired wife idea as ridiculous. They had all laughed about the absurdity of it. Then, the following days had been so hectic for him, he had not given it a second thought.

Now, here he was, watching Mollie talk about it. She was offering herself up to him as his hired wife. He had listened to her plan for almost two hours now, observing her, fascinated. A well thought out and meticulous plan for his success. It impressed him!

She bit her bottom lip, and at that action, he wondered what it would be like for him to nibble at her lips.

So, his mind wandered off while she was still talking. The image of how it would be to bed her as his hired wife distracted him, and his eyes twinkled—to caress that flawless skin, to kiss every little inch of her.

Then, he shook his head, and he returned his thoughts to the proposal. He tried to focus again on what she said, harder.

But the girl had done well! She had even compiled a contract of marriage, with roles and responsibilities for both of them. She'd written a report to rebuild his image in the eyes of the Board.

There must be close to a hundred pages in these papers, you clever girl, he considered with a smirk. *Unbelievable!*

And she was still in full flow on the details of her plan, her soft, angelic features alive with excitement while pouring her theories out on the matter. She was unstoppable, and he was enjoying studying her.

The highlight of my day! Hell, no! Of the month! A laugh escaped out loud from deep inside him.

She stopped in her tracks and stared at him, frowning. "Am I amusing you, Mr. Sorensen?" she asked with a glare.

"Oh, no, no. Please go on. Zac, please call me Zac," he said, forcing himself to steady his features.

"Sure, Mr.… Zac…" Mollie ignored his amusement and struggled to concentrate again. It would be dangerous for her to be deterred from her focus. So, she kept on talking animatedly on how her plan would work. She didn't want to lose her nerve.

"I have also studied the accounts of one of your businesses. I didn't find everything in the public domain. But I have a report with suggestions for operational efficiencies and a cost reduction exercise. This may save the company around £2 million pounds, if my hypotheses are correct. A superficial study of the accounts, though. Please ask me anything once you have read it."

She stunned him. At that stage, he lost his cool for a second, and his eyes went big at her. He recomposed himself. *Save two million pounds?* Now, that was tempting! His business head was now making more of an entrance!

I bet the Board would like that! he pondered. *I must be confident about this girl, though.* He didn't know her at all.

"Fine, fine, Mollie. I hear you. I will look at your papers. But tell me, was this your idea?" Zac asked. As much as he liked the young woman, he was cautious. It came with the territory.

"It is my idea. You mustn't worry," she lied, trying hard not to tug at her sleeve.

"Are you sure? Shall we say, a friend or a young man helped you on this? With the papers I mean, or with the idea?" he asked, *I'll tell Fin to check her background!* he mused.

"No, no young man. I did it all. I wrote all the reports. I

told you, this is my idea." She was sitting erect in her chair now. At least part of it was true; the papers were her work.

"Did you share your thoughts with anybody else? A boyfriend?" He persisted with this line of questioning.

OH, that word again, boyfriend. She felt guilty.

"No," she said. She didn't know how much longer she could take this, how long she could lie.

His eyes were in slits, piercing at her. A deep frown took over his handsome features.

Can he see through my lies? she fretted.

"Anyone, shall we say, *encourage* you to do this?" he persisted, with his eyebrows almost in a flat line.

"No. No one. Only you and I know about this," she lied again but stared at him. She forced herself to think of something else to avoid lowering her eyes and giving her game away. So, she steadied her gaze on him and raised her chin. Her lover had told her that he would challenge her.

She felt ashamed. She realised it was disgraceful, the way she was lying to him, but the boat had sailed, no going back.

Although she didn't know him, Zac had been charming and welcoming to her, encouraging. Not to mention, the flutters in her belly every time his eyes settled on her. So, he didn't deserve her lies. She hated lying. At that moment, she despised every lie she'd told him. She loathed lying to him with a vengeance. Guilt overwhelmed her, wrenching her guts in knots. She felt faint as she perspired and blanched.

"Are you okay, Mollie?" he asked, concerned at her turn in colour.

"I'm fine, just tired is all. I'll take a glass of water if you don't mind," she replied with a gloomy smile.

"Sure." He stood and poured her a glass of water from

the sideboard and handed it to her. Then he went back to his chair.

She sipped it, peering at him through the glass, struggling to calm herself.

He studied her.

Oh God, what have I done? What I gotten myself into! She silently cursed herself. And for an instant, she glimpsed at the door behind her and almost contemplated leaving. For once, she realised she might have bitten off more than she could chew. Her lack of common sense and her lack of prudence was high on her mind. *Silly girl!* But it was too late now, no turning back.

Zac smiled at her, and she relaxed for a moment.

"Better?" he asked, concerned.

"Yes. Thank you." She nodded, taking a deep breath.

"Excellent!" He winked at her, and butterflies danced in her tummy.

THIS GIRL HAS DONE a lot of work for me. Incredible! A contract of marriage and how it would work, she had even given him a business report for one of his father's companies which, if correct, could spare them millions of pounds. She had taken all of this seriously; no wonder the girl had made herself ill. *She must have worked tirelessly on this.* But above all, she was captivating, and well… *foxy.* And he loved watching her go through it all. He had scrutinised every slight detail of her face. *Her quirks, adorable! The passion in her face, lovely.*

She was after money for the arrangement, and he realised that. Way too well! But he must turn the Board around. Would her plan be worth his time? *If it works, maybe,* he reflected.

Would it work? Zac wasn't certain. But this girl, as his hired wife, had an undeniable appeal, regardless of the proposal. And he wasn't sure why. So, he focused on the business proposal instead.

A lot of reading and studying to do. He forced himself to recover control of his thoughts.

The £2 million pounds cost saving exercise would have the attention of the Board, and by default, now Mollie had Zac's.

Chapter 4

"**M**ollie, you were against my plan from day one. Your heart wasn't in it," her boyfriend accused her.

"The papers were perfect; you know that. I did the best I could."

"Psst..." he hissed, annoyed.

"You need a beautiful woman for him. I'm not his type. I told you it wouldn't work," she sulked.

Two weeks had passed since her meeting with Zac. She waited for his call every day, but she heard nothing, not a single word, only silence.

Her boyfriend asked her for news every day, and he was fretting.

Her mind cast back to when she was writing the papers; she'd worked on the reports tirelessly. Even if she didn't want to do it, she had put her heart and soul into it to please her lover. She spent days writing the proposal. She had worked on every facet of the plan.

To get inspiration, she studied him. But when she looked at footage of Zac during charity events and society parties, he was with gorgeous women on his arm on every occasion. When she stared at those women, anxiety got the best of her. They were far too beautiful. She wouldn't be able to compete with them! Not physically, anyway. This thought rooted in her mind.

She had watched Zac's interviews on TV; she'd read articles and seen hundreds of pictures of him in magazine and newspapers. She analysed his background. She learned about his humanitarian side, his business achievements, his bachelor's lifestyle, and his womanising too.

Not much about the private Zac. *Is there a private man? A man no one knows?* Who knew!

Except… that one photograph.

One image captured by paparazzi when he was sitting on the outside space of a coffee shop; the caption said it was in a Mediterranean foreign land. That photograph fascinated her.

It seemed that the photographer had taken Zac by surprise. He looked gorgeous anyway, even if he seemed just out of bed, with a rather rakish look. In that picture, Zac lifted his head to glare at the paparazzi, the moment the picture was taken. His eyes stared into the camera, with intensity and annoyance.

It captured his beautiful eyes well, at his best, passionate and brooding light brown eyes, like mellow cognac. She watched that image of him for a long time. The expression in those eyes had a sexy, magnetic, and menacing glint mingled together. Alluring!

She couldn't forget those eyes, and she had loved them from that moment.

She wondered if those eyes, with that same expression, were to land on her for an instant, what emotion would she have? She tried to imagine it for a moment. And her body shivered. Warm flutters caused havoc inside her.

She inhaled sharply. *Wow! What the hell was that?* But she smiled to herself.

"Mollie?" her boyfriend interrupted her musings, exasperated, bringing her back from her lascivious thoughts. Oh, yes, despite that photo, she had worked hard on her lover's idea. It was a perfect plan.

But she had heard nothing from the man.

Her mind was wandering, *would she do for Zac? As a woman? No*, she didn't think so. *Not even as a hired wife.* Perhaps a woman with a sexy, voluptuous body was all he wanted, which ruled her out.

"There is nothing wrong with my work; he doesn't want me!" she snapped, "I don't fit his womanly standards," she concluded with a scowl.

"Shut up, Mollie," her lover said with vehemence.

WEEKS LATER, she was in a tutorial, though she was not listening to Professor Blake or the discussions of her fellow students in her class. Her thoughts troubled her.

It was almost the end of March, and Mollie had given up hope on hearing from Zac.

Where did I fail? she thought from time to time. *Perhaps, he changed his mind or, more likely, I am not beautiful enough for him.* She sighed.

Her lover became more agitated every day. It frustrated him. He blamed her for the failure. He'd even yelled at her a few times, which he had never done before.

In her mind, she convinced herself that Zac had not wanted her. That was that! She felt relieved, though. She had dreaded the crazy plan. Something in her mind kept niggling at her. She was only doing it for her lover. But now, she was relieved it had all fizzled out, that nothing would happen.

At least, I won't have to do it, not have to lie. Things would go back to normal, no strange situations. No deceit! Though, sometimes, she couldn't help but wonder if her proposal would succeed.

Interesting, she reflected with a peculiar grin on her face, only for the purpose of trying out her theories, nothing more... Or was it the fact, deep down in her unconscious, she had relished the opportunity to know a man such as Zac?

No, no... hmmm... nothing to do with Zac, she went on, just pure scientific interest. She tried to persuade herself that her interest was purely empirical, nothing to do with those brooding, sultry eyes.

She smiled. It was a ridiculous plan, anyway! It would have been a disaster!

But, alas, I'll never know now. She felt relieved, though her lover blamed her for the failure.

"Well, the end for today." Professor Blake dismissed the class, interrupting her musings. As the class began to disperse, he said, "Mollie, wait a moment please," while her fellow students left the classroom.

"Yes, Professor?" Mollie asked, still with a distant air.

"Next time, Mollie, I would like attention and participation from you in the class. Is that clear?" Peter said in reprimand.

"Oh, I am sorry, Professor." She blinked twice and blushed while one of her fellow students pursed her lips to her in sympathy.

"Never mind. Run along, I have another class in a minute," Peter said with a wave of his hand, dismissing her with annoyance.

She fled the room, embarrassed.

After her tutorial, she was to meet with friends at a coffee shop.

She crossed the road from the university's building, when she heard a man's voice behind her, "Miss Belloc?"

She turned.

"Yes?" Mollie answered, looking suspiciously at him.

"My name is Jim; I am Mr. Sorensen's driver. I have instructions to drive you to his office."

"Mr. Sorensen?" Mollie's eyes grew wide.

"Yes, miss."

She glanced at the car then at the man. She didn't know what to do. She hesitated. *Get into a car with a stranger? No!*

"I'll dial in Mr. Sorensen. You will see him through the camera, so he can reassure you," the man said, reading her hesitation.

"Mollie, I thought as much! It is safe. Please, if you have time now, Jim will drive you to my office, and we can talk," Zac said, looking at her through the mobile phone camera.

"MISS BELLOC, Mr. Sorensen will see you now," Gladys said, knocking on the oak doors and motioning her in.

She entered his office. Mollie, standing now in front of him, was the girl with a green baggy sweater and tight jeans, no makeup, and her hair in a messy ponytail. She was tugging at the sleeve of her sweater and blushing when her eyes landed on him.

He smiled at her.

He liked the sexy, well-groomed Mollie who first came into his office with the proposal. But he realised he liked the Mollie standing in front of him now even more—the clean-faced girl, with a shabby sweater and messy hair.

This girl was far more endearing, *a sweet girl.* She looked charming, *adorable! God, that word again. Why the word leaps into my mind when she's around? Cool, man!*

It astonished him.

She was nervous, he could tell. He had studied her last time. Besides her furious blushing, the fact she bit her bottom lip or tugged at her sleeves gave her away. It made him chuckle. *She is cute. Delightful. Bloody hell stop that!*

Her eyes darted from Zac to the men in the room and back.

In a flash, he saw vulnerability in her eyes. Perhaps, even panic. For a moment, he was sure; she had contemplated running away. So, he had the urge to put his arms around her, to reassure her.

"Miss Belloc, can I get you something to drink?"

"Water please," she said, her stomach in knots. His secretary poured her a glass of water and then left the room.

"Miss Belloc—" Zac started.

"Mollie, please," she interrupted him in a whisper.

He nodded. "You met Alex West, and this is his partner Florian Kirsh. Alex is my lawyer and handles all of my business deals," Zac stated, while the people in the room extended their hands to greet her.

A CELEBRATED LITIGATOR in the English courts, Alex had become a senior partner in a law firm at the tender age of twenty-eight, two years ago. With a brilliant future, he was a clever lawyer. The fact he was handsome, a bonus! *Not the arresting beauty Zac possessed,* she realised, comparing the two. Alex was tall and slender, elegant with classic good looks, and a strong jaw.

So, the combination made him attractive to women, and to some, irresistible. I bet, on a night out, the two men would be like Genghis Khan on a rampage. No chance for women.

And a green-eyed pang hit her.

ZAC COUGHED, bringing her attention back to the room. She blinked several times, returning her focus back to him with a blush.

Does she like him? Hell, no! he wondered, not missing her attention on Alex. He cursed silently with a scowl and didn't even know why. A feeling, a sliver too close to jealousy, assaulted his senses. *No, no, this isn't.* Zac's frown deepened, but he shook his head.

He motioned her to sit, his movement jerky and author-itative.

She winced at him and sat.

"Mollie, there are several points that we must clarify. Alex will talk you through the contract. Florian is here to instruct you, to consider your rights. You can have it examined by your own lawyer if you prefer." Zac relaxed, now that the bitter, baffling moment had subsided.

It was Mollie's turn for her mouth to fall open. "Does this mean you agree to my proposal?" she questioned him in disbelief.

"Well, hmm, it has potential," he said, cocking his head, "providing we both conform to all the terms and conditions in the proposal. It might just work."

Though, if he knew anything about women, Zac was not convinced she would grant approval to one specific stipula-tion in the agreement.

He motioned to Alex to go ahead.

"Mollie, your straw-man contract was impressive. A few tweaks here and there, and it became workable. Good work. I have introduced pre-nuptial clauses to ring fence Zac's financial assets. I am sure you realise it is unavoidable, but we will go through each section. Let's begin." Alex stated, passing her a copy of the contract. She grabbed the substantial agreement with wide eyes.

The lawyer then led her through the various sections in the contract, one clause at a time, including the pre-nuptial ones.

While Alex talked her through it, Zac's eyes riveted on her. Observing her, scrutinising her while her focus switched from the contract to the lawyers and vice versa.

She listened intently to every word they said. She asked all the appropriate questions.

Zac adored the expressive frowns on her face when she tried to absorb a difficult section of the agreement. He delighted in her baby blue eyes when the particular strict obligation on monogamy surprised her. He loved the wrinkle on her forehead when she focused on reading.

He kept glancing at her over his papers.

At one point, she bit her bottom lip in concentration. His eyes grew at her lip movement, and his gut clenched. He craved a taste of those sensual lips. He wondered how her mouth would feel if he ever got the chance. He found her sexy and endearing, and he lost his concentration for a moment.

Her smile charming, it lit up her face. A *smile to die for! Captivating. Wow, down, boy.*

She laughed at something Alex said, and the melodious tone of her laugh made Zac's hair stand at the back of his neck.

Bloody hell, this girl…

Mollie kept court with Alex on the agreement, which left him with no doubts how clever she was.

As they went on with the reading, Zac found himself spellbound by her. It took some effort to rein back his thoughts to focus on the contract just because he liked the sound of her soft giggles so much. Her smile made him gasp every time.

A tenderness grew inside him, something no woman had achieved in years. And he didn't even know how.

Occasionally, she would glance up at him, sensing his eyes were on her, and she would bite her lower lip. But she would turn back to the lawyers quickly.

Zac missed nothing, and she blushed when he caught her looking at him.

This amused him no end. The women he was used to, didn't blush. Nor were they endearing and sweet, like this one. He enjoyed studying her. He absorbed her every little detail. A beautiful and bewitching face, as it became to him at the end of three hours of contract reading, etched in his brain.

Alex described the complexities of the contract, while Florian gave her help and advice as and when she required it.

SHE REALISED Zac's scrutiny on her was intense, and it was making her uneasy. Mollie had no time to dwell on him; she needed to focus on what the lawyers were explaining to her.

Once or twice, he rewarded her with his devilish smile, and she almost wet her pants.

To his delight, she blushed furiously. And she dropped her face deep into the papers to conceal her face, which made him grin from ear to ear.

Alex was summing up now.

Mollie would accompany Zac to parties, dinners, charity events, public engagements and such, whenever he needed her.

There would be a two-month courtship, followed by a wedding.

In public, she would be the devoted and adoring wife and impress the Board with her actuary work. He would marry her for three years, which the contract expressed. That was sufficient time to rebuild his image and ingratiate the Board. Then an amicable divorce would give her the sought after pay out at the end of the term, or a pro rata following the first eighteen months.

The penalty, if she demanded out before this period: she would have nothing.

However, Alex said there was one issue her straw-man contract had not touched upon. And it was covered in the contract.

"Sex?" she said in a sharp cry that startled even her. She glanced at Zac and at the lawyers. She flushed crimson.

There was a section on sex in the contract. She inhaled and rummaged through the pages, chewing her lower lip. She stared at them and then at the pages in front of her. She caught a fleeting amusement in Zac's eyes when she glanced at him, but he said nothing.

Bastard! And vile, silent curses burst into her mind. He had ambushed her, and her face reddened again.

"Yes, Mollie, sex," Alex replied.

"Nobody said anything about sex," she eventually cried out in a high-pitched tone, with a scowl on her face.

"You didn't, Mollie, but the contract does," the lawyer repeated in a deadpan tone. At that point, though, he seemed apologetic. The lawyer knew his friend was stubborn and would not back down.

"But no one told me..." she attacked again.

"That's the position, my dear," Zac stated, raising a handsome brow, but she shook her head.

She stared at Florian for help, but her counsellor pointed

out that Zac would be her husband. Sex is expected in a married couple, unless both sides agreed to remove the section on sex, but this was not the case with him.

"Mollie, these are my terms. You must comply if you wish to do this. If you don't agree, then it renders the contract void, no harm done," he pointed out, shrugging his shoulders.

"But that's absurd; we can discuss this," she emphasised.

"Sex is an intrinsic part of the proposal. You will either agree, or we can part ways, your decision! No more to say about this. Without sex, there is no agreement, and you will go back to your life," Zac said with finality in his strong masculine tone. She didn't miss his intense eyes on her.

That look! She recognised it. *Sexy, magnetic, and menacing!* This glance had passion in it. *Ahh, that look!* She gulped and coughed. Her eyes locked on him.

Zac turned to Alex with a slight bow of the head, who warned Florian. The two lawyers excused themselves and left, leaving Mollie and Zac alone in the room.

"Mollie, the contract says we must be monogamous for the term of the marriage. That means no lovers, or it will defeat the purpose," he emphasised, once alone.

"I know what monogamous means," she said, flaring her nostrils, but he overlooked her comment.

"Besides, lovers are unreliable. So, monogamy is the key! That's the only way I can rebuild my image; otherwise, it will be meaningless. I might as well carry on womanising as a bachelor. No need for a wife. So, monogamy is important if we are to succeed. Now, do you understand?" he explained.

"Yes, I do, but—" She tugged at her sleeve nervously, with her tone a pitch higher, but he cut in.

"You don't believe… I would have no sex for three years!" he added in his bass voice.

She inhaled. His deep tone and *that look* on her was

sending mixed signals to her brain. She rubbed her forehead with a shaking hand.

"I assumed—" She paused, pursing her lips.

"Well, you assumed wrong. No chance! Not giving up sex, not when I would have a legitimate wife. Take it or leave it. Your choice!" He was brutal.

Her eyes grew big in astonishment at his stubborn reaction.

But he smiled warmly.

The colour flowed from her face. *He won't give up!*

"But, but—" she stammered. She grabbed a loose strand of her hair and toyed with it, rolling and unrolling it around her fingers, anxiety getting hold of her.

He followed the action, enthralled, and he wondered if her hair was as soft as it seemed.

"No buts," he said, regaining his self-possessed nature. Leaning forward in his chair, he stopped her from toying with her hair with his big hand on hers. She withdrew hers abruptly, but the strand of hair remained in his hand.

"No, I can't…" she blurted out.

Yes, soft silky hair, and it unsettled him. She pulled her hair from his hand, and he resumed. "Mollie, I don't share. Is there a young man? Is that it?" he whispered but with an icy mask.

"No! But—" she lied and flushed.

He glared.

"No buts! End of story," he stubbornly dictated.

Suddenly, she became furious. She narrowed her eyes on him and glared. Her nostrils flared. "Mr. Sorensen, I will not have sex with you," she said.

Oh, it's Mr. Sorensen now, is it? he thought, watching her stand unexpectedly.

She gave him a dismissive wave of her hand.

Well, perhaps… I could, no… no sex! she thought, shaking her head with a deep frown at her own hesitation.

"Please, call me Zac," he said with delight in his eyes, noting a hint of indecision in her face.

"*What?*" *I must be nuts, no… no sex!* She cursed at her faltering thoughts, disappointed in herself. Then her spirit took over, eclipsing her doubts. "Well, Zac, get this! I will not have sex with you," she blurted out, clenching her fists.

"I see," he said. She was standing there in front of him, blazing at him, with her chin up.

A gentle smile curled on his lips, which made her even angrier. On that note, she seemed younger than her years.

"Goodbye, Mr. Sorensen," she whispered, returning to his last name, to emphasise the clash between them remained firm.

"Think it over, my dear! You have two weeks, or I will find someone else," he yelled after her, staring at her firm ass in those tight jeans as she moved towards the door.

She got hold of the door handle, but she paused. She turned to him, her eyes flashed, darting fire. "Psst," she spat then turned back and slammed the door shut. And she was gone.

"WHAT DID you say to her? She looked furious," Alex asked, once he was back in the room.

"She'll come back," Zac replied with a grin.

"What if she doesn't?"

"She will."

"My friend, I am not comfortable with this. This time, you may have outdone yourself. The whole thing is absurd. You should reconsider. It could all go wrong," the lawyer stressed.

"Nay. She's cute."

"What? She didn't look that sweet right now. Fiery is the word if you ask me."

"Yes, if eyes could kill..." Zac chuckled.

"Hey, it's a beastly sum you'll pay her, but the idea is crazy. You know my opinion on this. As your lawyer, I have to warn you against it, again! This is a mistake," Alex emphasised, but his friend wouldn't change his mind, no doubt.

"Bloody hell, just her business paper alone will save my father £2 million on one of his companies. We checked; she is damn right! The Board is ecstatic. Imagine what she can do in three years. So, her pay out at £5 million is a bargain! I would have given her more if she had asked." Zac smiled.

Besides, what he had not said to his friend was that he liked this girl! The more he watched her, the more he liked her, and the more he was looking forward to seeing her. *But what if she is not back?* His eyes clouded with doubt. For the first time in his life, he doubted his charm.

Alex looked at him in disbelief, sensing something in his eyes, but Zac recovered his composure.

"And a hefty sum of fifty thousand pounds in monthly expenses while married. Don't forget that," the lawyer pointed out, still searching his eyes, but he couldn't see that fleeting moment anymore.

"Still a bargain. She will need clothes, pocket money, things," he said instead, dismissing Alex's concerns.

Besides, he enjoyed watching her blush. Zac's thoughts were on her beautiful smile, her quirky mannerisms, her baby blue eyes, and her adorable ways. And he grinned to himself.

Yes, he couldn't wait.

"I think you scared her with this sex business," Alex pointed out.

"Nah, she will be back. She has guts. I feel it."

MOLLIE WAS SPITTING FIRE. *How dare he?* She was sure she had seen a glint of humour in Zac's eyes.

The bastard was making fun of her too.

I cannot accept such a thing, she thought with a scowl.

Well, perhaps… I could, hmm… hell no, no sex! I am not a slut, she considered with a sad grin.

In all the discussions with her boyfriend, they had never considered that possibility.

Her work on the contract had never touched upon it, either.

It had never occurred to her that Zac might want sex.

Despite her cleverness, her naïveté was sometimes outstanding. For all her intelligence, she always slipped on the obvious, at the most practical of things. How, with all her hard work, could she have miscalculated that?

'Clever, yes, for learning, for books! But, Mollie, you have not an ounce of common sense. Your head is always in the clouds,' her mom always told her with a sigh, and she was right.

First, she would kill her if she learned of this crazy plan. No doubt her mom would kick her boyfriend for putting her up to it.

Second, a man like Zac, and no sex? Her mother would laugh at her nonsense and with good reason. *I am a fool.* How had she missed such a crucial point? Misjudged his need for sex. It hadn't even crossed her mind.

She didn't consider herself pretty enough to worry about it. As a woman, she believed herself ordinary for a man like Zac. Too plain! He wouldn't look at her twice. No appeal for him.

Well, wrong! He likes sex, regardless! He won't go without it. Nothing to do with me! she convinced herself.

She cursed under her breath. A docker would sicken at her swearing! She was raging, frantic! Her face was red. She didn't know if she was livid because he'd smiled at her refusal or if she was offended by his request.

Anyhow, this couldn't happen.

Though tempting, she couldn't do it. She would not make sex a part of her marriage of convenience.

The problem... he was dead set on it. *Oh, sweet Jesus!*

Besides, she was certain her lover would not allow such a thing.

It was one thing, marrying Zac for a profitable transaction, but this... another issue altogether. She would become, for all intents, his real wife. Or maybe it would make her his whore instead? Who knew? She couldn't tell, but it was not right! She couldn't stoop so low for money! Not even for her boyfriend!

It was dangerous enough to lie. All those false statements... The shame at her deception was draining her, and she had signed nothing yet. But to add sex into the equation was madness.

No, no, no!

She exhaled in irritation and yet... a smile suddenly appeared on her face. She had seen a glimpse of lust in his eyes when they'd talked about sex. Briefly, but she had seen it.

She grinned at Zac's temerity, and for a millisecond, she considered how it would be to make love to this infamous womaniser... *Make love? Hell no, just* sex! But she dismissed the thought as horrid. *Bizarre even to think about it.*

She fretted for nothing. Her boyfriend would not allow another man to touch her.

My lover won't tolerate this, she believed, calming herself. *He will never agree to such a preposterous idea!* Surely, he would never consent to her having sex with another man!

Never! He wouldn't!

It would scandalise him, horrify him!

"DID you think he wouldn't bring up sex? Jesus, Mollie! Have you learned nothing about this man?" her lover asked, shocked.

"You never mentioned a word about this," she said, puzzled.

"Sex was implied, implicit. Zac must want sex!" he said bluntly.

"Implied? Implicit? Are you insane? I can't." Her tone was shrill with horror. She paced the room with purpose, like a caged animal.

"You'll offer him your body, but he will not have your mind or soul," her boyfriend told her.

"Bullshit!" she cried out.

"Mollie—" he sighed, changing tactics.

"I can't believe you are saying this to me. Don't you care at all?" Mollie blurted with tears in her eyes.

"Think of it. It is our only chance."

"No, I won't do it. I can't," she murmured. *As tempting as it may be,* was her fleeting thought.

He looked at her with a frown.

Suddenly, it was too much for her, and she started crying.

"Please..." He put his arms around her shoulders and held her to him. Standing in the middle of the room, she cried on his chest for what sounded to him like an eternity.

Her tears finally subsided, and he said, "I wouldn't be asking you to do this if I didn't think you could do it. You are strong; you can do it. Our future depends on this. We will be together forever, happy and free." He sighed. He caressed her cheek with the back of his hand. But she moved away from him and crashed on the sofa, feeling dejected.

She shook her head, unable to speak. She squeezed her eyes shut. He followed her to the sofa. He went for her lips, and he kissed her.

"I am not a slut," she whispered almost in his mouth, with another sob.

"No, not a slut. You will be his wife, his lawful wife. Please." He started kissing her, savouring her for a long time.

How can he ask such a thing, so unashamedly? She had been naïve, expecting no sex from Zac. But for her lover to ask her to have sex with another man, for money, it was beyond comprehension to her. It hurt her. She was devastated by his insistence, by his lax attitude towards her.

"Do you love me?" he whispered in her ear, implacable.

"You know I do."

"Then, please, do it, Mollie, for me."

"Why are you doing this to me? To him?" She wept, closed her eyes, and sighed.

"Three years will fly by, and meanwhile, you'll have a wonderful life. Think of it."

"I can't. How can you even say that?"

"Mollie, every woman on earth would give her right arm to be in your place. Just do it." He spat the words at her with such vehemence that she blinked, recoiling from him, but she had guts. She stood up.

"As tempting as it might be, no! I won't!" she bellowed, with her fists clenched.

"You are a fool!" he said. He stood up and paced. He was angry.

"Find yourself another woman. You are selling me to him," she sulked and returned to the sofa.

"No. You will do this!" he shouted, standing over her. His

voice was hard, no emotion in his eyes. It sent a shiver down her spine. She winced at him, but then he smiled tenderly, and returned to the sofa. He caressed her hair back. He kissed her forehead.

"You are exchanging me for money; you are! Do you know how this makes me feel?" she repeated disconsolately.

"The daily grind will swallow us. We'll be unhappy, thinking we missed our only chance for a good life. We'll hate each other. Just think about it." He started kissing her again.

She looked at him with pleading eyes, but he was relentless. He stood up and paced. She watched him move around the room.

He may end up hating me if I don't, but, how can I?

"You are strong. You can. I know you can," he said, and kneeled in front of her, taking one of her hands to his lips, kissing her wrist. Then he sat next to her and put his arms around her, and he buried his lips on hers. They didn't stop kissing until it engulfed them.

He kissed her ravenously then bit her lips. She responded with the same force. He lifted her into his arms and moved to the other room, placing her in his bed. He continued kissing her, giving her no respite. He opened her blouse and bit and sucked on her nipples, and it made her wet.

She remembered the first time he had done this to her. Her first real boyfriend. Her first lover. And her world had changed! But how could he ask this now? How could he give her to another man?

"Please," she pleaded, wanting to forget her pain.

He stripped her naked, and then he took his clothes off. He made passionate love to her until their bodies were raw with pleasure and sated. She kissed him. Her body quivered with strong sensations in the aftermath of their lovemaking.

"Will you do it?" his voice demanded instead, "will you? At least, think about it?" He stood up from the bed, parading his nakedness but denying her any more pleasure. She pleaded again, but he stood firm.

She couldn't bear it. "Oh, bloody hell! Fine, I'll think about it…" she shouted, with black curses flowing out of her mouth, but her lover ignored them. He was relentless.

For the next two days, they made passionate love, her body sore with lovemaking. And between lovemaking sessions, there was only one topic of conversation.

She must marry Zac.

Her lover pleaded with her, cajoled her. He seduced her into it, but still, she resisted. He demanded it of her. Her lover dictated it to her. He pushed her to the extreme. She had to marry Zac and accept his request of sex in the midst.

"Our love will survive it," he said, though Mollie was not so sure. For days, he virtually bullied her into it, using passive tactics, until it exhausted her. And finally, she relented and stopped fighting him.

But Mollie knew one thing. *I won't have two men at the same time. I am not callous enough for that.* So, she gave her boyfriend one more chance to back out.

"If I marry Zac, then my relationship with you will be on hold until the end of my marriage with him. Can you wait three years?" Mollie said to her boyfriend.

The man smiled, cupped her cheeks, and kissed her nose. "Hmm…"

"I am serious. If I marry Zac on his terms, I am not prepared to two-time him. Besides, the contract is clear on no extra-marital affairs. Zac was categoric on monogamy. It's one of the conditions. You do understand that, don't you?" she stated, hoping that this would change his mind.

He laughed. "We'll be careful and discreet, but we will continue as usual," he said firmly.

But Mollie was adamant. "No. The monogamy clause is

strict. Otherwise, we will risk losing everything. It will be all for nothing," she spat.

She would help Zac rebuild his image and gain that coveted CEO spot. So, she clung to the flimsy conviction that it was a good deed after all… but that meant her boyfriend had to disappear into the background. She was not prepared for two lovers in her life. If she had to marry Zac, then he would be the only one for her until the divorce. If she had to do it, she would do it her own way.

So, she made up her mind! Her man would get what he wanted, the money, even her monthly allowance. She would marry Zac, but her lover would have to wait three years to have her back. Mollie was adamant, if she had to do it, she would be faithful to Zac.

She wondered what her boyfriend was thinking, but at that point, she was past caring. It was self-preservation.

MOLLIE'S LOVER knew she was stubborn. So, he played along. He had no alternative. She was headstrong, and that was as far as he could push her.

She was under his spell, and she wanted to please him, but he had to be careful. There were certain things she would not contemplate, that she would never do, not even for him.

She was a clever girl, but she was naïve, and she had no common sense. So, he manipulated her. He needed to be cautious, or she would run a mile.

Besides, he would watch her relationship with Zac, not for nothing, women flocked to Zac. Though Mollie was not like any other woman; that's why he had chosen her.

He would be mindful. She needed to remain under his spell.

He had achieved his purpose. He had what he wanted. Mollie would marry Zac. *It is a good start.* The marriage agreement provided a great deal of money, and he wanted it all. *But there is much more…* If he played his cards right, a great deal more from Zac.

Way more. Don't worry her for now.

He could have it all. But if his plan was to succeed, he needed her at the centre. His plan had to go without a hitch, and Mollie was his precious pawn to play with.

He had planned it for a long time, and now he was so close.

Chapter 5

Mollie couldn't say how she made it to her wedding day, but she did. The two months prior to it passed in a daze.

From the minute she agreed to wed him, Zac took charge. "There is too much riding on this. We must not fail," he often said in a conciliatory tone when he pushed her too hard. But those months flew by.

The fake courtship went without a hitch. Zac's image improved, with Mollie at his side. Gradually, the Board of Directors commented on the positive effects she had on him.

He was pleased. He complimented her often. She assumed he liked her. Though she had a major control freak on her hands, and perhaps for the best.

Mollie was thankful for his support and guidance, meandering a society she was not familiar with. Give her an advanced algorithm to work out or study theories of subatomic particles or a complex business balance sheet to deal with, rather than mingle in his world.

But she did it.

From the moment he introduced her to his family and

the Board's members, to his social circle, even when Zac met her own mother and friends; it had been in a controlled manner. And she guessed, she would not have survived it otherwise.

She was grateful to him for helping her navigate all the complexities of his social status, the people and the many high-profile events and functions they attended before the wedding.

Thus, two months down the line, after a long wedding day, she was Mrs. Sorensen, although she was tired and mentally exhausted by then.

Navigating her new life, wed to one of the wealthiest men in the country, would not be an easy task. But she willed herself to succeed. He seemed to care for her, and they got along fine.

Those months culminated in a ceremony where she felt like Cinderella meeting her prince charming, a ceremony so magnificent, so overwhelming, but there was light at the end of the tunnel. And she had reached the other side.

If it wasn't for her mother, her childhood friend Clarissa, for Kathryn, George, and a handful of other friends, she would not have known a single soul at her own wedding, despite seven hundred guests attending it.

Zac helped her navigate through the day, but it had not been simple. It had ended in the early hours of that morning, with enough time for them to change clothes, dash to the airport, and head to France. So, now, here she was, on her way to Antibes, with her new husband, about to start her honeymoon!

Finally, his wife... Mollie relaxed, looking forward to a few days of tranquillity on the French Riviera. She reflected for a moment. *Well, perhaps not tranquillity...* at least, she would only have to deal with one person, just Zac and nobody else for a few weeks. *Thank God for small mercies,* but now that her adrenaline had dropped, she felt exhausted.

During the flight to Nice, in his private plane, she tried to sleep, but she couldn't. Mollie picked up her book instead, but she was too restless to focus on anything, although she looked forward to getting to her destination. As they were about to land in Nice, his bride of a few hours, Mollie wondered what else was in store for her in the forthcoming days.

Sweet Jesus! My wedding night! She gulped. She felt curious and uneasy. She closed her eyes for a moment and took a deep breath.

"No sex until after the wedding," she had dictated.

Zac had consented but had taken several weeks to agree on these delicate negotiations about sex. He yielded, despite his many attempts to change her mind, but Mollie remained firm on this decision.

By then, Zac had learned that his new bride was stubborn, and when she decided on a matter, there was nothing that could change her mind.

After months of putting it off, her wedding night was now upon her.

TOUGH OUTWARDLY, she seemed to have conquered all. The two months before her wedding had also been the most difficult of her life. Emotionally, she was at her lowest.

In the solitude of her own bedroom, Mollie cried long and hard. The lies were too much to bear. She lied to everyone around her. She had lied to her family, to her friends, and most of all, to Zac.

Her mother and friends had taken the news of her impending marriage wonderfully.

But she couldn't tell them it was an arranged marriage, a pretence, a fake—a business transaction! Worst of all, she couldn't explain to them her boyfriend had pushed her into it, demanded it of her. Her mom and friends would not understand her actions; they would deplore her deeds. So, she had hidden the truth.

It had been difficult for her to pretend to be the happy bride at all times. In particular, with Kathryn and George, with whom she shared a house. Above all, she hated lying to her new husband.

Zac believed the arranged marriage to be her own idea. He thought she was a willing participant, but it was not so. Far from it! She didn't want to do it. Therefore, she deceived him on the premise of their arrangement. And if this wasn't bad enough, Zac was unaware of her lover's existence and of the manipulation. Her boyfriend had masterminded the plan and propelled her into it unceremoniously.

Thus, it was difficult to surrender herself to the deception. She felt neck deep in trickery, wretched and guilty, but there was nothing she could do.

As time went on, she cursed herself for having allowed a man to rule her life. All that cleverness, but lately, she was not the master of her own destiny. Her universe seemed upside down. Her lover had controlled her and pushed her into this marriage.

She hoped her new husband would never find out about her boyfriend's ploy, or even of his existence. Worse, who he was. She prayed to the heavens that Zac would never know. Somehow, she sensed he was not the forgiving kind.

At times, she couldn't see the light at the end of the tunnel if her life depended on it, when her labyrinth of thoughts drove her crazy.

She had done it for her boyfriend, so she wouldn't lose him, and though she had always been uneasy about her lover's plan, now two months down the line, she had doubts. Enormous doubts, and through the months leading to her wedding, her fears about her callous man increased in her mind.

She was not an expert in love matters by any means, but the more she thought about it, she doubted a man who truly loved his woman would ask her to do such a thing.

Alas, it was too late to backtrack. The boat had sailed, and she had no choice but to sail in it.

Besides, the more time she spent with Zac, the less she missed her ruthless boyfriend. In fact, less and less every day. By the time she got to her wedding day, Mollie's feelings for her lover had evaporated in a cloud of suspicion and doubt.

Her feelings for him were doomed, the moment he pushed her into this. She had felt it then. Something had broken in her soul, and so, steadily, her love for him died. More each day, until there was nothing left.

In addition, the differences between the two men were outstanding, staggering!

The more she was with Zac, the more she wanted to be with him. He made her feel good about herself, confident, and beautiful. He was supportive and full of encouragement, while her lover had been selfish and venal. He'd used her, sending her into the arms of another man. *For money! That can't be love!*

Her lack of common sense had let her down again, but now, as if she had awakened from a nightmare, the revelation hit her.

Her heartless lover had not kept his word, either! In the weeks leading to the wedding, he had broken his promise. He texted her again, wanting her back. His amorous messages flooded her mobile phone, but she disregarded him. She understood her lover was not to be trusted, a liar...

She left his messages unanswered, but for how long

would she be able to ignore him? She would have to be strong and distance herself from him. She knew it now, no doubt. She had been blind!

So, in her own mind, she referred to the awful man as her ex-lover. *Yes, ex-boyfriend now. I don't want to see him again. Not if I can help it.* She hadn't told him she was done with him. She couldn't. It would be best not to, at least for now.

But he persisted. Her ex-boyfriend wanted to rekindle their dangerous liaison behind Zac's back! *Madness. He must stop!* She was ashamed as it was.

So, she ignored him. There was nothing she could do. *You silly girl!*

She began thinking, if her ex-lover's reasons were so simple, she had realised who and what he was. Was it just money he was after? She wondered why she had accepted this crazy proposition. She cursed herself, time and time again. But alas, too late. Her path was set, even with her change of heart.

She contemplated telling Zac everything. But it would have been disastrous, now that his reputation was finding a balance. Now that the Board of Directors had acknowledged a change, she couldn't backtrack! It would ruin Zac's position and it would be her fault.

It would spell the end of her relationship with Zac, even if it was a pretend one. That alone, Mollie couldn't contemplate. She was getting attached to Zac, perhaps too much.

'YOUR LIES WILL ULTIMATELY CATCH up with you,' her granny used to say to her when she was a child. And this had her guts in knots.

God help me, if he finds out!

Somehow, she didn't believe Zac would take too kindly to

it. Besides, he would never share his woman in any circumstance. She knew it too well.

She recalled an instance of his possessiveness during their fake courtship period. She remembered a particular evening, when news of their engagement first hit the press. She had attended a ball with Zac at the Norwegian embassy in Belgrave Square, one of the grandest and largest nineteenth-century squares in London.

It was a beautiful party. It thrilled her, a ball full of finery and great music. At the event, Mollie had danced with a dashing young officer from the embassy. She danced with the gallant young man more times than it was perhaps appropriate in the circumstances, given she was a newly engaged woman with a dazzling ring on her finger.

The officer was handsome, and in uniform, he reminded her of *Count Vronsky* in *Anna Karenina's* story. They danced well together. So, that evening, they swayed to the music.

At the event, Zac behaved like the seasoned businessman and the charming socialite that he was, although she couldn't miss his eyes narrowing on her until she felt self-conscious.

"Do you mind if I dance with my fiancée?" Zac asked with a hand on the young man's shoulders, suddenly appearing at her side, thus interrupting her dancing in the middle of the ballroom.

"No. Of course, not," the young lad responded, but a flush crept up on the officer's neck. Then, he kissed Mollie's hand and left them with a swift bow of his head.

That evening, Zac had attempted to smile. But Mollie sensed it looked more like a scowl when he took over the dancing.

"Were you enjoying the young man?" Zac asked her in a whisper close to her ear. His arm circled her waist and pulled her close to him, while they started moving to the rhythm of the music.

"Oh?" She squared her shoulders when his words hit home. She shifted from one foot to the other, missing her dancing step.

"Were you?" he repeated, dead calm and tightening his arm around her waist.

"We just danced. Kurt is a good dancer," Mollie mumbled.

"Kurt? Kurt, is he?" he asked but went on, "I bet he is, but if you dance with him one more time, I'll spank your sweet little ass." He'd whispered the peremptory words with a rawness in his voice that left her no doubt about his command.

No more dancing with Kurt.

A shiver ran through her.

It took her by surprise. She was not expecting him to be possessive, since it was all a pretence, a fake relationship. She stared at him with wide eyes. But he gave her a roguish smile and leaned forward and kissed her. A public kiss for the cameras. She couldn't avoid it. But she kissed him back. With his possessive words still ringing in her ear, and his kiss ravaging her mouth, she felt a warmth engulfing her in a way that she felt weak at the knees.

That surprising evening had stayed in her mind.

On one hand, Zac's possessiveness pleased her no end. On the other, he made it clear he didn't like to share her, pretend romance or not. His words made her belly flutter, a tiny bolt struck at her core. She felt wanted, desired.

And she liked the emotion.

The complete opposite of my ex-lover, who, on the contrary, has been lax and casual towards me. Shame on him, the weasel! Her ex had no qualms sharing her with another man. *Blasted man!* She concluded her ex-lover was *a bastard, a scoundrel, a brute.*

But she couldn't share that sentiment with anyone. At least, not yet! Not for now. It had to remain her secret!

Her hideous ex-lover was now history to her, and in his place, her subconscious had replaced him with Zac. She would never admit to it, but she had. Mollie was not sure when that happened exactly, but it did.

Zac's possessiveness scared her too. *What if Zac finds out about my ex-boyfriend? What will he do?*

She could only see doom and gloom; she was in an impossible situation.

She would need to tread carefully.

Chapter 6

"We're almost there," her husband told her when the flight was ready to land. His voice interrupted her musings. Zac looked at her and winked. He had read a business report for the duration of the flight, while she pretended to be engrossed in her book.

Mollie's musings unnerved her. But she smiled back at him and fumbled with her seat belt. He leaned over to help her and fastened her in. In doing so, his knuckles brushed under her breast, a light touch, like a tender caress. She held her breath. For a moment a warmth spread from the underside of her breast to the tip. Her nipple became tight as a bud, rising to the occasion. She was not expecting her body to react to his touch in the way it did, and she blushed.

He side-glanced at her, and his lips curled up at one side.

The flight was ready to land in Nice, in the South of France.

Mollie had never been to France. In fact, her worldly experience was limited and mostly through the internet. She hadn't travelled outside of England much, too engrossed in her studies. For years, mountains of homework had swamped her, and she had hardly taken any time off.

So, she was expecting a wonderful break and to discover a new country, though this would be her honeymoon. Their destination was his grandmother's villa in Antibes, on the Cote d'Azur on the French Riviera.

HIS HAIR STOOD at the back of his neck. She wanted him. He was not expecting her body to respond that way.

She was an amazing girl. Zac had to take his hat off to her. During the last few months, this young woman had withstood the onslaught of meeting his mother and his grandmother, no less. She met his father and the Board of Directors, with the charm and *savoir faire* of a seasoned royal princess. She had astonished him.

Mollie absorbed everything in her stride, all he threw at her. He only said something once, a name, a face, a place, a fact, and she would not forget it.

He approved of most things she did; she learned fast. Though, occasionally, she couldn't help but put her foot in it, but she was endearing. So, he forgave her blunders.

During their flight to Antibes, he'd noticed her tugging at her sleeve constantly. He stopped her twice, but soon she returned to it. So, he allowed her to do it since they were alone, not without a big smile on his face.

He liked Mollie's little quirks. He suspected his bride was nervous, with their wedding night upon them.

He felt protective towards her, and he hadn't even realised it. He had been protecting her since she'd agreed to marry him. He couldn't help thinking, under all that cleverness, there was a rather shy girl, adorable and vulnerable in the midst. She was pig-headed as hell and feisty, but people could take advantage of her. *Clever, yes! But she is too young. Too naïve in many respects.* So, he was there to protect her, to guide her.

He adored the way she beamed at him; her smile captivated him. When her cheeks flushed, it made his heart miss a beat.

Even though she allowed him kisses for the cameras, he loved those short moments of closeness. He revelled in her company more than he would admit to. He enjoyed spending time with her.

She got under his skin. So, sometimes he occupied himself with work to keep the distance between them, but it was difficult.

He had endured over two months with no sex, the longest he had been without since he was a young lad. Not for want of trying, but Mollie kept firm. So, now after their wedding day, he was looking forward to spending time with her, alone.

In the weeks leading up to the wedding, he noted that she was getting nervous, but Zac thought it was pre-wedding jitters. Little did he know that his bride had secrets.

Though, he soon came to realise his new bride was not a pushover.

She was stubborn. Something he would have to work on. But he wanted a woman with spirit, with character. And Mollie had lots of it. He appreciated a challenge.

He was proud of her and thanked his lucky star for throwing this woman into his path. Was he getting too attached to her? He needed to be careful. This was a transitory situation, just for the Board's purposes, just long enough to turn his image around.

This relationship was not a real one, not a real marriage. It was all fake. He reminded himself often enough.

He knew she was aware of the transitory nature of their relationship, rather more than he was. He wondered why. Most women would have capitulated to him long ago, but not Mollie. Though sometimes, he sensed her hesitation; it had tempted her… several times!

But something held her back.

He had to keep his wits about him, or he could risk falling for her.

He looked at her when he heard her sigh and wondered what had gone through her mind.

A few weeks of relaxation on their honeymoon were now looming ahead of him. He intended to get to know his young bride better, and at some point, he would have her in his arms. Perhaps even tonight! He desired her with a passion.

THEY LANDED IN NICE.

Mollie stepped outside the aircraft and stopped for a split second on the top step of the stairs.

It was the end of May, and spring in its purest and delightful form hit her. She looked up at the bright, blue sky. Sparse and wispy white clouds floating aimlessly on the horizon, while the sun caressed her face. She smiled a languid and contented grin. After the harsh winter, and all her troubles, she welcomed the spring sun. It felt snug and cozy.

Zac offered his hands to help her down the stairs. She inhaled, closed her eyes for an instant, and then took it. And as she went down the stairs, her heart lightened. Her hand in his, the radiance of the sun, and the limpid blue sky made her feel at ease, cheerful. It calmed her.

At the heart of Europe, where the southern Alps meet

the Mediterranean Sea, protected from the cold north winds by the Alps in its hinterland, the Cote D'Azur was magnificent. And she was ready for it.

Spring came early to the French Riviera, with flowers in full bloom wallowing in a soft, warm breeze and gardens filled with an explosion of colours and exhilarating scents. In particular, at the height of spring, and that year, it was just the perfect season.

So that day, as Mollie entered the car which would take her to their honeymoon's home, the warm breeze and the sun filled her spirit with joy for the first time in months. The French Riviera would be a real treat for her.

Perhaps this won't be so bad, she thought with eagerness.

And her body responded to the lovely effect of the dazzling sunshine. She wondered if, to that warm day, would follow a hot night.

Will Zac keep me warm tonight? she mused when he would claim her. *Do I want him to?*

She knew he had every intention of doing so. She could sense it. She had seen lust in his eyes. She smiled to herself at the prospect.

She didn't venture such fantasies often. But a lascivious thought, in which she saw her body wrapped around Zac's frame, came to mind. She blushed. Her face glancing out of the car's window, she avoided embarrassment.

They had half an hour's drive from Nice Airport to Antibes, on the Riviera. The car bordered the spectacular scenic route on their way. Suddenly, the Mediterranean Sea opened up in front of her, powerful and majestic, its crystal aquamarine waters giving way to slight changes of colours as the sunlight hit its surface. It was so glossy and vibrant and laid out like a cerulean mantle in all its splendour. The view of the sea, with its backdrop scenery, was extraordinary.

The French Riviera was a land of contrasts. In places,

she saw a rugged coastline, high mountains, and steep, rocky cliffs, while in some other areas, golden sand blessed the coastline.

Her first reaction, it was to die for! She loved it, a smile on her face all the way to the house.

After months of stress and unhappiness, she was enjoying herself. A giggle escaped her lips; she couldn't help it. She covered her mouth with a hand to stifle it, but the excitement within her made it drift into the air.

It enchanted him.

She pointed eagerly at famous landmarks as the scenery unfolded on her way.

She was light-hearted, like a child in a candy store. She side glanced at him and saw an amused look on his face, but she didn't care. For once, she was jubilant, and no one could spoil it.

They entered Antibes, a smart Mediterranean resort in the Alpes-Maritimes department of southeastern France, on the Cote d'Azur between Nice and Cannes. Antibes was a fascinating place, with its charming old town and its classy marina full of magnificent yachts and sailing boats.

"The town has fine beaches and museums, and it even has plenty of night life," Zac emphasised.

I bet he experienced plenty of nightlife here, she mused with a slight pang of jealousy, despite her admiration for the landscape.

As they drove along the coast towards his grandmother's villa, Zac asked his driver, Henri, for a diversion to town for her.

They stopped, got out of the car, and walked towards the marina with expensive yachts. Zac gave her a peek of his father's large sailboat, a magnificent Grand Soleil 50 sail cruiser, complete with living room, shower room, kitchen and sleeping berths. She gasped at the splendour and refinement of its rosewood interior. She launched herself on a sleeping berth. He laughed, kissing her hand. To her delight, he promised to take her sailing during their stay.

Then, they moved on to the old town, behind the ancient and impressive stone walls, to the many squares that housed elegant cafes and restaurants. They entered the market with all its aromatic spices and delights. Everything about this quaint town was mesmerising. Antibes seemed magical to her.

Back in the car, they drove along the Promenade Amiral De Grasse, above the coast, with an amazing view of the bay and Cap D'Antibes.

It is glorious!

Zac pointed out to her the Archaeology Museum sitting atop the promenade in the magnificent old Bastion of St Andre, a seventeenth-century fortress.

Stunning!

As she looked out to the sea on Cape D'Antibes, she noticed yachts and sailing boats gliding on the water.

Enchanting! And here she was, too. The place inspired her. It lifted her spirit.

No wonder Picasso spent six months here, painting masterpieces, she thought in awe.

"Can you see the Museum?" Zac said on cue, as if he had read her mind. He pointed to the impressive building as they passed by the Chateau Grimaldi, which housed the Picasso Museum.

"Oh, wow." He spellbound her.

"You'll love it. It houses one of the best collections of Picasso's in France. You'll adore Antibes; you'll see," he said, animated. He caressed her face, and without thinking, she leaned into his hand for a moment.

"Do you have one?" she asked, glancing up at him.

"What?" he questioned.

"A Picasso," she said with laughter in her eyes, expecting him to call her silly.

"Yes, my father has one in his vault. My great-grandfather bought it from the artist himself."

"Really? From the master himself?" she cried out.

"Honest!" He chuckled at her astonishment and crossed his heart with his fingers to make the point.

She smiled, but her eyes went big, like moons, with incredulity.

"Wow." She shook her head. She had married into a family that owned a Picasso, incredible.

But she couldn't bring herself to believe it, so outlandish. It didn't ring true, even to her own ears, but if he said so…

"True. I assure you," he said, recognising her doubt.

"Oh, yes, if you say so," she said, blushing.

"Remind me to show it to you one day," he said.

She nodded eagerly.

"Amaze me! What else do you have that will surprise me?" she asked, staring at him with her baby blue eyes wide.

But Zac gave her a playful look and a boyish grin, and he glanced down at his groin, raising an elegant brow.

She followed his eyes. And she snorted with an unladylike noise when her eyes landed on his groin, with a hand over her mouth. He winked at her, and she laughed and blushed at the same time. He couldn't help but laugh with her. Instinctively, he raised a hand to caress a strand of hair out of her face and kissed her hair.

His naughty schoolboy humour was a revelation, and it had them in stitches all the way to the house. It was a side to Zac that she hadn't seen before. He was playful and charming, a welcome surprise after months of stress. He put her at ease.

She wished she had the guts to go for his lips, hard and fast! But she didn't. *Sweet Jesus,* she cursed silently.

He was even more handsome when he laughed. With a carefree, unreserved, and relaxed air about him, he was so lovable and dashing.

Maybe that's the real him? A playful and charming rascal.

She accepted the fact that he was gorgeous. But she couldn't look at him without pinching herself. And this glorious man was her husband.

Good God! The realisation hit her, and her breath hitched.

Sometimes they had gone to a gala event, and he'd looked so handsome, it had taken her breath away.

She once saw a woman trip, flat on her face, when she missed a step looking at him. The effect he had on men and women!

And he was her man. *At least on the surface, don't forget!* She forced herself to breathe.

He had charm too, and plenty of it. So, she liked him. In particular, he was irresistible when he was playful like that day.

With his eyes focused on her, it seemed like the world ceased to exit. As if for him, there was only her on the planet.

His brooding eyes were so sexy, she would have to watch herself.

Ahh, how revealing that photo had been. *That expression in his eyes!* She knew now how it felt to have that look on her.

She sighed. It was as if his eyes caressed her skin, igniting her with pleasure and fire.

How would she manage him? She realised perhaps she was out of her depth with this man. And then she reminded herself that this was transitory; he was not her man.

It would be difficult to keep her wits about her, she knew, but she would have to try hard. She had entered a world where everything was flawless and perfect. A world to bring her happiness, the company of this handsome and playful man, the gorgeous landscape, the emerald sea waters on her doorstep, and the blazing sun caressing her skin.

It was a place to brighten her darkened soul.

But would it last? *No! Not when he knew the truth.*

Chapter 7

She had a glimpse of his home in the distance as they were about to enter the gates to the property. The white-washed villa with colonnades stood large and imposing in a quiet private road off the Boulevard du Cap, in the heart of Cap d'Antibes, close to the beaches at Garoupe, Oden, and L'Ilette. The house, a massive structure with eight bedrooms, stood in extensive and beautiful gardens. It also boasted a tennis court and a magnificent pool.

On the long drive to the house, she had a view of the gardens, which featured a small Moorish pavilion with internal and external mirrors; it reflected the light and the water beautifully, like a celestial glow. From there, steps led to the landing area of a private marina, where a speedboat docked.

The splendid waterfront loggia, meshing with the sea, offered its far-reaching views.

The terraced gardens boasted a harmonic coexistence of old trees and plants, such as palm trees, scented citruses, shrubs, multicoloured azaleas, and roses. High hedges of pink and red camellias bordered the perimeter walls, while flower beds of every colour, shape, and intoxicating scent enclosed the footpaths.

Marble statues decorated the gardens. A stone fountain provided water for the resident birds in the grounds. It was enchanting. The villa was remarkable, splendid! *If there is a heaven, it must look like this.* She felt delighted. Her eyes were wide with amazement, capturing it all in.

She had been in his elegant town house in Oxford where they would live, and it was grand, but this place was something else. The place was surrounded, on a one-hundred-and-eighty-degree radius, by deep waters that changed from blue to turquoise, and every shade in between, as far as the eye could see. It was magical, and she had not even set foot inside the house yet.

She grasped his hand, as she did when she felt nervous.

He smiled at her.

For a second, he let go and put his arms around her shoulders, tightening her to him protectively. With a natural gesture, he kissed the top of her head.

The car stopped in front of the house.

They got out, then he took her hand in his again, and he led her up the three steps to the portico.

Marie Therese, his tall, white-haired housekeeper, was standing outside the front door of the house.

He smiled at the woman, kissed her cheeks in greeting in the local manner, and said in perfect French, "Bonjour, ça-Bonjour, ça va bien?"

"Ça va! Félicitations et bienvenue, monsieur. Congratulations and welcome, madame," Marie Therese responded in typical French fashion, and in English for her with a tender smile.

"Félicitations, madame, monsieur," Henri, Marie

Therese's bald and rotund husband, echoed after driving them home, mirroring his wife's enthusiasm.

Mollie smiled at the couple. "Thank you," she said. But before she had the chance to say anything else, Zac lifted Mollie into his arms and stepped over the threshold.

Mollie let out a squeal, halfway between a scream and a giggle. She was not expecting to be lifted into his arms.

And the melodious sound of her giggles echoed around the house, striking a bolt in his guts.

"For good luck," he said to her, his face so close to hers that she could breathe in the intoxicating whoosh of his aftershave. It was that tangy, spicy, and pleasant scent that was so him. She inhaled and closed her eyes. Suddenly, he brushed his lips on hers.

It took her by surprise, but he winked when she opened her eyes. She rewarded him with a blush. She got a warm and cozy feeling.

For the first time in months, she felt his kiss. He had brushed his lips on hers for the cameras at galas and such occasions before, but she had been too self-conscious and nervous during those situations to notice it.

This time was different. Even though it was just a light kiss, just a sweep of his lips on hers, the softness and warmth of his lips pleased her. And suddenly, she had butterflies in her stomach. A giddiness ran through her body.

At that moment, she would have gladly kissed him, hard and fast, like she had done that time at the Norwegian embassy, but she held back.

She gave him the sweet smile he adored so much instead. Looking into his large and brooding eyes, something warm burst into her heart. She didn't understand what it was, but it was there all the same.

He gazed at her in his arms; and she knew he felt the

pinch too, but Marie Therese said something to them. He released her back down, the spell broken.

She would have to watch herself. *This is not real.* Perhaps if she kept repeating it to herself, she would be fine. *We are not a couple.* But then, he took her hand.

"Let me show you around the house," he said. Her palm felt small and snug in his, but she liked it there. She got used to holding his hand a lot. It reassured her. It made her feel safe in her new uncertain world.

The house dominant colour was white. It was a rather feminine house, but then it was his grandmother's. Over the years, he'd used the house as much as his granny. Of all the houses in his family, this was his favourite. He loved the house and Antibes; thus, he had chosen it for their honeymoon.

There was white everywhere, in the massive kitchen and in the grand sitting, dining, and living rooms, except for his study. His grandmother had carved a study in the house for him. His space, so, he could spend time with her even when he had work to do. His study was a sedate and masculine affair, but the rest of the house seemed almost ethereal if it weren't for blue and orange accents throughout the ground floor lifting it to reality.

Mollie loved Antibes, the house, the gardens, but mostly him. The way he kept touching her hair, caressing her face, and planting little kisses on her forehead or nose, fascinated her. His kisses warmed her toes, and she didn't mind it one bit.

Before the wedding, she thought she would dread this day. Now that it was upon her, she rather enjoyed it, *a lot!*

This house was to be her home for a few weeks. *And Zac is my husband.* She pinched herself on the arm to make sure she was really there, and she smiled the widest grin ever!

An arrangement! She reminded herself again, it was fake.

Remember, we are not a real couple. It's an illusion! Don't get carried away by fleeting moments like this! Keep yourself grounded. She cursed silently. *All of this is transient, short-lived. Don't forget!*

His kisses had unsettled her. She was not his real wife; he had hired her to do a job. She had a task to do, that was all. She couldn't allow emotions to get involved. It was too risky.

Mollie recalled her ex-lover's words when he'd said she would have an amazing life. He could be right. But God would not allow her to enjoy all of this. Not when knowing of her falsehood and deceitfulness. She was not a religious person by any stretch of the imagination, but she believed in Karma. Somehow, she felt guilty and ashamed, out of her depth with her deception. She wasn't used to telling lies. She felt like a rat for having lied to this caring, lovely man.

She gulped and shivered. But she put the depressing thought out of her mind.

His wife now, she would make the most of it. There was no point in fighting it. She was where she was, and she needed to do a good job at being his hired wife.

She wanted to make Zac proud of her. That was the least she could do for him, after telling him blatant lies.

The perfect wife for him, to please the Board!

For the next three years, *if it lasts that long,* she would remove any thoughts of her ex-lover pushing her into this and his vile behaviour. She wouldn't think about what he might say or do when he discovered she didn't want him anymore. *Or, God forbid,* if Zac were to find out about her ex-lover and who he was.

So far, it had not been difficult to push these thoughts aside with Zac at her side. Easy, in particular, with his kindness and thoughtfulness, it gave her strength.

They reached the pool with its beautiful surroundings.

"Oh, this is so beautiful. The house is a dream, and the

gardens are so luscious. The view is amazing! Even the pool is so inviting," she blurted out.

He gave her a big hug.

"I have a conference call for an hour. Why don't you change and lie by the pool with a drink, relax for a while?" he suggested.

"Oh, I would love that."

"You deserve it. You have worked so hard, and you've done well. I'm proud of you. You fascinated the Board, and that's not an easy task!" He kissed the tip of her nose.

She beamed from ear to ear, but a flush crept up her neck. Why did she always blush every time he touched her or looked at her? *He must think I am a giddy schoolgirl.*

"Marie will show you to your bedroom, then you can get changed and go down to the pool. Enjoy yourself. I'll join you when I'm finished."

"Sure."

"But, Mollie, beware; the sun may not seem strong, but it is. So, be careful. You are so fair," he warned her protectively.

She smiled. It felt nice to have someone care for her for a change.

BEDROOMS HAD BEEN one of the many arguments they'd had before the wedding, their sleeping arrangements a bone of contention.

Zac wanted her in his bed every night, but she had insisted on having a separate bedroom. He'd refused for weeks until they reached an impasse. Then, he yielded and agreed.

She had won the battle. But he'd manoeuvred other

aspects of her life. It couldn't be helped; he was her boss. She had a job to do.

So, she allowed him to have control, but also because she felt guilty about lying to him and needed to expiate her deception.

Though, she had the distinct impression that he might end up controlling sex too, when they got down to it. Soon, she dared hope for a moment.

In the weeks leading to the wedding, she had noticed that he became bolder in his touches and kisses. *Would he take control of that part of her life?*

To be honest, she'd gotten too attached to him, so she didn't mind it. Sometimes she craved his touch, and when he did, she wished his hands would linger on her longer.

He was a handsome man with genuine charm, a playful personality, and she liked his company. Through the months, he had grown on her, and she hadn't even realised it until the day they arrived in Antibes.

Once she got past his somehow arrogant and confident exterior, he was a caring and thoughtful man. Little details delighted her. He would ask her if she was *okay*, often. He held her hand in public, put his arms around her, picking up the mood when she needed a hug. He also came to her aid when people had been unpleasant to her. He seemed to sense when she needed him. But he was not overwhelming her. Though he liked control, she didn't feel like he confined her. She was free to be herself. He reached that balance where she was comfortable with him; protected, wanted, and still free.

But she shouldn't read too much into it. It would be too dangerous.

I am his hired wife; that's all I am, an employee!

NOW, in her magnificent and massive white bedroom with scattered turquoise and lavender touches, she looked around for her luggage. Marie Therese explained that her clothes were already in the wardrobe. She smiled at the woman and glanced around the room.

The centre piece was the enormous bed, with a small, triangular canopy draping softly down its sides. The bed was bigger than a king-size, elegant in white pristine covers, and masses of pillows in lavender and turquoise, coordinating it with the canopy overhead. Similar colour accents could be found across the room. Sea landscapes, framed in soft gold, adorned the walls.

She studied the beautiful white dressing table, an antique Louis XIV. She brushed her fingers along it, admiring all its sinuous forms. *Stunning!* She noticed the white sofa at the other end of the room, with inviting turquoise and lavender cushions too. She smiled. Her beautiful and elegant bedroom was bigger than any place she'd ever had, and she marvelled.

A giggle escaped her, but she tried to repress it in her throat.

Even a drink cabinet in my room, well, what can I say... wait until Kathryn sees this!

Then she opened the balcony. With the view of the sea displayed in front of her, she giggled without constraint with a hand over her mouth, and the array of colours and the intoxicating scents coming up from the garden flooded her senses. It seemed to her; she was in Paradise, a long way from her student shared house in Oxford or her mother's provincial hotel in Devon.

Marie Therese then left her to it.

Mollie took out her black bikini and changed into it. She stared at herself in the mirror, but she didn't like it. Her skin was too pale, so she changed into a light, leafy green bikini instead. She looked at herself again. This one seemed more suited to her fair skin and red hair.

She was anxious. Zac would join her later, so she wanted to look her best for him. She glanced at herself in the mirror one last time, and then she sighed—nothing she could do about her figure; that was it.

Oh dear, he will have one look at me and… she started thinking, but then she concluded there was no point in dwelling on her body. She could do with colour. She was naturally pale, more so after the long winter.

Well, at least there is plenty of sun, she mused, contented.

She thought of Zac. They got along fine, but she doubted he liked her physically. *Will he appreciate my body? No, if the women he usually goes for are any sign. Too bad for him now. He married me, and he was the one who demanded monogamy. So there!*

She speculated how he liked his women. But she didn't think he had a type, as long as they had big tits and big asses, all things she didn't have.

Mollie was willowy with small, pert breasts, and a small but perfectly formed ass. *Zac will have to do with small and willowy.* She sighed. It was useless trying. She should be past that, but she wasn't. In reality, she worried, like any other girl.

She went down to the pool and sat on a lounger in the sun, but she felt tired again. The last few months of hard work were catching up with her. She needed to relax and clear her mind. She had a book with her, so maybe that would help.

A short time later, she was resting in the sun, with a delicious drink that Marie Therese had prepared for her. She liked the drink. *No idea what it is, but it's yummy.* The sun was caressing her skin, and the beautiful scents of the garden were all around her. So, she made herself comfortable reading, while she waited for Zac.

Chapter 8

Zac was in his study, on a call. He stood, pacing while he listened to the caller at the other end of the phone.

Finley Harman was his number two in his security firm, and one of his longstanding friends. The son of the driver in the Sorensen household, he had known him forever.

When Zac's grandfather died, he'd left his friend a small legacy.

So, they had grown up together. But the man would protect Zac with his life.

Sometimes, he joined Zac at galas or events whenever he needed a bodyguard. He was unobtrusive, despite his height.

Finley went into the army after university. His athletic body made him an expert soldier in the special forces. His tall frame and his strong, manly features gave him a handsome but rugged look.

Zac always wondered when the man slept. It seemed he was up all the time, day or night. Sometimes, he wondered if his friend was human at all.

But the man was clever too. He had risen to the rank of

captain while in Iraq and Afghanistan, during hair-raising assignments. Three years ago, wounded on a mission, Finley decided that a desk job in the army was not for him.

So, he'd returned home and joined his friend's business instead; his cleverness made him a brilliant strategist and intelligence specialist, his expertise useful to the company. So, when Finley left the army, it was a natural conclusion to join Zac's security firm.

That day, the two men were on a business call. He looked out of the window. While his friend was still talking over the phone, Zac saw Mollie near the pool.

"Fin, hold on for a second, please," he said.

"Sure."

Zac called his housekeeper.

"Marie, can you check with my wife, so she doesn't burn herself in the sun? I have work to do, and I'll be in the study for a while."

The call took longer than expected, and he sighed, *unavoidable.*

Looking at her in the distance in her green leafy bikini, he lost his train of thought. He hoped he could untie those strings holding her bikini up. When he glimpsed her beautiful backside as she changed positions on the sun-lounger, he desired her. He wished to get his hands on that pert and firm little ass of hers and do naughty things to her.

He inhaled. *She has to change her mind on separate bedrooms,* he thought. He wanted her with him, in his bed. He was confident he would win her over, but Zac would need to go slowly. His wife was not like his previous women. He would take his time with her, be patient and gentle.

He had kissed her for the cameras, though, lately, he felt something he had not experienced before. In the last few months, he had grown to love the mellow sound of her voice, the sweet tingling of her laugh. He loved when her face flushed, the way she smiled. She was clever, no doubt. She was his equal but for money; he was proud of her. But most of all, he found her *adorable. That word again!* He couldn't help it.

She had done an incredible job for him in the last few months. Everyone felt their charade was real. Even his formidable grandmother believed it. But lately, Zac had a problem separating facts from fiction. *It was not real love. Right?*

His mother liked her. His dad told him he had been a lucky bastard to meet someone like her.

"This young woman is a rare pearl. The Board likes her, and they are not easily pleased. She is doing miracles for you. Please don't screw this up," his father ventured with a warning in his voice.

So, it had not taken long for his family to worship her, and he agreed on that point.

When he kissed her, Zac couldn't quite explain why, but he liked it. He hoped she would too.

While his feelings blossomed for her, she was his hired wife. *A business arrangement, pure and simple. Not true. I must not forget that.*

Was he getting too close to her, too attached to her? He reminded himself this would be short-lived. Long enough for him to build up his image for the Board's purposes, but transitory.

He referred to the file Finley had compiled on her when they first settled on the marriage proposal. Finley assured him, she was suitable, and everything was in order, even though his friend warned him it was a crazy idea.

His three close friends were the only ones who knew the truth about the arrangement with his wife. He never kept any secrets from them. They'd tried to warn him, but he wouldn't listen. They told him to be careful. Or, at worse, it was a damn foolish idea, as Alex repeated endless times. But

Zac skimmed over their worries with little interest. He had always known what he wanted, and somehow, he wanted this slip of a girl. How he came to that conclusion, he didn't know.

So, now, two months later, he wanted to read her file again, to study the woman who was now his wife, to discover details of the woman who put his feelings on new grounds, in unchartered territory. The girl who, even if temporarily, had upended his life. He wanted to know everything about her.

The monogamy clause in the contract had thrown her. He realised that. *She didn't expect that!* Though she didn't object, she was pensive afterwards. Did she have someone else then? She had said, "no." She'd reassured him that she had no boyfriend.

Regardless, he was confident she would comply with the monogamy clause. He couldn't say why, but for the duration of their contract, he knew she would be his and his alone.

She would give him her devotion. He couldn't define the reason, but his gut instinct told him so. No other reason! But his companions warned him not to get too carried away, to be vigilant. So, they had agreed that Finley's team would watch her for a while.

But now that he'd found her, Zac had no intention of sharing her with anyone.

"Zac? Are you listening?" Finley asked twice, returning Zac's thoughts to the call.

―――――――

"MRS. SORENSEN, do you have sun lotion? The sunlight is hot." Marie brought her another drink.

"Yes, I do. Please, call me Mollie," she answered with a grin.

"He said you would ask me to, but Zac stressed we must

call you Mrs. Sorensen, until you get used to your new name."

"Huh? Well, that's silly," she replied, lifting her head from the sun-lounger to look at the housekeeper, but the woman grinned at her.

"Do you need anything else?"

"No. I am fine, thank you."

Marie left her to bask in the sunlight. She watched the lady walk away.

Mrs. Sorensen, um… it sounds good, Mollie smirked. She put sun cream on her tummy, but she hated how sticky the lotion felt on her skin. So, she decided against it. She left it alone with a grimace and shrugged her shoulders. She would not stay in the sunlight long, a few minutes at most. So, it wouldn't be a big deal. *Besides, after the long winter, the warmth feels lovely on my skin.*

So, she placed herself more comfortably on the sun-lounger and continued to read her book with her back to the sun. But soon she yawned, slouching. She felt too comfortable, and her eyes got droopy.

It could have been the heat, or the drinks, or all those months of hard work and stress, or a long wedding day finally catching up with her, perhaps all of those things combined, but she fell into a deep sleep.

HOURS LATER, Zac was still at his desk. He wanted to cut the call short, but a few loose ends needed his attention. He was thorough in his business, a workaholic. So, he hopped onto another business issue, then another, and another again.

"Jesus, this is your honeymoon. We've been on the call for nearly three hours," Finley warned him with a laugh.

"Three hours? No!"

"Yes, man. If I were your bride, I would be annoyed by now," Finley taunted.

"Well, that's why you are not my bride then. Besides, this is an arrangement…" he responded drily.

"Seriously, man, business is under control. I am sure, she hoped to be in bed with you by now." Finley chuckled.

"Hey, hey, that's my wife you're talking about."

"Well, maybe it will get your ass into gear. Go shag her." And Finley cut off the call.

"Fin? Great." Zac sighed, a bit annoyed! Though, it was true; he should return to Mollie. Besides, he was hungry by now. *Whoa, way past lunchtime,* he thought, staring at his watch. He had spent way too long on that damn call. He rolled his eyes. He must leave work aside for the honeymoon if he wished to get to know her better.

As he stepped outside his office, Marie told him lunch was ready.

"Great, I'm starving. I'll get Mollie."

He found her by the pool, still on the sun-lounger, lying on her tummy. She was asleep. He sat on the border of her chair and caressed her hair back from her profile. There, asleep, she seemed so sweet and peaceful. Angelic, and he smiled, *adorable!*

"Mollie, wake up." But he noticed her skin was bright red. Her shoulders and back seemed to be in flames. Her beautiful, shapely legs were scarlet. He tried to wake her up again.

"Huh?" She opened her eyes, but they were fuzzy.

"How long were you in the sun? Your skin is bright red!" he exclaimed, now standing and scanning her body.

She looked at him but couldn't focus; she kept squinting. She struggled to get up, but halfway to a standing position, she practically fell. Zac caught her just in time.

"Easy," he said, steadying her, but she leaned heavily on him.

"Sorry, I feel dizzy... a headache," she mumbled, but she struggled to rise on her own two feet again.

"Jesus, how long have you been lying in the sun?" he asked again, but before she could speak, her legs gave way. She lost consciousness, and he caught her.

He sat on the sun-lounger with her in his arms. "Mollie, can you hear me?" Zac tried to focus her, patting her face, but she opened and closed her eyes. *Good God,* he cursed.

"I, my head... my legs, cramps..." she mumbled incoherently.

"Mollie?" he repeated, fretting.

It all happened quickly. She tried to stand up again, but she stumbled. She felt too dizzy, and she vomited right there. Then, she fell down on him, unconscious.

He cursed, alarmed that something was wrong. He pulled her up gently and ran to the house with her in his arms. "Marie, Marie," he yelled.

The housekeeper came out of the dining room, and it scared the life out of her, seeing the young girl like that.

He ran up the curved, marble staircase with Mollie in his arms, and Marie followed. The lady opened the bedroom door for him, and then he placed his bride down on the bed.

She was still unconscious.

He lifted her eyelids. "Was she in the sun all this time?" he asked as he touched her forehead.

Mollie was burning up. Her translucent skin was blazing red and hot.

"I don't know," Marie responded, wringing her hands with concern.

"Get the necessary items to cool her skin, then call the doctor to come immediately," Zac ordered.

Marie returned a few minutes later with two flannels and a bowl of fresh water.

Zac placed a damp flannel on Mollie's burning forehead. Then, placing her on her side, he started sponging her red skin with cool water. Her shoulders first, and then her back, to cool it down. He followed it with a lotion containing aloe vera to sooth her reddened skin, something his grandmother had done countless times when he was a young boy and had overindulged in the sun.

Mollie's skin felt burning and clammy to his touch. She was feverish, her forehead hot.

"Doctor Fernier is on his way," Marie said a few minutes later.

"Thank you." But he was frantic now. What the hell, had he not told her to be careful in the sun? Zac cursed, black foul-mouthed words. Almost three hours in the sun, the likelihood was high that it had made her ill.

After a meticulous visit, Doctor Fernier confirmed that Mollie had severe sunstroke. She had complained of a headache and dizziness, and she had a rapid heartbeat and shallow breathing. Her pale skin was as red as a fire engine. But worst of all, she had developed a high fever. Those were the symptoms of sunstroke.

The doctor said to watch her for the next day or two and to keep her temperature down. If her fever rose any higher, they were to call him or go to hospital. He prescribed a remedy to lower the high fever and told Zac to continue to keep her skin cool and hydrated. He would have to be vigilant.

Zac's stomach was in knots with worry.

Several times during the weeks leading to the wedding, Mollie had complained of tiredness. The stress of it all had taken a toll on her. He had pushed her too hard. *It's my fault,* he fretted but tried to be calm. Still, he cursed so obscenely that an old sailor on a pirate ship would have learned a new word or two.

ZAC DIDN'T MOVE from the chair at her bedside for hours, changing often a damp flannel on her forehead to lower her temperature. She was in and out of consciousness as the day wore on because of the fever, intermingled with sleep. Her temperature had not risen, but neither had it dropped. A small consolation, but she was stable.

He kept caressing her face with his fingers, a feeling of tenderness creeping up inside him. He would protect her now. He had pushed her too hard. Yes, the sun, the heat, the hot weather, all contributed to it, but he couldn't help thinking if she had not been so tired, this wouldn't have happened.

He reached the drink cabinet and poured himself a brandy. He took a good gulp of it, the sensation in his throat, as the warm liquid made its way down, soothing him.

So, he kept a close watch on her. He didn't want to lose her. She was too precious.

He heard her soft voice. She mumbled something in her feverish state, but he couldn't quite make out what she said.

A few hours later, when the first signs of sleep crept upon him, he stepped out onto the balcony to get some fresh air for a few minutes. He needed to keep alert.

Suddenly, he saw her standing in the middle of the room as if in a trance. He rushed inside. "Mollie, bloody hell! What are you doing up? You are burning up again." He took hold of her and placed an arm along her waist.

She glanced at him with wide eyes, as if she had not recognised him. But she went with him as quietly as a lamb.

He smoothed the bed covers over her, but she shivered uncontrollably.

"I'm cold," she whispered, despite the warm night and her high fever. So, he shut the balcony. He got into bed with her and wrapped his body around hers to keep her warm. Zac cradled her in his arms until her shivering subsided. She closed her eyes, but she was still burning with fever. He caressed her face with the back of his hands.

"Please read to me," she whispered in a moment of clarity. He took the book from the nightstand and started reading to her. A few minutes later, he put it down, back on the bedside table. She had drifted to sleep. He was still holding her. She looked delicate and fragile in his arms. His heart warmed to her and missed a beat.

But it troubled him. "*It'll get worse before it gets better,*" the doctor had said.

So, he prepared for a long night.

Early the next morning, when it was barely light yet, he was sitting by her bedside when there was a knock at the door. "Come in," he said.

"This is Nurse Louise. She looks after your granny when she is in town and needs her injections," Marie Therese said when she introduced the other woman.

"Yes." He smiled, recognizing her.

The nurse greeted him.

"Why don't you let Louise look after your wife while you get some rest and something to eat?"

"Well, I—"

"Go on; she will be fine with me." Louise grinned, but he seemed hesitant.

"Zac, it's dawn and you haven't eaten or slept at all since your arrival yesterday morning, and after the wedding too. So, it must be two days now. You need to eat," the housekeeper insisted.

She was right; he was hungry and exhausted, so he agreed.

But the night had revealed his feelings for Mollie. Feelings he hadn't known he harboured. There was the concern as a friend, sure. But the tenderness, the devotion, the affection for his bride were new to him. Probably there from day one, but they came to the fore now that she needed him. They became real to him, nestled inside him.

"How is she?" he asked the nurse when he returned to her room after a good breakfast, a shower, and three hours' sleep.

"She is stable. No change. I suspect we might see an improvement tomorrow; I hope," the nurse said. He smiled, but the strain of several nights with barely any sleep was evident despite his rest.

"Do you want a break? I'll watch over her," Zac said.

The nurse nodded. She was a plump and jovial woman, and she had known Zac, through his grandmother, for many years. The woman could be crude. She was forthright, knowing Zac and Mollie were newlyweds.

"What were you making her do?" she asked with a mischievous grin.

"What?" he asked her with a puzzled look.

"Your wife kept mumbling in her sleep. The high fever is making her delirious, which is to be expected in the circumstances. At first, I didn't understand what she said, then I figured it out."

"Delirious?" he asked, but he knew Mollie had mumbled incoherently through the night too. "What did she say?"

"*Please, stop it,*" Louise repeated as she raised her eyebrows.

"Umm?"

"*Please, don't make me do it.*" The nurse continued, mimicking Mollie's melodious voice again with a wink.

"No idea," he said, shaking his head, annoyed. A flush crept up his face. Zac had not made love to Mollie yet, not even a passionate kiss since the one at the Norwegian embassy's ball over a month back, so there was no reason for him to flush. Perhaps, it was more about his desire for her, the lustful thoughts about her that had tormented him for the last few months that gave him away.

The nurse smiled at his momentary boyish flush.

"Oh, never mind. I will be half an hour," the nurse said and left the room.

Tired and worried, he ignored the woman's words. He didn't know what to make of Mollie's mutterings. She was sick, and the high fever was making her mumble nonsense, perhaps a dream? A nightmare? So, he shrugged it off and dismissed it.

He settled into his comfy chair to watch over her. Fifteen minutes later, he sat on the edge of Mollie's bed, drying her perspiring forehead. His heart knotted to see her like this. His sweet Mollie was ill, and he was powerless. He missed her sweet and beaming smile. He missed her company, her laugh. He missed her! He hadn't realised how attached he had become to her until then. He sighed in frustration.

Mollie's fever was still high. He caressed her sweet face, but it agitated her in her sleep. She was restless, her head bobbing. She started mumbling again.

At first, he couldn't make out what she said, but soon her voice became high pitched, frantic. She sounded frightened, but her meaning became unequivocal. "No. I don't want to. Please," she muttered in her sleep. She was in a state of delirium because of the high fever. She tossed her head left to right and back again, droplets of sweat visible again on her forehead and upper lip. She was clearly agitated.

"Shush, you're fine. I'm here," he whispered tenderly, mopping her forehead.

"I don't want to do it, please." She tossed out the words in her frenzy.

"Please, don't make me do it. I'll be good," she murmured, trembling in delirium.

"I beg you, please," she pleaded, then she became incoherent again. She perspired again and there were tears streaming down her face. Distress was visible on her face.

Zac's face hardened. He sat motionless, listening to her while she continued mumbling in fear and confusion in her delirium, but there was no mistaking her words.

It dumbfounded him. *Is it possible? No. No, incoherent mumblings of a sick, feverish woman, that's it. The delirium is making her utter nonsense.* He picked up the odd word here and there after that.

He had not realised he held his breath. Then he released it. He sat closer to her still, on the edge of her bed, and caressed her face.

"Shush, you are safe. I won't let anyone hurt you," he whispered to her.

Her murmuring continued soon enough. "No wedding. Please, I beg you," she kept mumbling, but this time her words clear to him, unmistakable. "Don't make me do it... I don't want to marry him," she said in her fever. Then she repeated it in a whisper, sobbing in her sleep.

He froze. His sweet Mollie was shaking, but her remarks pierced his heart. Her mumbling was now frantic.

Could it be? No, no! Am I wrong? I must be. A spark of hope still crossed his heart. But it was short-lived.

"Please, I implore you..." she stressed with a pause, "...I don't want to marry Zac." And he stilled when she said his name. But her fervent pleading lingered in her delirium, "No, no, please, don't make me marry Zac." Her words were chopped but clear as the sky. Her agonising plead went on for a few more moments. It was heartfelt.

He was powerless and struck by the revelation! If there was ambiguity to her mumbling before, there was none now. She had uttered his name. Mollie had blurted out her secret in her feverish mumblings.

"Shush, you are safe now," he whispered, despite his hurt. He cradled her in his arms. His arms were still around her when she calmed down and went back to sleep.

Suddenly, it all fell into place. He realised it had been a scam. His Mollie had not wanted to marry him. She had someone else. This person had put her up to this. His face set in a controlled mask, but it gutted him! Now, it all made sense to him. When he thought she suffered from pre-wedding jitters, she was despairing, about to do something she didn't want to do.

Someone had forced her to do it, pushed her into this. *Who had used her? Why? For money?*

Zac's heart bled, but then anger built inside him. One, he was furious with himself for getting too attached to her. His friends had forewarned him. She was dangerous. Two, he was furious with that man. He had no proof, but there was a man somewhere, whoever he was. *What kind of man would do this to a young girl? Who is he?* Three, what would happen if this came out? It would ruin him; *it would be a disaster!* And last but not least, he was indignant with Mollie for lying to him. Though theirs was an arranged marriage, she had lied to him on the premise of their arrangement. She had assured him this was her idea, when it wasn't!

He trusted that she wanted to do it, willingly! But no! Far from it. And someone controlled her. He clenched his fists. An intense feeling of anger mingled with anguish, and now jealousy, got hold of his soul.

Oh Mollie, what have you done? he thought in despair.

Chapter 9

Mollie slept peacefully again; he didn't. The problem unsettled him.

All those months ago, she had said there was no one else involved in this, other than herself. A lie! She'd told him she had no boyfriend. Another lie! Given what he'd just learned, she had lied, over and over!

Someone had dubious intentions over her, and now over him. This didn't sit well with him. His anger was simmering, and he could do nothing about it.

He left Mollie with the nurse and went to his study. He pinged Finley a new message. Two minutes later, he had her updated file.

He read Mollie's file a few times, but nothing new caught his eye. Not a thing out of the ordinary, nothing suspicious. There had been no boyfriend. It confirmed what he already knew. She was a gifted scholar. She had dated two young men before their marriage, but not serious relationships. No real boyfriends to speak of! There was nothing unusual in her life.

And yet, her mumbling during her fever had been clear.

The file must have missed something, someone—a man! Someone had pushed her to marry him against her will. The reason was obvious. Money! It had to be. Or were there other, more sinister reasons?

Zac rubbed his neck with his hand, in frustration, and cursed. Against his better judgement, he picked up her phone and had a look at it. It was necessary, given the circumstances. It didn't take him long to unlock it. It confirmed his suspicions. He read text messages on her phone. Someone had sent her them under a nickname, the number withheld.

These confirmed her rumblings, and his suspicions. But it seemed she had not answered those messages. The first few were rather loving, *"Mollie, I miss you so much. I thought I could stay away, but I can't."* Another, *"Please come back to me."* And there were others. They left him no doubt it was a man. The last two messages were not so loving, though.

"I'll tell him the truth." And *"Don't even think of double crossing me!"* The threatening notes were unmistakable. But as far as he could tell, she had answered none of his messages. She'd received the last one the day prior to the wedding; nothing after that.

Had she contacted this man? Who was he? Zac wanted to beat him to a pulp, violently, the bastard! His rage spilled from inside him. Somewhere out there, a man was pulling his wife's strings. Like a puppet! *Why has she agreed to do this? Does she love him?* The idea made him miserable.

So, the realisation of her words came crashing in on him —the likelihood that Mollie was in love with another man. Those words should not have mattered to him, not hurt him, since theirs was only an arrangement, not a real marriage, but they did all the same.

He hurt, and hard. Was it Mollie's lies, or was it Mollie's love for another man that pained him the most? He wasn't sure. He wished to get his hands on that bastard, and when he did...

Zac was furious. The fact that she had lied to him, unashamedly, hurt.

He was fuming at the position he found himself in. More so, it dismayed him, he had allowed a slip of a girl to get under his skin.

"Hey. How is she?" Finley asked when he called in.

"Stable. Fin, is Mollie's file complete?" Zac asked bluntly.

"Yes, why do you ask?"

"Are you sure?" he persisted.

"Yes, what's up?"

"Find out who put Mollie up to marrying me."

"What?" Finley cried, but he understood in a flash.

Zac told his friend everything. He charged him with finding the man. Was that man after his money? Or did he want more? That man was trying to claim his bride back, but Zac had no intention of sharing her with that man or any other man. His mind was clear on that point.

"Can someone pick up her phone?" he asked.

"Did you search the contents?"

"Yes, text messages but untraceable. No name. Can you hack it? Find out where they came from? Who sent them?"

"I can try."

"I need to identify the bastard! Do what you must," he articulated flatly, but he was hurting.

"I'll send two men down to you."

"No," Zac refused.

"Listen, if what she mumbled is true, and not some delirious, feverish nightmare of hers, someone has put your wife up to this. You need protection," Finley said, outlying his concern.

"Umm? Do you take her words as the result of a

delirious nightmare? Perhaps… No, I don't think so; she was too upset!"

"Well, hallucinations can feel realistic, you see. Listen, I don't know, but we need to talk to her."

"No. She is not well," Zac replied, combing a hand through his hair.

"Will you at least try as soon as you can?"

"I'll do it when she is better. In the meantime, please explore all angles."

"But you won't be able to avoid it. You must talk to her, eventually. Or would you rather I do it? Best if I do it."

"No. I will," Zac snapped.

MOLLIE WOKE up the next morning to great relief all around. The fever had lowered, but it had taken a toll on her. She was still frail. When she opened her eyes, his face was the first thing she saw. He sat on the edge of her bed, next to her. She launched a tentative smile at him, and he caressed her face tenderly despite the bile churning in his stomach.

"How are you feeling?" he whispered, still caressing her face. He placed a kiss on her forehead.

How could it be? He was so mad at her. And yet, he had all that tenderness for her, all that gentleness. *I can't understand it!* How could he feel this dichotomy for her? He couldn't say.

Any other woman would have been a different story and would have been crushed out of his life unceremoniously. Fever or no fever! Not Mollie!

He convinced himself that he couldn't divorce her because of the damage to his reputation. This would destroy his image. Perhaps true, but he was glad he couldn't divorce her. He wouldn't, even if he could. He couldn't understand the power this girl had over him.

"My head hurts," she mumbled.

"You had a sunstroke," Zac responded with a sour smile, still caressing her face.

"Sunstroke?"

"You were in and out of consciousness for two days."

"Two days?" she mumbled and turned as if to get up, but he stopped her with a hand on her shoulders.

"Don't move. Stay in bed." He didn't mean it to sound like a military order, but that was precisely the intonation in his voice. She flinched and stared at him. The warm smile was off his face, but then it returned to him.

And she smiled back. "I need a shower," she mumbled and closed her eyes.

He caressed her nose with his finger. "Not just yet. But the nurse will help you wash."

"What nurse?"

"She is on her break," he informed her.

"Oh God, I am so sorry. I am a nuisance." Her voice was low, but she rubbed her forehead with her hand.

"No, but you scared the hell out of me."

"Sorry."

"Now that you feel better, Marie and the nurse will look after you. I must return to Oxford today," he told her, getting up from the bed.

"Oxford? No. Why?" she protested, her voice more audible now.

"Unavoidable work. Marie and the nurse will take good care of you. The doctor will see you later. You must rest now, and that's an order. I'll be back in two, maybe three days."

"I'll come to Oxford with you," she said, starting to rise and sulking like a child.

"No. You won't. You need rest," he said and stopped her again.

"Why not?" The fever somehow had dropped her inhibitions. She was speaking her mind.

"Mollie, you are too weak. You can't go anywhere." He kissed her forehead.

The nurse came in with the doctor.

"Mrs. Sorensen, so good to see you awake," the doctor said.

"I need to go; my flight is in two hours," Zac said.

"But I want to come with you," Mollie pleaded.

"You will stay here and rest, discussion closed." And with that, he pecked her on her forehead and left.

What Zac had not said was that he knew her secret. She had not wanted to marry him, and she had someone else. Yet, he couldn't bear himself to say it. It was too painful. So, he retreated, establishing distance between them.

BACK IN OXFORD, Zac met with Finley. He demanded to know who had manipulated his beloved wife. But by being away from her, it would allow him time to absorb the truth. To understand his feelings for her. He could clear his mind and make a decision as to how to deal with her.

He wanted to scream at her, to shake the truth out of her. To ask her why? What was in it for her? But he couldn't. He would need to be gentle with her if he wanted her to trust him with the truth. But it pained him. There he was, in a pretend marriage, and his soul seemed ripped out of place. *Flipping heck!! What the hell am I going to do with her?*

They looked at all the leads, but it was getting them nowhere. They didn't have a clue as to the identity of Mollie's man.

"Jesus, she didn't buy a lavish wedding dress with the money. Wow, this is beyond me," Finley mentioned.

"She was beautiful anyway," Zac said. He thought of when she had arrived at the church, looking radiant and heavenly on their wedding day. She had taken his breath away.

"No, it seems she has used little of the money I gave her," Zac said when they investigated her bank account. Was she keeping it for her lover? Zac had given Mollie fifty thousand pounds as a monthly allowance, during the months preceding the wedding, but they were still in Mollie's account, minus modest expenses.

So, the considerations on who and why went on. Two days later, and they were no further forward. The leads were red herrings, leading them nowhere, so Finley had to start again.

"You must ask her," Finley finally stated.

"I told you; she is not well. We must not fatigue her. She's too weak."

"Zac, you don't know what this bastard is capable of. Money, yes, perhaps, but who knows? We need to talk to her, find out who he is, what he wants. I'll speak to her."

"No!" Zac said.

"I've been protecting you for years, but I can't do it like this. You may be in danger." But his friend perceived that Zac was in unchartered territory with this girl.

"Fin, leave her to me," he mumbled.

But Finley was certain Zac would go easy on her.

Chapter 10

"Where is my wife?" Zac asked his housekeeper, when he returned to Antibes a few days later.

Marie Therese stood by the stove in the kitchen, dishing out *Coq Au Vin* on a plate, a French dish of chicken braised with wine, mushrooms, and garlic. He whiffed the delicious aroma as he entered the house.

"Zac!" she exclaimed upon hearing his voice. She dropped the ladle in the saucepan and turned to him. But soon his housekeeper became uneasy. She started fidgeting with her hands and glanced at her husband.

Upon seeing him, Henri rose from his seat at the table and took his cap off. Then, he began bending the peak of it back and forth nervously in his hands.

Zac stared at his housekeeper when she didn't answer his question. He was not in the mood. "What is it?" he asked, sensing their nervousness. His eyes darted from Marie Therese to Henri and back again.

"I am sorry, but Mollie wanted to go out today. Henri drove her into town," the housekeeper told him.

"Is she out?"

"No. She is back now," Marie Therese said, still fidgeting.

"Is she okay?" Zac could tell something was wrong.

"Oh, yes. Mollie is fine. She is feeling much better. Her skin lost that awful redness and has a golden glow to it, nice... She is still weak from the fever, though. But good food and rest will help. She is in her bedroom now, but..." She paused anxiously.

"But what?" he snapped, impatient now.

"She met someone in the old town. I saw her," Henri murmured the words. As if by murmuring them, they would be less ominous.

"What?" Zac asked with a frown, and anger flashed across his eyes.

"She met someone in a cafe downtown," Henri blurted out.

"Who?" he barked.

"She met a man," Henri mumbled.

"What the hell are you talking about?" His tone was harsher now.

"I have photos of them," the old man said, aware of Zac's increasing wrath.

"Photos?" Zac asked, surprised, lifting his eyebrows. He lost his cool and cursed, alarm bells going off in his head. He knew where this was going.

"Yes, on my phone," Henri mumbled.

MARIE THERESE LIKED MOLLIE. She had gotten to know her better while Zac was in Oxford. She thought the young bride was a sweet girl, the perfect wife for her impetuous, strong-willed young master. Marie Therese felt awful doing this behind Mollie's back. But Henri had insisted they must tell him, a man's honour and all that... *poppycock!* She lowered her eyes, fidgeting with her hands.

The old woman had known Zac since he was a child, as she had been the housekeeper in his grandmother's house for over twenty years. She was protective of him too. But somehow, she felt they were making a mistake. She knew this would hurt Zac. *Perhaps there is another explanation.* She could have sworn blindly that Mollie loved her husband. A woman noticed these things, so she felt awful. She was convinced; they were making a mistake in telling Zac his bride had met a man downtown.

Alas, too late now.

"Give me the photos," Zac said impatiently, beckoning the old man with his hand.

Henri handed him his phone.

Zac glared at him while taking it, but soon he regained his composure. He inspected each photo, his eyes widening, slowly taking his time. He glanced from Henri to Marie Therese for an instant and then returned to the photos.

Zac's face was now composed—a controlled mask, self-restrained and calm, as if made of stone. With a mammoth effort, he was trying to keep his self-control while looking at the photos. In reality, he was dying to scream and shout and break every piece of furniture in his path. His rage seeped through every pore, but looking at him, no one would have guessed.

"You took the photos?" Zac asked with a steady poise in his voice, as if those were holiday snapshots. He was glad his voice sounded calm. He trusted the housekeeper and her husband with his life, so he knew this was no mistake.

"Yes. I thought you might want to know," Henri concluded.

Zac had recognised the man in the photos. "Did she tell you she was meeting him?" he asked.

"No," Henri answered.

"Send the photos to my phone now. And delete them from yours," Zac commanded. He received them on his phone a moment later. Then he put the phone in his shirt's chest pocket.

I must divorce her, Zac thought bitterly. He made his way to her bedroom. *How can she be so sweet and so duplicitous at the same time?*

He had desired her for months, from the moment she had waved her hand at him in Peter's chambers when he first met her. He had enjoyed every day they'd spent together over the last two months, but he was now fuming at her. He was vexed and furious; no one treated him like this, and this was his wife no less.

He had always been the one calling the shots, the one to make the rules. He had been the one commanding, the one pulling the strings. *Not my hired wife. Not this girl!* He cursed under his breath.

It hurt his heart and pride. His blood was rising to his head. *She will have to go. No one will take me for a ride! Not this slip of a girl.*

He rubbed the back of his neck and stood outside her bedroom door for a moment, swallowing in deep breaths. He needed to control his temper. Then, he burst into her room and slammed the door shut.

She was sitting by the bed, reading.

At the sound, she turned to the door. She rose and faced him with a sweet smile, from the other end of the room.

"Zac, you're home!" she squealed with warmth and pleasure.

The sound of happiness in Mollie's voice kicked in his guts. Her joyous squeal and the melodious note of his name upon her lips, made his hair stand at the back of his neck.

It was an aphrodisiac. He was not expecting it. He had

heard no one say his name in such a heart-warming and harmonious melody, with so much delight and joy. The mellifluous voice raised his pulse.

Her face lit up with that charming smile, the one he liked so much. Her entire face beamed with tenderness and adoration for him.

He closed his eyes for a moment and threw his head back, his hands akimbo. He cursed under his breath but didn't move or say a word.

When he opened his eyes again, she was upon him. He remained standing there motionless, but she circled her arms around his waist and put her head on his chest. Thus, she clasped him for a moment.

"Oh, I missed you so much," she said, raising her face to him, her eyes shining with happiness and heartfelt delight at him. She settled her head back on his chest again, tightening her embrace even more.

"Oh, darling, I am so glad you're back," she whispered.

His heart sunk.

Either she is genuine or an inveterate actress. The thought burst into his head. *How can she be so loving? So pleased to see me? Is it even true? Has she engineered this?* He shook his head, but he saw her exquisite smile beaming at him again.

So adorable? And yet so deceitful, a bloody liar. She seemed so genuine to him, though, or… was he willing her to be?

He still had the photos in his pocket. He touched his phone to remind himself why he was there, so as not to waver from his purpose.

"Oh?" he said instead, but he stood still. His arms were now in mid-air, as he didn't know what to do with them, not moving, not touching her while she was clinging to him.

He was not expecting such a heart-warming burst of welcoming joy from her, and it surprised him. But if he had to be honest, it delighted him no end. It was bliss!

Somehow, the contact of her skin on his chest seemed a glorious explosion on his senses despite his anger, her arms around him bliss. Cozy, where they should be, her cute face on him radiating a warmth of pure pleasure through his body.

But he touched his shirt pocket again, the phone with the photos, to remind himself he was there for a reason—what he *needed* to say, what he *should* say to her, to send her packing.

His arms were still not touching her.

"Oh, I didn't think I could count the days until you were home," she whispered, raising her face to him, and she stood on her toes to reach his face. Then, she brushed her lips on his, but she flushed. His body froze, as if turned into stone.

The warm flesh of her plump lips touched his again. And this time, she lingered on them longer, tenderly, deliciously.

And he never stood a chance. His defences melted, quickly, against her warmth.

Her lips kindled him like a torch that had just ignited a fire that spread ablaze within him, enveloping his senses. His arms came down and circled her waist. He drew her closer to him, and he kissed her.

It was no kiss for the cameras. For the first time since the Norwegian embassy's ball, they kissed like true lovers do.

Everything in his mind went blank. The pain, the lies, the anguish, the photos, the hurt, the jealousy, all forgotten. It disappeared, never existed.

He took her mouth, gently kissing her, tasting, savouring her lips. His tongue pushed into her mouth. At first, softly, exploring her, then with a resolve that turned into a ravenous hunger. A burning desire exploded within him which had no equal. He had subdued his feelings for her for some time, but now, he couldn't contain them any longer. His lust erupted in all his senses. It burst out. All his anger and suspicions over her went out of the window in an instant, even her lover, the photos, all gone!

All he knew, she was in his arms. He had desired her for months, but he didn't realise the passion for her was so strong and so forceful until then. She was his. He didn't care about anything else.

They kissed each other with ardour.

Her mouth reminded him of honey, catapulting him into seventh heaven, by savouring her delicious and sensual plump lips.

The kisses that turned lovemaking legendary, divine kisses, fervent and sensual. Her luscious mouth, her giddy jasmine scent, her soft skin, and his senses were exploding with a love for her, an intense destination. They kissed with raw emotion, again and again!

For a moment, she felt rather shy in his arms, with her guilt twirling in her mind. But he was so delicious, his kisses so electrifying, so passionate that she didn't mind them one bit. And she didn't stop.

She hadn't realised how badly she wanted him until that day, until that very minute. She hadn't known how much she craved him until then. And once he kissed her, she melted in his arms, like a bomb had exploded in her heart! She was utterly in love with this man!

And she kissed him, again and again—and more.

They were only aware of each other, their kisses the only thing that mattered, while the universe stood still. The awareness of their mouths meeting was exhilarating, a sensual flame exploding and expanding within them, full of consuming yearning and seductive charge that rose to the occasion.

It was like their mouths were making love. Her body quivered with every little move of his glorious tongue. She gasped in his mouth, and he grunted, deepening his kiss.

His hands roamed over her, leaving a blazing trail on her skin, on her hair, on her breasts, her arms, and on her back. His big and super confident hands rolled over her body repeatedly. And she was enjoying his touch, his caresses, every lingering finger on her skin.

He grabbed her ass, pushing her hips to him. She felt his erection, and it was rock hard and massive.

Then they slowed down.

He settled his forehead on hers for a few moments, glancing at her angelic face. She smiled, and he took her mouth again, with powerful force, as she whimpered little moans of anticipation, while a guttural sound came out of his lips. A groan from deep in his belly, almost primitive, bellowed out of him with want and desire for her.

She had never been kissed like this before. It was the only kiss that mattered. Thus, she kissed him back like her life depended on it.

They stopped to catch their breaths and he caressed her face with his knuckles.

The longing in his eyes was roaring. His brooding and sultry eyes were dark with passion in that look, the one she adored so much, but it just about matched hers.

He grinned, seeing desire in her eyes too.

She unbuttoned his shirt. She craved to touch his skin as she tugged it off his shoulders.

She stopped to admire him. She planted her hands on his skin, caressing him. His wide shoulders were strong and taut, his chiselled torso perfect.

She started kissing his chest, soft kisses here and there with soft sensuality. She licked each of his nipples too, and he grunted, with blood flowing forcefully to his shaft.

He had his hands in her hair, and he inhaled her scent. "God, you smell so good. Your hair, it's so soft," he whispered in his deep, guttural and lustful voice. She was alluring, and he took another strand of her hair in his fingers.

She raised her head to kiss him again.

"I should warn you; I am no expert," she said in a breathless whisper, almost in his mouth.

"Expert?" he asked, out of breath himself, full of desire.

"You know!" She raised her eyebrows in quick succession with a quick nod towards the bed. "I don't want to disappoint you," she mumbled, lowering her eyes.

He laughed and pulled her closer to him. He caressed her hair back, kissing her forehead. "Disappointed? No. I don't believe so," he whispered. *At least not in the physical sense, not in the passionate kisses,* he reflected for a second. And he kissed her again, but the pain in his heart at her deception was something else—something that was there, simmering, bubbling underneath.

But he felt too good holding her in his arms to bring that up. Her kisses were too sweet, and he didn't want to break the spell! He was enjoying her lips on his skin, enjoying caressing her, having his arms around her. It was like Heaven on Earth, so much so that he added, "You are better at it than you think. Trust me."

As he pulled her to him, she was aware of his erection rubbing her tummy.

He caressed her arms up and down, and she shivered. He kissed her again. His ravenous and passionate kisses, and the light sensual touches of his fingertips were creating a burning sensation throughout her skin, waking up all the senses in her body.

He aroused her; she was wet. She wanted him so much, she could no longer wait.

He pulled the hem of her sundress up and off, over her head. She was wearing cotton panties, not lace, not sexy underwear. But again, he would not have expected Mollie to wear anything else.

He chuckled but kissed her until her lips were raw.

"What?"

"No lace panties?" he said almost in her mouth.

"Lace?" she breathed out with questioning eyes. But she had no time to think; he took her in his arms and walked her over to the bed. His mouth never left hers. He placed her on the bed.

He pinched her breasts one at a time and then put his mouth on her nipples over the cotton bra. He touched her mound, her clit with his other hand.

It was pleasurable torture to play with her breasts and mound over the thin material of her bra and panties, but she wanted him to touch her skin. She wanted nothing to prevent her bare skin being touched by his hands, but she felt self-conscious. She didn't want to ask, but she glanced at him with longing. It soaked her panties, the intensity and anticipation building inside her.

She went for his trousers and unzipped them, but he stopped her. *Sweet Jesus, I want him so badly*, her only thought.

He knew and smiled. And he loved the way she was looking at him, full of lust and adoration, the way he had aroused her. He loved seeing her like this.

Bloody hell, she is so sexy!

But he continued his amorous torture, roaming over her body. Only then, he removed his trousers and stood at the edge of the bed. Left only in his boxers, the material was straining under his erection.

She looked at him adoringly.

She had seen nothing so beautiful in her life. A gorgeous man with a perfect body. A face so masterly sculpted that she took a deep breath at the captivating sight of him.

She kneeled on the edge of the bed and reached for him.

She caressed his chest with her open hands, down his body, trailing kisses on every inch of his torso.

"You see how good you are? And improving every second." He smiled, but his voice was a low rasp, his eyes dark with intense desire.

She grinned at the compliment, but he laid her back onto the bed.

He touched her again over her bra and panties. So, when he removed her underwear and touched her bare skin, she screamed at his touch. He stopped dead and looked at her in concern.

She smiled. "No, darling, please go on. It feels marvellous," she mumbled between breaths.

He grinned, and slid a finger inside her, and then another, moving them expertly in and out, while she gasped at the intense pleasure.

"Wow, Mollie, you are so wet. Gorgeous!" he breathed out, removing his fingers from her while she mourned his touch. But then he buried his face between her legs.

She cried out, but a smile spread on her face from ear to ear, with another loud gasp leaving her mouth.

He placed his tongue at her opening, teasing and probing. Then his tongue burst inside her, making love to her. All the while, her climax was building to a crescendo that she hardly contained. When he sucked her clit, she exploded into a sensual orgasm, so intense and powerful, an explosion of pure pleasure. It was as if an earthquake had suddenly broken inside her, releasing seismic waves of pleasure within her body.

He lapped up every bit of juice within her. Then he moved up on the bed next to her and kissed her lips tenderly.

He tasted sweet and salty, and of sex. The smell and taste aroused her, just thinking of what more he could do to her.

That thought just followed an almighty orgasm. *Wow, this man… How could it be? And I want him again.*

She kneeled on the bed alongside him, and she started kissing his eyes, the corner of his mouth, his jaw, his collarbone, and down to his chest, along his ribcage and hip bones.

The randomness of her kisses was sending intense pulses down to his shaft. The more she kissed him, the more his erection was throbbing.

"Mollie, you are glorious. You are!" he blurted between breaths.

"You are very glorious yourself!" She giggled, pinching him on his abdomen. He shifted, "ouch" he said, but then she placed a tender kiss on the pinched skin. He chuckled.

She pulled his boxers off, and he appeared to her in all his glory, hard and massive. On his back, now lying naked on the bed, he was a vision of manhood. She couldn't resist and put her hand around his shaft and licked the tip.

This is heaven! And a loud groan escaped him.

She swirled her tongue around his erection. And he groaned again, a bass, primeval sound. He put his hands in her hair, caressing her, grabbing little strands to help her with the motion, suggesting how deep to plunge her mouth on him, up and down his shaft.

"Suck slowly," he murmured.

She glanced up, and she saw his eyes were closed and his head back. She smiled at the power she had over him at that moment, at the intense pleasure she was giving him.

She got wet again just by doing it. She felt so aroused so soon after an almighty orgasm!

Oh, this man!

"Mollie," he murmured, but he would come undone if she continued this way. So, he stopped her, pulled her up, and laid her down on the bed. And his body followed her. He took her mouth again.

He tasted his saltiness, and he kissed her, hungrily.

"Bloody hell! What are you doing to me?" he breathed out, looking at her. And she rewarded him with the smile he loved so much.

A beam of pure love shone on his face. He had made love to countless women in the past, but nothing came close to this, to the feelings she unleashed in his heart. And he knew, from then on, he would make love only to her. No other woman would ever do.

He placed himself over her.

He took one of her legs and hooked it over his hip. He lifted her pelvis up to give him better access and inched inside her.

She gave a soft cry, and he rejoiced in her pleasure.

"Oh, sweet baby!" he murmured.

He slipped in and out. He was big and hard, and she felt every bit of him when he started thrusting inside her, every inch of her tightening around him, the sensation sending wild pulses down his shaft.

He began thrusting with long strokes. Her climax was building inside her with each stroke.

"Oh, Zac…" she said in a shiver, digging her nails down his back. Her hands grabbed his hips, pushing him towards her. He thrust deeper and faster. It was at that point, she screamed his name while lingering waves of wild ecstasy took hold of her body until her senses left her for a few seconds.

Even in his deep arousal, he was manly proud at the intensity of feelings he provoked in her. He grinned at her exploding pleasure.

Her emotions were powerful, incredible.

But she soon focused on him trailing behind her, wanting to return the favour. Her own body was still fervent with raw emotion, shivering with lingering pleasure.

And it was not long before he followed suit. His climax

came long and protracted, his body alive with sensations so fervent, like a passing of raw emotion between them. It was exhilarating until their bodies stopped shuddering with pleasure.

He rolled off and towards her. Side by side, facing each other, they kissed tenderly. He kissed her on her eyelashes, her nose, her hair. He nipped at her shoulders.

"Ouch," she said and nipped his earlobe.

"Well, I just happen to like that," he teased her, and she smiled at him.

He caressed her face and hair. They wallowed in the warmth created by their passion for a while. He had just experienced a lovemaking that was thrilling; it had never felt so intense, so beautiful, so meaningful with a woman before.

He had wanted to make love to her for months, but he had not expected it to be so wonderful. She was a revelation to him. He adored her, and it amazed him that he did. But he wallowed in it. It was a new feeling to him, and he liked it —a lot.

As the feelings in his body subsided, and his common sense returned, his eyes landed on his shirt on the floor. The photos in his phone returned to his mind, still burning him.

Mollie's revelations while she was sick came back clear and present in his brain. His bride had secrets, and he must know the truth. He needed answers from her. But he felt too good to ruin the moment. He was greedy for her and wanted more of her, all of her, again.

Besides, he felt Mollie's lovemaking had been genuine. He could tell. She had enjoyed it, loving him as much as he did. So, he gave her the benefit of the doubt and pushed all his worries aside for the time being.

Perhaps now that she is learning to trust me, dare I say, like me, maybe she is even fond of me? Perhaps their intimacy would levy out all her secrets. He hoped she would come clean with the truth of her own accord. He wished she would tell him everything unaided.

Thus, he would wait until she opened up to him, until she was ready to share the truth and her secrets with him.

So, he made love to her again instead. They made love again, and again.

For the next three days, their passionate lovemaking continued, only interrupted by gentle strolls, hand in hand, through the gardens. By moonlight walks on the beach, whispering sweet things to each other, or by earthy meals which Marie Therese prepared for them with motherly pride. An afternoon on the speed boat, at a low pace, cruising along the French Riviera was a romantic interlude too, and it brought them closer together.

They shared sweet moments, and the languorous and amorous days made him think he was in a real relationship for the first time in years—a real honeymoon, the impression he was one-half of a loving couple.

He had to admit; he was in love with Mollie! *I adore the minx!* He had fallen in love with his bride. Completely!

But it is still a fake marriage, a business arrangement. Not only this, but a sham marriage, with despicable secrets overshadowing every second, he thought to himself. He had let himself forget that not so small a point in their relationship and, instead, he allowed himself to live *"in the moment"*. He knew it wouldn't last, but he enjoyed the moment too much to deal with the truth. He was enjoying being with Mollie too much to question her about her secrets.

So, they continued their love interludes.

Often, during their lovemaking intervals, he would ask, "Mollie, do you have something to tell me?" He was hoping she would open up to him and tell him. But she would smile at him, and her cheeks would redden.

"Oh, the best time of my life!" she would respond

instead, with delight, and she would pull herself up to reach for his lips for a sweet kiss.

He couldn't resist her kisses, so he carried on. *Only for a little longer,* he told himself, hoping she would reveal everything unaided. Although he loved spending time with her, he got irritated by her silence and her secrets. He knew he should ask her outright, but he enjoyed her company too much to spoil everything.

He had fallen for this girl, like a ripe tomato. So, he waited a little longer instead. But he was getting frustrated by her silence.

Bloody hell, three days, and she has not even mentioned meeting him in town yet! he thought repeatedly, but one sweet smile from her and he was gone.

He would have to ask her the inevitable, but he kept hoping she would tell him. He wanted her to trust him. He wanted the whole story from her, the truth. But above all, he wanted her, all of her, warts and all.

SIMILARLY, in her heart of hearts, Mollie knew she would have to tell him. She would have to open up and tell him everything, that blasted truth lingering at the back of her mind. But things had taken an unexpected turn. Love had gotten in the way. She was aware now, she had fallen for Zac; she loved him to distraction! But it would not last once he knew; she was sure of it. So, she ignored the truth, her guilt, and her remorse and enjoyed the sweet moments with him instead. Because once she told him, it would spell the end for them.

On the fourth day, it was early morning when the warm sun filtered through the windows caressing their bodies. They had made passionate love, their bodies still tingling with pleasure so sweet and so exhilarating, it took them some time to calm down.

He wanted this woman with a passion so strong, it was never felt before in his life. And he couldn't have enough of her. He loved her with a burning so strong, it scared him.

As incredible as it was, and as the sensations in his body were slowly subsiding, all of his worries and suspicions about her came rushing to the fore—with a vengeance.

Something she'd said, "I wish there was just you and me in the world," mumbled with a sigh, brought him back to the notion... there was someone else. She had secrets! He must not deny it. She had fed him a pack of lies since the moment they met.

She had lied on the premise of their marriage of convenience. It had not been her idea, and someone had pushed her into it. *Another man lurks between us, for starters.*

She had seen George in town, four days ago, and she had

not even mentioned him yet. What was George doing in Antibes? *Is he her lover?*

Once the amorous tingling eased, once Zac's quivering and shuddering lovestruck body returned to normal, so did these questions in his mind—forcefully. He tried to put these worries aside again, to enjoy the moment as he had learned to do in the last few days, but he couldn't do it any longer. Not this time! He must know his wife's secrets, whatever they were, and all of them! As the thoughts refused to abandon his mind, his caresses became stilted. His body tensed next to hers, and his shoulders tightened.

Sensing something was wrong, Mollie gazed at him. "What is it?" she asked, still in his arms in the aftermath of their explosive lovemaking, caressing and kissing his chest, sprawling her legs along the bed next to him.

"Do you have something to tell me?" Zac ventured again; his body stilled as he uttered those words. He must not let go now.

Again, she smiled and kissed him, but he didn't relent this time. "No, Mollie, I mean it! You have something to tell me, don't you?" His words were harsh, with tension in his shoulders, but he tried to control himself.

"Like what?" she asked, raising her head from his chest, looking up at him. At that moment, Mollie was blissfully unaware of anything else around her but Zac.

"Take your pick," he drawled with annoyance.

"My pick? I don't understand. The last few days have been amazing—" She started snuggling up in the crook of his arm with a smile on her face, her skin still feeling the delicate shivering delight of her body's pleasure.

"As much as these last few days were thrilling for me too, I need the truth." He said it outright, waving his hand. He couldn't hold it any longer. But, looking at her face, he now wished he had eased her into the matter. Too late now.

"What truth?" She bounced abruptly to a sitting position, despite her nakedness, her eyes round and big, staring at him.

"You met George four days ago, and you haven't even mentioned him yet. And that's for starters."

"George?" she snapped.

"Yes. George. Why?" he said, passing a hand over his face in a quick, jerky movement.

"Well, I…" she mumbled.

"Why?" he repeated severely.

"I… George." She leapt out of bed and looked for her clothes, her back to him.

He closed his eyes, and his head went back. He cursed under his breath. "Come back to bed," he said. And even annoyed, he couldn't avoid a good look at her pert little ass.

"No," she snapped, pushing her hair back from her face.

"Mollie! Come back to bed."

"No. You knew I had seen George, and you are just telling me now? After four days?" she replied, while her eyes were searching the room for her clothes.

"Why did you see George? Is he your lover? The one that put you up to this?" he asked with vehemence, while he leapt out of bed. He stood up, glorious in his nakedness, but he did nothing to cover his modesty.

At his words, she froze. She stood perfectly still, with her back to him, and gulped. Then, she turned slowly, stilling herself, and watched his face. *Does he know?* Her face flushed.

"What? No. No, George is my friend." She recovered a few seconds later.

"Then why did you sneak out to go to him without telling me?"

"I didn't sneak out. You weren't here. You were in Oxford, remember?" she said with a touch of annoyance.

"What did he want from you?"

"I was sick; he worried about me. That's all. Then when you came back from Oxford, when I saw you, well... I forgot all about George."

"Is he your lover?" His voice was calm now. His face showed no emotion, as if made of stone, but he clenched his fists at his side, betraying the growing turmoil inside him.

He was naked and looked divine, at ease with his nakedness. She gulped at the gorgeous sight of him. But then a fleeting veil of fury went across his eyes, and she scurried along the room, picking up the rest of her clothes.

"No. I-I already told you, G-George is my friend," she stammered; anxiety getting hold of her. She dressed quickly. She didn't wish to have this conversation naked.

"You mumbled during your fever."

"What?" She whipped round to him. The colour drained from her face. *Mumbled? What did I say?*

"Well, let me enlighten you..." he cracked on with blazing eyes, like he had read her mind. If those eyes could have spat the fire they had in them, they would have covered her in burns.

Zac told her about her mumblings, her exact words.

Mollie's face became ashen, but her first defence was denial. "The mumblings of a sick woman. Meaningless. I was delirious!" she retorted.

"Do. You. Or. Do. You. Not. Have. A. Lover?" This time, his voice uttered every word harshly. Loud enough for her to wince at him, with more than a hint of demand in it.

She knew it commanded a response.

"No, I don't. You are my l-lover. My only lover, given what we have been doing for these past four days." She rushed the words out.

"I want the truth. Now, please," he snapped, short and crisp, and about to lose his patience. He was now dressing as fast as she had.

"George is my friend, not my lover," she repeated in a murmur.

"But you have a lover who pushed you to marry me. It was not your idea, was it?" He glared at her. She bit her bottom lip.

"Huh?"

"Mollie, please... talk to me," he repeated, this time with more tenderness, but she averted his eyes.

"I don't understand what you mean," she lied again; she didn't know what to do.

This time, he lost his patience. He walked to her, grabbed her wrist, and dragged her towards the bed.

"Hey, stop, let me go!" She tried to flee, but his grip was strong.

"Sit," he commanded. And when she stood there looking at him with defiance, he continued furiously. "Sit, I said," he bellowed.

And she jerked into action. She sat, and she gulped. "I am not your dog," she whispered under her breath, but he ignored her comment, raising his eyebrows.

"I will ask you one more time," he drawled, towering over her, wagging a finger at her. His tone was calm but icy, and she knew his patience had run out. "Who pushed you to do this? Or would you rather talk to Fin?"

She opened her mouth to protest, but she saw the resolution in his face.

"Fin? George is my friend. I swear, he is my friend. I told you, I was so surprised and happy to see you back from Oxford that day that I forgot about George," she blurted out. Her voice pitched and edgy, almost in panic.

"And?"

"George came to visit me because he was worried about me, because I was sick. He is nice like that," she sighed.

"And?"

"Oh, Jesus! Stop saying *and;* it is so bloody annoying!" she snapped in defiance, and cursed. His eyebrows shot up, and he glared at her in disapproval. She lowered her eyes and looked at her feet instead. *Don't challenge him; don't make him angrier than he is.*

"So? Is this better?" His words mocked her, but his eyes narrowed on her.

"Yes, thank you," she said with a nod. More than a show, to prove she was not intimidated.

"So? Go on. I am waiting," he hissed, and she had nowhere to go but talk.

"I *had* a boyfriend. Notice the past tense? *Before* we were married! Before we were even engaged!" she said, side glancing at him for a moment. "He is not my boyfriend anymore. So there, are you happy now?" She rushed out, fidgeting with her hands, but then she looked down at her feet again. She was sorry and embarrassed. She peeped at him and saw the hurt in his eyes. The hurt she had caused! And her bottom lip quivered. Her eyes softened on him and pleaded forgiveness from him. But he stared at her, unmovable.

How dare she look hurt when she is a liar, Zac thought. His eyes were dark with fury, and his insides were churning in anger.

"Who is he? And what does he want?" he asked with a steady voice, raking a hand through his hair, but the icy tone was unmistakable.

"N-nothing."

"Mollie, I am warning you. Tell me who he is and what he wants. Now," he said while he clenched his hands at his sides and his nails dug into his palms to keep his self-control. But his tone and his stance didn't give her any doubts that she must tell him.

"You knew about George, about my ex-boyfriend, all

these things, and you said nothing to me? So, we could roll around in your bed for days? How dare you?" For a moment, she tried to revert the tables on him as a defence mechanism, trying to divert the conversation, but he was not having it.

"Mollie, I am asking you one last time. Who is your lover? What does he want?" he asked, spitting the offending words. He knew she was trying to test if she had a way out, but she had none.

"*Ex*, ex-lover. You are my lover now. Only you!" she bellowed and paused, but she went on, "and he wants the money you will p-pay me. That's all." She rushed out these last words, half mumbling and half stammering them. Then, she blushed and grabbed a strand of her hair and played with it, tormenting the luscious strand.

"That's all? You bloody fool!" he quarrelled and glared at her while pacing the room. He walked back and forth for a few moments and ran his hand over his face and hair. Her eyes followed his every movement.

"I am sorry, so sorry," she whispered.

"You are sorry? *Now* you are sorry?"

"I *am* sorry. I really am. I never came to you professing my undying l-love," she whispered with a tremor in her voice, even though her feelings for him had changed. Her feelings for him were too strong, her passion for him too powerful, but he would not believe her now.

He whipped around and watched her with a stony face, unreadable.

It tugged at her heartstrings. But she was walking a tightrope.

"You lied to me," he said with venom this time.

"This was... is... a business arrangement," she corrected herself and then added, "it was a fake marriage. Why do you act as if I betrayed you? What does it matter if I give the money you will pay me to somebody else?"

She tried to salvage her very dim situation. But it was no use.

"To him, you mean. You will give the money to him! Who is he? Tell me everything, from the beginning."

"Oh, Zac. Please listen to me. That was then, all those months ago. But things have changed now, haven't they? I know they have; you must sense it too. You and I are happy together, aren't we? We've found each other. Why do you care how it all started or whose idea it was? Hey? What does it matter?" she pleaded.

"What does it matter? Christ, you are a silly girl! I bloody care! It bloody matters!" he yelled at her, still pacing the room, and a pack of crude curses bellowed from his mouth.

"But—"

"You didn't want to marry me! You lied. Someone urged you to do it. We could be in danger… for money? It wasn't even your idea, was it?" he persisted. "And George? You didn't even tell me about George."

"I forgot about George; I didn't hide it from you. I am sorry."

"Sorry? Mollie, your lover wants you back while you are married to me!"

"Have you been spying on me? Reading my phone messages?" she snapped, knowing too well about her ex-boyfriend's messages. Why had she not deleted those texts? Was she willing Zac to find them?

"Clever move, but it won't wash. I want a name," he spat.

"I am sorry I lied to you, I am. I feel awful, but this does not change things. No one will harm you. He is not a bad person. I know he is greedy; I have to admit—" she ventured, but it changed things now that her real feelings for Zac had burst open in her heart.

"Not a bad person? Oh, Mollie, for all your cleverness, you are remarkably silly and naïve! He wants the money, and now he wants you. He used you, you foolish girl. This is bad, Mollie. Fucking awful!" he bellowed, and there was no mistaking the chastisement in his voice.

"Well, I…" she whispered, lifting her chin up but feeling so bad for him, she didn't know what to say. She wanted to beg forgiveness. Her eyes welled up, but she was trying not to cry.

Mollie was stubborn. It frustrated him.

She refused to give him a name. She told him nothing. He got annoyed at her foolishness for believing in a man who used her.

"Did he force you to do this?" he asked her.

"What difference does it make? It shouldn't matter to you now," she mumbled.

"Oh, Mollie! It matters to me," he whispered with emotion.

SHE LOOKED AT HIM, and for a fleeting moment, she saw a flush of longing in his eyes, but he didn't act upon it. She wanted to run to him and cocoon in his arms, make it better again. The girl wanted to turn the clock back, but she couldn't.

"Oh?" It was all she managed instead. Guilt and remorse clenched at her guts. *Zac hates me now; I can sense it.* She was thoroughly ashamed, but there was nothing she could do.

Zac was hurt and furious. And all her fault!

Despite everything, her love for Zac was booming in her heart. The last few days had been the most loving, happiest of her life. Alas, she had destroyed the relationship.

She saw it clearly now. Her ex-lover had manipulated her into marrying Zac. He'd masterminded her into it. She had foolishly believed in his love, but he didn't love her, no, no, no! The bastard had used her.

She presumed herself in love with that greedy and vain man! He had been her first lover. She understood now. She had not given herself to her then-boyfriend, but rather to the sublime ideal of love itself. And it had backfired on her.

She would give her ex-boyfriend the wretched money. Mollie had never wanted the money. And she couldn't overlook the fact that her ex-lover could make matters worse for her, given the chance. So, she thought of him with contempt and disdain.

Oh God, what have I done? How did she not see it coming? She had been blind.

She cursed herself for it, *Mollie, you are a fool!*

She sighed and touched her temple, massaging it. She peeked at Zac for a moment but lowered her eyes again. She was distraught.

He was still pacing around the room. Silence descended between them, but she knew he was thinking what to do with her!

Now that she had found the ideal love and sampled it, it would be lost to her forever. Watching Zac so hurt, it tugged at her soul. She felt his pain. Her mother was right; she failed in the most elemental of things. She had no judgement, no common sense. *I am an idiot.*

She was in a mess, but she kept her mouth shut. She couldn't tell Zac the name of her ex-lover. It would only make a bad situation worse.

If she had known her husband to be so caring, so thoughtful, she would have agreed to marry him in a flash. All by herself, for nothing! *And oh, such glorious sex, well, fat chance now! He hates me now; he despises me.* There was only one outcome! Her husband would divorce her straight away.

She glanced up at him. He stood by the balcony, looking out, rubbing his neck.

"Some fucking pimp you got yourself there," Zac spat at her after a long silence, and her eyes welled up.

"I am sorry. Please, don't say that," she pleaded with a crack in her voice.

"Who would stoop so low with a woman? Your boyfriend sold you to me."

"Please. I—" she pleaded, but she knew he was right. *Her ex-lover, the bastard, the weasel, the scumbag!*

"Bloody hell, Mollie, for a clever woman, you are awfully irresponsible and misguided. Bloody reckless," Zac cried out fervently, but he went on, "he used you. Don't you see that?"

"I... sorry!" she murmured, fidgeting with her hands. She was squirming.

"Are you seeing him?"

"No. What do you take me for?" she responded indignantly.

"Do you really want me to answer that?" he snapped flippantly, turning his head.

"Please. There is only you, no one else. From the very first moment, I swear!"

"Why should I believe you?"

"Because it's true."

"Do you love him?"

"No. I did, past tense. Well, I thought I did, but it was an illusion. I thought I loved him, but I was wrong. I know that now. I made a mistake, I am foolish; I am aware of that!" she whispered with tears in her eyes, trying hard not to cry.

"What does that mean?" Zac's eyes were on her, a spark of hope bearing on him. Was the love he had for Mollie his punishment for all those women's hearts he had broken through the years? Was this Karma's way to get back at him?

He felt miserable, but a flash of hope made his way into his heart.

"Oh, God. What a mess. I hate him now. I am so sorry; I didn't mean to hurt you," she whispered.

"A little late for that, don't you think?"

"Zac, I lo… like you. A lot! You know that. And you like me too, I know. Can we start again?" she sighed, and then her eyes welled up again. She wouldn't use big words with him; he wouldn't believe her. She limited herself to say she liked him, but what she wanted to say to him was she loved him. So, tears stained her face.

HE CRAVED to go to her, take her in his arms and stop her from crying with his kisses. But he needed to know. She might be in danger, and he as well. Besides, he felt too raw.

"Who is he?" he asked instead, ignoring her statement.

"Please, don't…" she responded stubbornly.

And then he saw red!

"Tell me, Mollie." Zac came closer to her and grabbed her forearms with his hands, lifting her from the bed where she was still sitting. He dragged her a few steps with him. She cried out and tried to wriggle out of his clutch, but he held her in his grip.

"You are hurting me, please. I'm sorry, but I can't tell you who he is," she pleaded.

"You can, and you bloody will. Tell me!" he yelled as he shook her.

She screamed. "No. I won't. You are hurting me," she said, her eyes flooded with tears.

"You will tell me. Make no mistake," Zac hissed, but he let her go.

His frustration and anger were so palpable that it clouded his mind, so Mollie took a few steps back from him.

He sensed fear in her eyes. And he cursed, for scaring her. So, he turned on his heels and left the room, afraid of his temper.

———

WHEN HE LEFT, Mollie threw herself on the bed. She cried and cursed her ex-boyfriend.

When her crying subsided, she craved to soothe Zac. She wanted to tell her husband she had grown to love him so much. He had swept her off her feet, and she couldn't bear to see him hurt.

Too late for us now.

In her mind, there was only one person at fault, and it was herself, for lying.

She couldn't tell him what he wanted to hear, the name of her ex-boyfriend. It was too dangerous. Her silence was imperative.

But why had she not mentioned anything about George? She had genuinely forgotten about her friend's visit.

She'd screwed up big time with Zac, and soon her family and friends would know too.

Bloody hell, Mother will go ballistic!

But above all, she was heartbroken about hurting Zac. After the passionate love of the last few days, she adored him.

But what now? What will become of us?

Chapter 12

Zac left the room before he lost his temper completely. He was so frustrated with her that he had no option but to retreat. He took sanctuary in his study. *I never harmed a woman in my life, and I won't start now.* Despite this, he longed to spank the truth out of her.

It was inconceivable that she was the tender girl in his arms only hours ago. Now, she was his duplicitous wife. *The captivating and delightful girl of the past few months, the loving woman of the last few days, a deceitful minx! How can she be that enchanting girl? And fill me with made up stories, the mendacious cheat!*

The adorable creature he had grown to love and then the lies! *Plotting against me with a boyfriend, no less.*

Zac was livid but confused too. The problem was now that he'd savoured her soft, fleshy lips, her velvety skin, he had to give her up? He still felt the tingling in his body from the lovemaking. How could he forget her soft, mellow laughs? Her giggles were still echoing in his ears, her smile branded in his mind. *Now that he had tasted her sexiness, could he forget her? With her baby blue eyes staring at him full of lust...* His lips still burned with the heat of her sugary kisses. *How will I let her go?*

He was going out of his mind. An ominous growl mewled his way from far down in his belly and boomed over to his mouth. A primeval angry howl exploded for all to hear. It bellowed across the house. He cursed, so much so, an over-worked and underpaid old deckhand would be horrified at his sinful blasphemes.

Umm... no, no way! He shook his head. No, he couldn't, he wouldn't.

He paced like a madman. On one hand, he wished he could spank her backside so hard, until he would pull her lover's name out of her mouth, but alas, it was not possible. On the other, he wanted to make sweet love to her, until her body ached and swelled with pleasure.

Bloody hell! What am I going to do?

Thus, a naughty thought crept into his mind, the vision of spanking her beautiful perky ass, to teach her a lesson, then pinning her down and driving into her hard and fast. That thought got him rock hard in an instant, the tip of his shaft raising against his jeans.

Bollocks! He was confused and enraged... and now, he had blue balls too. He cursed again!

She would make his life a misery. *My well-ordered and enjoy-able life, a total misery!* The past few days had been a paradise for him, well worth it, the best of his life.

He still smelled her sweet jasmine fragrance on him. It was an intoxicating scent. But now he had fallen from the heights of Heaven to the darkest depths of Hell. *By God, the woman is infuriating, dangerous!*

He rubbed the back of his neck hard.

She won't give me his name. Why? It was exasperating for him.

He was getting even more frustrated about the impossible thoughts of making love to her again. How could he curtail them now that he'd had her? Impossible! He wanted to have her again. *But she is a liar, a duplicitous liar, but… I love her!* These thoughts surged and swirled in his mind like a violent storm unleashing darkness.

He sat at his desk. He raked a hand through his hair in frustration. He called Finley and told him what he knew.

"Pick up George and see what he says."

"Do you want me to speak to her too?"

"No, Fin, I already told you," Zac snapped.

"Okay, cool, man. Is she getting to you? We must have the truth! We need a name."

He knew Finley had guessed! He knew this girl had crawled under Zac's skin. He had never seen his friend troubled by a woman, not since they were kids.

Finley chuckled.

"What the fuck is so funny?" Zac spat, moving to the sideboard and filling a tumbler almost to the rim with cognac, even if it was only mid-morning.

"Nothing." Finley coughed, averting his question.

"Anyway. Start with George, and find out what's what," Zac repeated. He took the drink to his desk and sat. He had a swig, and the warmth of the liquid radiated down inside his body, making him feel better.

After the call, Zac started pacing the room. He refilled his glass at the sideboard and took it to his desk and sat there, dejected.

He recalled some tales her mother had told him of when Mollie was a child. 'She runs into mischief often,' her mother had said. 'She trusts people too much, and the result sometimes is disastrous for her.' Bringing to life some old stories from Mollie's childhood had caused him to wonder and smile despite himself.

No surprise then, but this mess… Mollie has surpassed herself this time.

He took a sip of his liquor and the hot blaze trailed down to his curling toes.

With all that cleverness, she is rather naïve, reckless. She puts her trust in the wrong people. Her mom is right, he thought, shaking his head. That man, whoever he was, had taken advantage of his wife. He gulped his drink in one go. He would have to take charge of this impulsive and mischievous creature who had come into his heart so casually but was now causing havoc with his feelings, with his life. *Oh, Mollie, what am I going to do with you?*

A storm of emotions was brewing in his soul.

Mollie… heavenly, bright, sexy but oh, so fucking dangerous. He closed his eyes and then glanced at the empty glass in his hand.

One minute, he craved to bed her, to ravish her with his kisses and his love, to fuck her senseless. The next, he craved to yell at her, to scold her, to punish her for the trouble she was bringing into his somewhat orderly life. So, he sat there, brooding about what to do. After hours of thoughts spinning in his head, he was sure of one thing. He wanted Mollie in his life, at all costs and whatever pain she brought to him.

Bloody hell! I must be nuts!

He had documents to read, but he was too rattled to concentrate. He couldn't think straight. So, he went for a swim, expecting it would help. That was his relief. Ever since his university days, swimming and water polo had been his passions. Up at five in the morning, he put in an hour of swimming every day whenever he could. That day was the perfect time to do some lengths, to tire his body and clear his mind with a long swim. No doubt it would settle and relax him. So, he went up to his bedroom, changed into his swimming trunks and headed down to the pool.

THE SOUND of his guttural growl had reached her in the bedroom, and she blanched. It made her blood ran cold. Why had she done this to him?

Mollie cried for hours after that. She hit the pillow with soft cries, and in the midst, she roared the crudest curses that came into her mind. She paced the room relentlessly. Thousands of thoughts flashed through her brain at the speed of light, until her head hurt. She was heartbroken.

His heart, it seemed, was in no better shape!

Then she cried and paced even more. She stopped at the balcony and saw him standing by the pool in the distance. She stood there watching him for a while.

Sweet Jesus, his body is glorious. Every time she looked at him, it never ceased to amaze her, as if sculpted in marble by one of those splendid Renaissance masters, down to the fine detail.

Zac's body seemed as if chiselled to perfection, tall and athletic, with wide shoulders, slim hips, and muscular thighs that all came together in flawless harmony.

Oh, the warmth of his body, the reminiscence of their sexual intimacy giving her a flush, making her panties wet again. She wished for his glorious hands to roam over her body again.

Sweet Jesus, I miss him already. She sighed, looking at him. His back muscles rippled as he was about to enter the pool. He was her gorgeous husband, but he hated her now. She had disappointed him, big time. If the roar that had come from his mouth earlier that morning was anything to go by… it chilled her to the bone.

She had seen it in his eyes, in his face. Probably, he had already called Alex and asked him to prepare the divorce papers.

Oh, dear God.

She cursed her ex-boyfriend under her breath for forcing

her into this situation. It was his fault, and hers, too, for accepting. It was her fault, for agreeing to this crazy plan. It would have never worked, she thought in anguish. *How ludicrous!*

A small comfort was that her secret was in the open. She wouldn't have to lie anymore. She was crestfallen, but relieved at the same time.

She paced the room, but then she stopped in front of the balcony's glass panes again. Mollie studied Zac once more. She wished she was in the pool with him, but she wouldn't dare. She moved away from the balcony but soon returned to gaze at him again. His lure was captivating. She stared at him swimming. His hairline cresting above the surface of the water, his neck and muscular back relaxed and rippling. His strong thighs were propelling him ahead, as slick and as graceful as a dolphin. Extending his arms to their full length powerfully, he was pivoting and rotating his sexy body and, with each stroke, pulling his perfect frame through the water majestically.

She enjoyed watching him. So handsome. So vigorous! His relentless strokes mesmerised her. He was powerful in and out of the water. He could swim beautifully, but Mollie was not an expert swimmer like he was. Not at all. He looked so natural in his strokes. He made it look easy, like no effort at all, and he was unrelenting. There was something mesmerizingly beautiful in watching him swim. *Surely, his umpteenth length of the pool*, she thought, when a knock at the door made her jump.

She turned towards the door. "Come in."

"Mrs. Sorensen, I brought you something to eat," Marie Therese told her with an impish smile.

"No, thank you. I can't eat anything." She shook her head.

"You must eat, Zac's orders."

"Oh, the hell with him," she said, but she deplored her words.

Marie Therese smiled at her outburst. "He will be fine. The swim will calm him down, though he is in a dreadful mood," the housekeeper said, assuming a lover's tiff had caused her young master's bad temper.

Mollie closed her eyes for a moment. "He has been swimming for an hour," she said, looking out again.

"He used to play water polo when he was younger, you know. He is a strong swimmer. Water is his thing; it will be good for him. He swims every day, more when upset. Why don't you go to him?"

"Me? No, I don't swim."

"Not at all?"

"No. I can't swim. Besides, he is upset with me as it is."

"Oh, Mon Dieu, change and go to him. A pretty girl like you, in a little swimming costume, will make him smile again. Ask him to teach you to swim."

"No, I couldn't," Mollie said, shaking her head.

"Mollie, do you want your husband or not?"

"Oh, Marie, if only it were that simple," she sighed.

MOLLIE WALKED towards the pool and stopped just at the edge. Now that her body was a little tanned, she was wearing her tiny black tie-side triangle bikini. She felt comfortable with it. She was apprehensive, given the circumstances, but she stood her ground.

Zac reached the edge of the pool, ready to turn back for another length, when he saw her silhouette standing there, flickering above the water.

He stopped, pulled his head out of the water and looked up at her.

"You swim beautifully," she said, while she toyed with the tie-side strings of her bikini bottoms. Her eyes couldn't hold his gaze, so she diverted hers over the landscaped gardens. She seemed self-conscious, awkward and mortified at the words they'd had earlier. He now knew everything except the name of her ex-lover. She had hurt him, and she was ashamed of it. But at least, the guilt she had carried on her conscience for months was out in the open. It didn't pardon her by any means, but it felt like a big weight off her shoulders.

But he was furious with her, and she was not sure what to expect next from him. She flushed crimson under his scrutiny, standing there by the pool. She felt hesitant, with him looking at her so intently.

She thought she saw that expression in his eyes again— longing. It made her shiver.

"What do you want?" was his curt reply instead.

It stung her.

She was counting on him being at least polite. But he would not make it easy for her. She wanted to make a swift retreat and looked over her shoulder towards the house, wishing to run back in.

"*Do you want your husband or not?*" Suddenly, Marie Therese's words played in her mind. She inhaled and took strength from these. She wanted him, so very much!

"Why are you not speaking to me? I am fully aware I upset you, but—"

"You are asking me?" he growled, astonished. "I don't believe you are standing there, daring to ask me! I am so mad at you, honestly; you have no idea," he went on, his nostrils flaring while shaking his head.

"Sorry I asked," she sighed, blinking. But she stood there. She didn't move. Zac stared at her, and she blushed.

"I am sorry. How many times do I have to apologise? I said I'm sorry. I am!" she stressed.

"Are you now?" His eyes burned on her.

Mollie was sure his next words would be about divorcing her, but she persisted. She would not retreat. "You were gone for so long, after this morning..." she paused, and then went on, "...I am worried about you."

"Really?" He cocked his head with a hint of amusement in his eyes, but he didn't smile.

"We must talk. Talk to me, please. Your wife... remember me?" she said, hinting a grin and making a little awkward curtsy, half with a remorseful expression and half with desire.

Ahh, his wife, but not for much longer, she thought, expecting him to say something along those lines. So, when he didn't respond, she started fidgeting once again with her bikini's bottom tie-side strings.

HE STUDIED HER IN SILENCE, still not smiling. After an hour in the water, his body was tired but had relaxed, the earlier tension gone.

How can she stand there as if nothing has happened? He cursed under his breath, ready to continue swimming.

But he looked at her contrite face and realised her eyes were bloodshot, and he froze. *She'd cried? Tears! No, no, no! I must be firm.* But he couldn't help feeling a tenderness for her. His heart pumped hard. *No, be strong, man! She is messing with you!* He tried to stop himself from succumbing to her. *No, don't yield to her, man!* His inner voice was unrelenting.

But then, his glance swayed to her swimsuit, her small hand playing delicately with the strings of her bathing piece.

His eyes moved to the soft mound covered by her bikini, to her delicious body. His firmness was wavering.

Seeing her there, standing at the edge of the pool, he had an overwhelming desire to untie the strings of her tiny bikini and reveal her naughty secrets in all her beauty. He recalled her warm and soft lips beneath his, her breasts quivering with pleasure, and he needed to touch her again.

The thought of her warm body tormented him regardless of her lying. Despite his wife's duplicitous behaviour, he wanted her.

No, I can't. I won't... no. He was trying hard. *Be a resolute man, for God's sake; don't give in.*

But his body had a mind of his own.

The flesh was weak... *Traitorous body!*

Chapter 13

All it took was a split second for him to use his body strength. In a complex body movement reminiscent of his water polo days, to lift himself up, he kicked his legs under the water in an explosive boosting action. These powerful kicks allowed him to spring half of his body out of the water and in mid-air. Just high enough, long enough for him to settle his big hands hard on her hips, and thus he pulled her down into the water with him, just like a predator tiger fish leaps out of the water to catch his prey in mid-air.

Well, that was not what Mollie expected! And not exactly what she was hoping for, not when she was a poor swimmer.

They sank under the water. Not a problem for a skilful athlete like Zac, but for Mollie, it was something else. Lacking air, she was not expecting to forgo, her body couldn't perform. Distress and panic took over and she thought she would drown as she took in water through her nose and mouth. Her arms started flapping wildly in an attempt to raise her mouth above the water to breathe, her head tilting back in desperation. She even hit Zac with slaps of her hands.

Zac didn't flinch, but he had underestimated her ability to swim, big time! He got hold of her and pulled her up from under the water like a drowning cat.

"I've got you. You're fine now," he whispered when he realised her distress. He held her arms to stop her from lashing out, but she wriggled one arm free. She latched her arm around his neck tightly to stay afloat and to get some air.

"It's okay. I've got you," he repeated in her ear.

She gasped for air. Her hair covered her face like a curtain. She coughed and sputtered, while taking in deep breaths, but her arm was holding onto his neck as if for dear life. She wrapped her legs around his waist instinctively, to keep herself from going under the water again.

"Are you okay?" he asked while pulling her hair back from her face with a hand. She was still coughing while clinging to him.

She nodded, but then she had second thoughts. She slapped his face with her open hand with all the strength she mastered.

"Ouch. Hey, that hurt," he said, frowning at her.

"You m-moron," she seethed in between coughing and wheezing sprees.

"Mollie, I thought you could—"

"Were y-you trying to d-drown me?" she stammered, her body trembling, while still gasping for air.

"Sorry, I didn't know—" he apologised, watching her in concern, their faces inches from each other.

"What's wrong with you? I can't swim," she was forced to reveal, still coughing but starting to recover. Her inability to swim had not come up in conversation; she had been ashamed to tell him.

"Hey, my face hurts," Zac said, massaging his cheek with

his hand, and then he cleared more strands of hair from her face. But an amused grin was taking shape on his face.

"Not enough." She took in a deep breath and said, "I know I pissed you off, but drown me? A little drastic! Don't you think?" she blurted out.

He laughed while he held her, and she tightened her arm around his neck. They couldn't have been any closer if they tried, their bodies almost meshed together.

"Are you okay now?" he asked her tenderly, but her warm body wrapped around him was bringing back images of their lovemaking. He struggled to put these visions out of his head.

She nodded, still frightened from her experience, unaware of the effect she was having on him.

"Please, get me out of the pool," she pleaded.

"You can't swim?"

"Didn't you see me? Did it look to you like I can?"

"Well, no—"

"Oh, I doggy paddle; does that count?"

"Nope. I don't think so." He laughed, shaking his head, an earthy belly laugh that made him look lovely. Despite her discomfort, she hinted at a smile too.

He cradled her in his arms, and despite all her lies, he had to admit that it felt good.

"Then, no. I can't swim. Please, get me out of here." She was hanging on to him as if her life depended on it. Water was not her thing.

This was news to him. Not that he had forgotten her lies, but it amused him seeing her like that.

"You need to learn to swim," he said encouragingly.

"Sure, but not right now. Please, take me out of here," she persisted.

"Just relax before you strangle me," he said, trying to release the tight hold she had around his neck.

"I can't."

"Mollie, loosen up," he repeated.

"Well, fine," she replied, relaxing her grip on him. But she was still apprehensive.

"Relax, otherwise, you won't want to enter the water again."

"I beg you, get me out of the water."

"Shush, loosen up. Extend your body," he replied with a soft command.

"No."

"Do you trust me?" he asked, caressing her face.

"Oh, my God!"

"Relax, I said. I'm holding you," he repeated, granting her a soft kiss on the nose.

Oh, man, what the fuck are you doing? his inner voice grumbled. *What the hell? Damn!* He couldn't resist her; that much he knew. He was powerless against his desire for her. Not that he had forgotten her mendacity or her deception, but the swim had quenched his immediate anger, and he relaxed. Besides, he still wanted her, with a strong passion. So, he had no wish to fight his feelings for her. At least, not now, not with her in his arms. Thus, it become another one of those moments where he forgot their disagreement... their problems.

NOT EXPECTING a kiss after all the upset she'd caused him, she mellowed. *If this is what it takes to calm him down after what I've done, then water it is!*

So, they were beguiled by the moment. They felt cozy in each other's arms. Neither of them wanted to let go or to stop.

"Okay, if you insist," she said, relenting. She softened her tight grip on his neck.

Then, he taught her a few rudimentary swimming skills. He asked her to extend her legs back and her arms in front of her, and he held her by the middle of her body.

"That's great. Good girl," he said.

"Are you holding me?" She trembled, but he encouraged her.

"Yes. You will be fine," he whispered.

Somehow, his strength, the gentle words, and his protective arms around her made her safe. Besides, she had missed him. So, she mellowed, even if water was not her thing. So, she did as she was told.

He asked her to extend her arms and to pull the water towards her in a scooping motion. He showed her how to cup her hands to do it. After several unsuccessful attempts, she was moving forwards. She giggled, glancing at him.

"Look ahead." He smiled at her eagerness now to do the right movements and to please him.

Zac was holding her with a hand under her belly, keeping her afloat. She enjoyed him so close to her.

While scooping with her hands, he asked her to kick her feet under the water. "Kick as if on a bicycle. Extend your legs out and kick your legs."

"Like this?" She kicked her legs out and propelled forward, but he followed her.

"Good. You are doing well," he encouraged her.

She giggled with excitement.

And for a while, forgetting their problems, they were both enjoying the moments in the water, like two school kids in love, on their first outing.

He asked her to practise the movements until comfortable with them. She did it for half an hour under his watchful eyes. He followed her around with his hands under her body and blurting out instructions.

"Come closer to me," she said at one point, when he was too confident about her ability.

"You are doing well; keep going." He smiled.

JESUS, I must be nuts! But I can't resist her; she has bewitched me.

And she rewarded him with biting her bottom lip with the effort. She was enthusiastically launching strokes of legs and arms, but then he winked at her. She lost her concentration, and for a split second, she sank under the water again, but she grabbed him. She launched her arms tightly around his neck and her legs around his waist, holding on to him fiercely as if a blowing gale was trying to pull her away. Her hair covered her face again.

"Relax, you are doing fine." He laughed at her fierce grip on him.

"I would if I could see anything," she said, with her face hidden under long strands of hair, and he chuckled.

He pulled her hair back with one hand and smiled at her. *Bloody hell, I adore this girl! Christ, she is my weakness! Who would have thought he, of all men, an inveterate womaniser, would fall for this slip of a girl?* She beguiled him. Not only this, but she had fibbed her way into his life. He, who always called the shots… he, who was powerful, was at the mercy of this young woman! *She's wrapped me around her little finger, like a schoolboy.*

But soon, he realised her long legs were circling his waist and her face was inches from his. He could feel her soft breath panting on his neck. His manhood never stood a chance with her body pressed on him like that and shot up to a standing ovation. So, he went for her lips and kissed her.

She hesitated, not expecting it, but soon she responded with ardour. They kissed again, fervently. They had only been apart for a short time, after their cross words over her lies, but they had missed each other like the earth misses the hot sun in winter.

He made Mollie forget she was in the water. And she made him forget all their problems.

What the hell! He preferred his womanising days. At least then, he knew where he stood. He was on safer grounds, but now? How would he ever return to normalcy with this girl? His peace of mind was broken forever. His old life, as he knew it, was no longer an option.

Oh, Mollie… Mollie, what have you done to me? he thought while kissing her.

He untied her swimsuit strings. First, he removed her bikini top.

"What are you doing?" she asked, putting her hand up to cover her breasts.

"I want you naked," he whispered in his bass husky tone, close to her ear.

"I can't swim; you are not thinking of…" And she waved her hand, showing her body and the water, her eyes incredulous at his suggestion.

He laughed, an earthy belly laugh. "No, but I prefer you naked in the pool," he responded, still with laughter in his eyes, while untying the strings of her bikini bottoms. But she gave him a glaring look which said she didn't believe him.

In fact, she should not have believed him. Within five minutes of swimming frolics naked, he got his fingers inside her folds. She gasped, taking in water through her mouth. She turned to wrap herself tightly around him one more time while gasping for air and bouts of coughing.

"Are you okay? You took in a little water."

"I can't do it in here," she splattered through a cough, but his fingers were still inside her, his eyes lashing lust on her.

"The pool steps. You'll be fine there." He pulled her with

him to the corner, where the wide custom-built steps delved into the pool and sat on one. He sat her on his lap, astride, facing him. Only half their bodies were in the water, so she felt secure.

"What if someone sees us?" she asked, breathing in hard, starting to sense the pleasure of his probing fingers inside her.

"We are not overlooked," he said, kissing her eyes.

"Are you sure?"

"Yes. Relax."

"What if Marie or Henri see us?"

"Not a chance. They know better." He kissed her fore-head and then her nose. She had an idea he had done this before... make love in the pool... and a pang of jealousy ran through her body.

She asked, "Are you certain?"

He could feel her tensing in his arms. "Relax," he repeated, and kissed her on the mouth, hard. At first, the kiss was meant to shut her up. But soon it deepened, and he didn't leave her lips until they were both gasping for air. Thus, she relaxed, like jelly in his arms. His lips went back to her eyes, then to the tip of her nose, her earlobe, her neck, and to her mouth again.

This time she felt nestled in a pool of pleasure in his arms. She let out a moan and wriggled her body.

He groaned in her mouth, his fingers expertly moving inside her, but he changed positions. He sat her on the top step, and her hands went to hold the ridge of the pool.

He took a deep breath and lowered his face under the water between her thighs, his mouth going to her clit, taunting it with his tongue. The water tickled her too as he licked her clit while thrusting his fingers inside her. He came up for air every few seconds.

She was enjoying the blissful amorous torture he was

lavishing on her, water and all. She felt every little movement of his fingers and tongue, his touch on her body powerful. She was going with the flow, the only thought in her mind the pleasure he was bestowing on her.

I love his tongue.

Teasing and thrusting under the water with his fingers and tongue, his other hand reached up for her breast, squeezing her nipple hard between his fingers, each touch raising her pulse to new levels, until she called out his name.

He lifted his face from the water to kiss her mouth.

"Hold it; wait," he warned.

"I am—"

"Wait," he groaned, and for a moment, he stood up on the step, out of the water. She looked up at his magnificent taut and tanned body, wet and gleaming with ripples of water, in full splendour. He dispensed of his swimming trunks, and his steely erection emerged in all his glory, long and hard, like a spear ready for battle.

Her eyes widened.

"Loosen up." He winked, with a lustful grin on his lips, in his low and seductive voice.

She gulped.

He pulled her up and sat on the pool steps. He grabbed her hips, positioning her on his lap astride him, then firmly, he guided her into a descending motion over his unyielding erection, their bodies half in and half out of the water.

She gasped as he entered her.

He caressed her thighs with the palm of his hand as he entered her slowly, with short thrusts of his hips while she was lowering onto him.

She made a whimpering sound as he thrust inside her.

He smiled at her, but his eyes were dark and full of desire. "Hell, you will be the death of me," he mumbled breathlessly.

"Zac," she moaned, looking at him, pleading she was ready. She had been ready and trying hard to wait for his word, so she bit her lips.

"Wait. Oh, fuck, I can't resist you," he said, kissing her mouth hard.

"Zac, please," she whimpered in his mouth.

"Wait," he commanded with a coarse tone, almost there himself but trying to hold his final pleasure.

He was pleasuring her, up and down his shaft, with a yearning intensity, his hands tight on her hips, guiding her motion. Her eyes were closed and her head back, as she tried to stop herself from coming, and just feel him inside her.

"Zac, I can't—" she whimpered once more, and sweet short moans escaped from her mouth.

He was thrusting deeper and faster now, again and again, until they couldn't hold any longer.

She gave a loud cry and called his name.

"My sweet baby," he mumbled with almost a guttural sound, and they both let go of their bodies. The delight enveloped every little nerve and muscle of their frames in intense rapture, and their bodies shuddered in orgasmic pleasure. It took a while before their bodies subsided.

When Mollie's stopped trembling, she wrapped her arms around him with warmth and affection. She wanted this man in her life forever.

She kissed him. Her hands on his face, touching his mouth with her fingers, she kissed every little inch of his face.

"That good, ha?" He smiled with manly pride, caressing her face.

And he kissed her back tenderly.

Zac had suspected that he had been on dangerous ground with this woman the moment she had come to his office, all those months back. *Hell no, when she'd waved her hand at me in Peter's chambers.*

He had experienced nothing so sweet and powerful with a woman, not like it was with her. He couldn't let her go. Despite her lying and despite her ex-lover lurking in the shadows, Zac loved her.

She was his, for now...

He still wasn't sure how she felt about him.

That morning, she had said she liked him. But that was not the same as loving him, as he loved her, like he wanted her—a long way from it.

She was a danger to herself and to him. He needed to protect her from her own dangerous actions. Her ex-boyfriend was still pursuing her. Would her man give her up so easily? In his place, Zac wouldn't.

So, he knew he had a battle on his hands, but she was worth it.

Chapter 14

"What took you so long? I'm famished," he said as she entered the dining room that evening. But one glance at her, and he gaped.

Mollie was wearing a purple dress, fitted from the shoulders down to a belted waist, flowing into a short A-line skirt. The dress was soft and feminine with a square necked front and back. The long sleeves, bell shaped, went wide from the elbows down. It was a stylish dress; it suited her slender and willowy frame to perfection.

Her belt matched her over-the-knee black patent leather boots, complementing the outfit and transforming it into a sexy little number.

"You look stunning," Zac whispered in a bass tone, his mouth brushing her ear, sending tingles down her spine as he pulled a chair for her at the table.

"Thank you," she mumbled as she sat, but her face took a flush of colour. *Hmm… But I take the compliment.* Then she added, "Oh, the warm shower felt good."

He sat opposite her, but he stared at her while images of her under the shower formed in his mind.

"Which reminds me... next time," he said in a raspy tone, waggling his eyebrows with a playful grin and a glint of lust in his eyes.

"Oh? No! Not water again," she murmured under her breath.

He snorted.

Marie Therese served them dinner.

"What is it? It smells delicious," Mollie asked, dilating her nostrils.

The housekeeper dished out the portions. The aroma spread through the room. "It's a light cassoulet. It is a traditional French casserole, with lean gammon and pork shoulder, slow cooked, an earthy meal," the lady explained.

"I love it. Marie always cooks it when I am here," Zac said, beaming at the old woman.

"I have also made your favourite potatoes," the housekeeper told him.

"Excellent!"

"Boulangere potatoes are light and healthy, perfect if you need energy," Marie Therese said and winked at him with a brief nod of the head towards Mollie.

He was munching on a piece of bread, but he practically choked on it, struggling to control his laughter. *Oh, the French...*

But it was Mollie who turned bright red at the innuendo.

Zac grinned at his housekeeper, amused. Marie Therese finished serving them then left the room.

"Oh my God, it tastes divine, but I'm not surprised. Marie's cooking is to die for," Mollie said, putting another forkful of cassoulet in her mouth.

"Can you cook?" he asked, and he realised, in all these months, he had never asked her the question.

"Umm, no. Not really. Only a few basic dishes," she replied, shaking her head.

"Maybe you should learn," Zac stated. *Cook? Why? Where did that come from?* he wondered.

"Cook?" Mollie repeated in shock.

"Yes, cook. At least my favourite dishes," he stressed, suddenly disconcerted at what his mouth had just uttered. A dull flush crept up his neck as he wished he could take his words back.

What is this? he thought. *Seriously?*

"What are you? A caveman? Your favourites dishes? Indeed!" she repeated, wide eyed, and at that point, she made an uncouth, unladylike snort.

But he wasn't finished. "Mollie, stop repeating what I say," he groaned, ignoring the "*caveman*" appellative, embarrassed at his own comments and where this conversation was going.

"Well, even if I wanted to… I didn't think I would have the chance, anyway," she ventured, now turning red at his serious face.

"Don't you enjoy cooking?" he asked. *Oh crap! What the hell? What's wrong with me tonight?*

"Oh, yes, I do. I cooked a dish or two with Marie while you were away, trying to entertain myself." She stared at him. He could detect the admonishment in her words for his "*caveman*" behaviour and also for leaving her alone in Antibes for days after her sunstroke.

Is she chastising me, when she lied her way into marrying me and into my bed? The bloody cheek! He glared at her with a scowl, but his mouth had other ideas.

"Then, why don't you learn to cook? Properly. Marie would love to teach you." *Hell, I should divorce her, instead of encouraging her.* His mouth had a will of its own. The sugary words tumbling out of his mouth made him wince, as if they belonged to someone else.

She sniggered and chuckled at his words.

Christ, what has she done to me? Who is this man talking? It wasn't the cooking he was after but a picture of domesticity with her. *A life of bliss with her. I must be nuts. What the blast? Have I lost my mind?*

He took a deep breath to get himself out of those dreamy, domestic lingerings with Mollie. Was this what he had always wanted? What he desired? A loving wife? A simple life with the woman he loved? *No, surely not. What the devil is wrong with me?*

But his actions in the pool had spoken louder. His words, following their lovemaking, had been sweeter. One, he had forgiven her for what she had done. Though, he still harboured concerns, upset about her lies and her ex-lover, he'd pardoned her. To let her off the hook so easily for all those lies, absolving her of all her faults, it was out of character for him. But he had done it. His feelings for her were too strong.

"Oh?" She paused with wide eyes, but she went on, "Are you sure?"

Two, he was now creating in his mind this picture of domestic bliss with her. *Am I crazy? I must be sick,* he thought. This was not him!

So, he shook his head and tried to focus on something else. He focused on the facts instead, pressing matters to deal with. Now that he was aware a third person lingered in his marriage, he needed to do something about it. He knew that. So, he placed his attention on her ex-lover and the potential dangers lurking on them. Those somber thoughts soon took control over his loose mouth and any picture of domesticity with the minx. It sobered him, bringing him back to reality with a vengeance.

"Well, I mean, I thought I didn't need to learn to do anything else because..." she ventured.

"Because?" he asked anyway.

"Well, you know..." She stopped, and he waited for her to finish her sentence, but she left it hanging.

"No, I don't know!" he said impatiently.

"Well."

"Oh, for God's sake, Mollie, what?"

"Well, I mean, you talked about forgiveness, but I guess it was on the spur-of-the-moment, wasn't it? I mean, after... ahem... our sweet moments. But you don't mean it, do you? I'll understand if you want to divorce me now," she mumbled, her eyes fixed on her plate.

"Divorce you?"

"Yes, divorce me—"

"Umm?"

"Yes, despite what you said in the pool about forgiving me. Will you divorce me? I mean, now that you know the truth! I'll understand if you do," she said, tugging at her sleeves.

"Do you want a divorce?" he asked with a steady voice. He held his breath for a second.

"No!" she cried out and blushed, surprised at her own vehemence.

"Good! Then, no, Mollie. No divorce." He voiced the words against his better judgement.

Stay married to her? Fucking crazy! He knew! *Well, there is my image to consider.*

He tried to justify his ludicrous decisions about his wife. *Yes, the Board, that's right! There is that,* he thought, that's why he had forgiven her. He convinced himself the reasons for not divorcing her were about the Board and about improving his image.

"No choice now, too late to backtrack from our arrangement. There's my reputation to think of. I have to appease the Board of Directors. I need to achieve my goal," he said, to keep a vestige of manly pride following his earlier sugar-coated words.

Now that he had savoured her lips, made passionate love to her, there was no turning back. After the last few days of bliss, he was addicted to her, despite her revelations. He wanted her in his life. He wanted to live and grow old with her. Besides, the thought of another man touching Mollie made his toes curl. He couldn't bear it. That was the truth. *I won't let her go. For my sins, I won't!*

"No?" she asked, surprised. *Seriously? No divorce?* Her thoughts were twirling in her mind.

"No!"

"But I lied to you," she said. *Oh sweet Jesus, thank you! He wants to stay married!*

"Yes, I know that, way too well. Though I have forgiven you, I've not forgotten your lies, understood?" he reverberated with an orotund tone.

Her fork rattled in her plate at the accusatory words. "Oh?" she said, lowering her eyes, picking up her fork again and toying with her food.

"But no divorce," he stated. Somehow, he had the feeling this girl was playing him like a schoolboy.

"No divorce," she murmured, more to convince herself of it than to him. *Thank you, Lord,* was her silent prayer.

"No. I hired you to do a job, to rebuild my image, and it's working. I have the Board to consider," he said with more self-possession now. *Yes, true enough.*

But his tone was less conciliatory now, vexed at his own weakness for her, at not being able to control his craving for her. All his life, he had been in command. But now, when it came to his wife, he was powerless.

"So that's exactly what you'll do. We'll stay married, and you will work to improve my image. You'll deliver on our contract," he said, his tone harsher and commanding. The reality, he was in love with her. She melted his reckless heart, like a schoolboy on his first crush. Though, every time her lies surfaced again in his mind, he couldn't avoid the dichotomy of misery and joy. It was driving him crazy, but he was utterly in love with her. Thus, he'd decided; he would stay married to her.

She lowered her eyes and toyed with a strand of her hair, noting the change of tone. "No divorce?" she mumbled more to herself and thrilled at the thought of it.

"Absolutely not!"

Silence descended.

"You want to stay with me," she whispered again after a while, like in a trance.

I cannot believe it! Good God!

"Oh, man, this cassoulet is divine," he said instead, closing his eyes. He munched on a piece of pork, savouring it.

She watched his lips, mesmerised, reminiscent of what those lips had been up to in the pool on her intimate parts. It made her wet. Until he caught her staring with her lascivious thoughts. She couldn't help it. He was too handsome, but something must have shown on her face as he grinned.

"Are you gaping at me?" he teased.

She coughed instead, looking at her plate. "Well, I was ready to pack, despite your forgiveness," she mumbled.

"You will not be so lucky, Mollie," he stressed.

"Umm," she murmured.

He watched her with amusement in his eyes. "Well, that's settled then, but I'll make you work hard for it now," he said, raising his eyebrows.

Marie Therese came back in the room to clear their plates. They fell silent while the old lady served an inviting platter of French cheese with crackers of different shapes and textures and served the rest of the wine. She placed the cheese board on the table and the dessert and coffee on the sideboard.

"The dessert is a super-creamy white chocolate soufflé. Henri has already eaten two servings. Zac, I put three on the sideboard, in case you want a second helping," the housekeeper said.

"Marie, tonight, you have ten out of ten. Magnifique!"

"Anything else I can do for you?"

"Thank you, Marie. That's all for tonight; we'll take it from here."

"Good night." And the housekeeper left the room.

"Would you like some cheese?" Zac asked her, when he started cutting big slices of cheese from the platter while the earthy and smoky aroma filled the room.

"No, thank you. I'll wait for dessert."

"Please help yourself, the soufflé is better when it is just out of the oven."

"No. I'll wait for you."

"Okay," he said, while he served himself Chabichou and Banon slices of cheese with crackers and red grapes. He took a gulp of red wine from his glass.

God, he loves the stuff, she thought, witnessing his gluttony for cheese.

"Besides, you enjoy sex with me. You like a good fuck, don't you?" he suddenly asked her, as cool as a cucumber.

She looked at him open-mouthed, not expecting such a direct question on sex on those terms.

"I-I—"

"Well, did you enjoy fucking me or not, all these last few days, ha?" he repeated, his tone dead calm. He may as well be asking if she had enjoyed her swim.

"Yes," she whispered, red in the face. She took a strand of her hair and rolled it around her finger.

"There you are. Sorted then. We'll stay married."

"Well, I was not the only one, I hope," she ventured coyly.

"The only one, what?"

"Well, you know…" she said with a quick raise of her eyebrows.

"What? And stop toying with your hair."

"Oh, Lord. What you said!"

"You marry for money and you lie! And yet, you are a prude? You enjoyed fucking me, but you can't say it?" He laughed at her contradictions, but his laugh was short lived while annoyance took over her.

She glared at him. "Stop this. I am not a prude," she boomed and stood up and cursed under her breath—a hefty, dirty mouthed curse.

"And you curse like a trooper! Yet, you cannot say fuck!" He shook his head with a grin, but she cursed again.

"Are you cursing at me?" he went on as an afterthought. He tried to tense his features, but there was amusement in his eyes.

"No," she mumbled.

He narrowed his eyes on her. Though he would not admit to it, he found it hilarious that his wife's curses were almost as bad as his. She was a deceitful liar and cursed sinfully but intrigued him. She couldn't even mention the words sex or fuck without a flush. The words themselves, in abstract, were fine for her. She used them and cursed with them, no problem. But when specific about the sexual act with him, she couldn't say them. They made her blush furiously.

"Sit down Mollie," he commanded.

She sat down again but gave him a fiery look. "Well, if are going to be so horrid to me, I—"

"Horrid? Because I asked you if you enjoy fucking me?" He laughed.

"You are doing it again."

"Well, if you think I am horrid, wait until Fin comes this weekend and asks you for his name."

"Fin?" she asked, astonished, turning pale.

"Fin, Alex, and Peter. They are taking my plane. Alex is fuming that I am not divorcing you and is dragging the other two with him. So, they have invited themselves down for the weekend."

"You are kidding." She stood up again, shocked. She started fidgeting with the sleeve of her dress.

"Don't worry. His bark is worse than his bite."

"Your friends cannot come," she said with vehemence, still standing.

"Why not?" he asked, frowning.

"Well, it is our honeymoon," she blurted out, to have some excuse.

"Oh? Don't you worry; there is plenty of room for everybody," he said, calmly munching on a grape, but a grin couldn't help escape him.

"Zac, tell them not to come."

"Mollie, sit down."

"Please."

"Why are you so upset at them coming? You said it yourself; this is a business arrangement. Not a real honeymoon." *In theory*, he thought, and funnily enough, so did she! Both of them were aware of the contractual arrangements but also of the tumultuous feelings they had for each other. But he couldn't spill the words, his feeling for her; he wouldn't. Neither would she. Though her vehemence surprised him, her sudden antagonism towards his friends made him suspicious.

"I am not upset. I know this is an arrangement, but, well, I… if we are to stay married, and given the amount of s-sex in the last few days, I…" she blabbered almost incoherently;

it was not like her.

It made him even more suspicious. "Jealous of them, are you?" he asked, raising another piece of cheese to his mouth.

"Why? No. No."

"They are coming, end of story!" he emphasised.

He would have told his friends not to come. He thought it ludicrous for them to visit when he was happy to be with Mollie, alone, despite her lies.

But seeing her so put out by them coming, he wondered what was going on in that beautiful red head of that wife of his. She looked so troubled and bothered by the fact he had mentioned his friends, that he had an idea she didn't like them. But his instinct told him it was not that simple. Something was bothering her. Big time! By now, he'd learned there was more to Mollie than she let out. So, he sat back in his chair and studied her.

Intriguing! As intimately as he knew his wife's body by now, there was a hell of a lot more he didn't know about her.

"Let them come some other time, not now. Please?" she insisted.

"No."

"But, Zac—" she pleaded.

"Mollie, it's settled. They will be here this weekend." So, he pushed the point instead, fascinated by her antagonism, intrigued by her resistance to it. He was curious now.

She frowned and looked away. Then, she turned to him again and sat back in her chair. Silence descended, each studying the other.

"Then if you don't mind, I'll ask mother and my best friends to come for the weekend too. I'll tell Marie and make the sleeping arrangements," she told him afterwards, not waiting for his approval, but as a given.

"It will be a crowd, but as you wish. The more the

merrier. Or is it safety in numbers, hey? It won't deter Fin, though."

She sulked.

THE LIGHT FILTERED through the blinds of the bedroom, and she blinked. She woke up next to him in his bed. She opened her eyes. A sudden warmth rushed through her body when she realised her head was resting on his perfect torso.

Mollie caressed him. She kissed Zac's chest, just barely touching him. One arm wrapped around his waist while one of her legs sprawled across his hips; she turned to face him, and she beamed languidly, her eyes somewhat hooded with sleep.

They were both like nature intended, naked.

He was asleep when she began praising his perfect body.

A beautifully sunny morning, and this handsome man next to her. *Oh, a glorious way to start the day!*

Mollie caressed Zac's face and kissed his jaw softly, not wanting to rouse him yet. She craved to enjoy the sight of his gorgeous body for a few moments, undisturbed. She wanted to caress those vigorous limbs. She trailed her hand up his arm and then over his shoulders and down his chest, barely touching him.

She raised her head again to study his face. He was gorgeous! And he would be hers for the next three years. *No Divorce! Holy cow! Whoopee!* She smiled, elated.

Three years of joyous, sublime sex with this god-like creature. That was not the only reason for her pleasure, though. She had fallen for him, and hard. The more she stayed with him, the more she needed him.

She sighed. *Ah, the loveliest of mortals. And he is mine!*

But her emotions kept varying with this man. He had

upset her at dinner. His friends were coming, and she didn't like that. Not one bit! It would spell trouble. She sensed it, but there was nothing she could do about it.

"Stop staring and touching me," he mumbled with half a smile on his lips, his eyes still closed.

"Oh." Mollie withdrew her hand, as if he had caught her with her hands in the cookie jar. She was about to move away from him, but Zac grabbed her by the waist and dragged her on top of him.

She giggled, facing him, and he kissed her lazily with his eyes still closed.

Then he opened them to look at her. "Nice. My lovely wife," he whispered, beaming a warm smile at her, cuddling her, kissing the tip of her nose.

GOD, this is heaven! He had not awakened with women in his bed too often. During his bachelor days, he would regularly send them home after the fact. But these days, waking up with Mollie in his bed felt right. Pure delight, his heart exploding with joy by being with her.

"You were rude last night, and this morning you are sweet," she said, smiling.

"I am never sweet. You'll learn that!" he growled teasingly.

"You were sweet just now. Yes, you were! And you cannot take it back," she smirked, jabbing her forefinger in his chest.

He wrapped his arms around her tighter, and in a swift movement, he turned them both, ending up on top of her. She squealed. He grinned and kissed her forehead, her cheeks, her nose, her lips, her neck, again and again. She got into a fit of giggles.

He held his weight by his elbows, but there was no doubt that his manhood had been on alert for some time.

"Damn, see what you do to me," he taunted, pressing his shaft to her belly, and then he took her mouth, this time owning her, delighting in the taste of her, teasing her with his tongue.

His hand went to her mound, and he slipped a finger in her folds.

"You are soaked!" He looked at her face. "You had a dirty dream about me?" he teased her again, and her cheeks burned.

"Stop it," she said, slapping him gently on his shoulder.

But he kissed her ravenously. He entered her in one forceful thrust, and they made passionate love. Alternating passion with a tender lovemaking, they explored every inch of each other's body. They couldn't keep their hands from one another until, finally, their bodies shuddered in a powerful climax.

Into the bargain, their hearts had a crucial role too, and they wallowed in it. Their hearts filled with that special once-in-a-lifetime love. But they were too afraid to word their sentiment, neither of them daring it first, still believing the other only coveted the arranged marriage, the business trans-action, for what it was worth.

It wasn't logical. How could she have fallen for him? She was afraid. She knew, eventually, it might all end in tears and sorrow. A powerful emotion for this man gripped her. She had given herself to him fully and uninhibitedly, and tears of joy came down her cheeks.

"Hey, what is it?" he asked her warmly, wiping her tears away with his hands, caressing her. But she held on to him and kissed him with love flowing out freely.

Chapter 15

That morning, Finley's team picked up George outside the Physics department of the university, off Park Road.

George had gone voluntarily, without hesitation. It intrigued him. He had met Finley at Mollie's wedding, and he wondered why this man needed to talk to him.

"Why did you see Mollie?" Finley asked him without preamble when he went to his office.

The young man raised his eyebrows in surprise but didn't hesitate in his reaction. "Because, I am her friend." But he tensed, shifting in his chair.

"Friend?" Finley repeated, sitting behind his desk opposite him.

"Is she sick again?" George questioned him instead, anticipating something was wrong.

"No, she is fine. But I need to understand why she saw you in Antibes, in secret."

"Secret? No. It's no secret," he replied.

"No?"

"No. I went to see her in Antibes, but Zac wasn't there. So, I met her in a coffee shop instead."

"Oh? Gentlemanly of you."

"True!" he said, scowling at him.

"But you went to visit a friend on her honeymoon? That's peculiar, don't you think?"

"Oh, come now. She was sick. I worry about her."

"Do you?"

"Zac has not known her long, otherwise he would figure it out that Mollie and I are great friends. We look after each other. We always have. How long has he known her, hey?"

"Umm." Finley looked at him.

"It's true." The young man continued, shrugging his shoulders.

"Is she your lover?"

"Lover? Bloody hell, are you insane? No!" he cried out as if he had insulted him, not to mention his astonishment.

"Not her lover?"

"No. I told you; we are friends." George wondered where this discussion was going.

"Umm…"

"Oh, man! What kind of questions are these?"

"Honest?"

"Yes. It's the truth. Mollie married Zac; why would she have a lover? Is there something wrong?" George asked, now dismayed.

"I ask the questions."

"And I say, I don't have to answer anything to you! But for the record, no. I am not her lover, and I never was, got it? She wouldn't do such a thing."

"Is that so?"

"Yes, really! I know her well enough to be certain."

"Oh?"

"I am her friend. I know her. Zac met her only recently."

"They met four months ago if you are really interested. Why are you so anxious to know this? Tell me!" Finley asked.

Four months ago! George realised it now. A year ago, Mollie's boyfriend couldn't have been Zac. *And he thinks she has a lover? No, I don't believe it.* Had she maintained a liaison with that man, despite being married now? *No. Not her, I am sure!*

Sometimes, Mollie had no common sense, true! But she was a good person. A sweet girl. George was positive of that, unless...

His heart sunk. His mind was running a hundred miles per hour with questions. Sadly, he had none of the answers. *What has Mollie done?* He suspected it had something to do with that boyfriend of hers, and he didn't mean Zac.

"Look, nothing more to say." George paused. "Now, if you don't mind, I am done here."

"You are free to go. We were just having a friendly chat." Finley grinned, but George turned a fierce scowl on him. Then he stood up, twirled on his heel and headed for the door.

As he walked to the bus stop, George had his suspicions, his mind in confusion. Mollie married Zac so suddenly, but now he feared something was up. *What had she gotten herself into? What the hell is going on?*

Mollie had to come clean with him. As a friend, he warranted the truth.

He needed to talk to her, and fast.

"WHAT'S GOING ON?" he said over the phone the moment she answered his call.

Her eyes widened at his question, not expecting it. "Hello, George, how are you?" Mollie said instead, not avoiding a crack in her voice.

They were having lunch in the dining room when George's call landed on her mobile phone. She looked at her husband sitting opposite her and smiled. *Blast, why the hell did I answer the call?* she thought, but it was too late.

"Finley interrogated me. He asked me if I am your lover. Why?" her friend hissed over the phone.

Mollie couldn't enter into that discussion while Zac listened and watched her. Not with her husband there. She couldn't excuse herself from the room, either. It would make him suspicious. *Damn!*

No choice, she had to delay the conversation with George, and thus answered the first thing that came into her mind, hoping her friend would understand.

"I don't know! The book is upstairs. I'll check later," she answered, instead, but went on, "we can talk about it over the weekend." She tried to keep her face relaxed and her voice calm.

"What the hell is going on? Zac was not your boyfriend, was he? I mean way back, about a year ago. They think you have a lover now! That I am your lover!" With George's awkward questions pouring over the phone, Mollie's face became crimson.

Zac didn't miss her flush, his glare on her. Mollie peeked at him from under her lashes for a moment, with a hint of a smile, and saw his eyes narrowed on her. As the conversation went on, her husband doubted her. She could see it in his eyes.

"George, we are in the middle of lunch. Can we discuss the book this weekend? How's Kathryn?" she asked instead. She tried, for Zac's benefit, pretending to have just a friendly conversation with her fellow student.

But Zac's scrutiny on her became incandescent, his eyes fixed on her. By his expression, she had an inkling he was not buying it.

She bit her bottom lip. And he didn't miss that, either. Her body language gave her away. And suddenly, a thunderous look clouded Zac's gorgeous features. But there was nothing she could do.

"I understand. Are you in trouble?" George sighed, exasperated.

"Yes, I am…" She paused and then said, "Let's talk over the weekend. I can't wait to see you." Mollie's voice had a hint of pleading, and she put the telephone down.

Then, she looked up and smiled at her husband. He turned away, and she knew it had annoyed him. She sensed his frustration and wondered what he was thinking.

But she turned to Marie Therese and said, "I meant to ask you about the cassoulet? I want to learn the recipe. We enjoyed it so much the other day; can you tell me about it?"

Mollie tried to avoid his questions after her call with George. And she offered no explanation, either, buying herself some time.

The housekeeper obliged and dived into the details of the recipe. The woman kept on talking, but as Mollie glanced at him, it was clear her husband had trouble keeping calm. At one point, a vein twitched in his forehead. The flashes of anger in his eyes burned on her, his eyes scrutinising her face. His beautiful features contorted in fury.

She tried to smile at him while Marie Therese blabbered on about the recipe, but he was not having it. He glared at her. Not a hint of a smile or tenderness left him. Every little frown and twitch in his face told her a story, and her heart bled for him. But there was nothing she could do. Her husband didn't trust her. She could see it in his face. She had to sit out the storm, for she was sure another one was coming her way.

HIS WIFE'S phone call brought back all of their troubles with the force of thunder, her lies uppermost, vivid in his mind. Zac knew of Finley's discussion with the young man.

George had tried to protect Mollie. So, the call had infuriated him.

If someone had to look after her, Zac was the man. *I am her husband, that's my job.* He was territorial, and that extended to his wife.

He scrutinised her while she spoke over the phone to her friend. His eyes examined every detail of her face. He saw her blush, and when she bit her bottom lip, he cursed under his breath.

Finley believed George to be the culprit, Mollie's boyfriend. But Zac didn't think so. Finley was adamant that, at the very least, George was hiding something. By the sound of the conversation between them there and then, Zac had to agree.

He understood she wouldn't talk in his presence. *Why?* The thought sent him into a rage he could barely control. She was hiding something! It forced back the concerns about his wife's lies and secrets.

I am not a fool. What more is there? He realised what she was doing.

She even held a loose tendril of her hair, rolling and unrolling it in her fingers, again and again. He recognised all the signs; she was nervous.

One thing was certain; his wife sought to protect her lover, whoever the man was. *How am I supposed to trust her?*

But if George was not her boyfriend, he knew more than he let out. Perhaps he knew who her man was?

She had said that her relationship with the man ended before they married. Then why did she protect the bastard? That thought begun to haunt Zac. He wanted a name, and she would not give it to him. Who was he?

Was the scumbag dangerous? Was she terrified of the man? She was a danger to herself and to him, he realised now.

What the heck! She is lucky she is with me now, Zac thought. *Another man in my place would not be so accommodating, for crying out loud!*

He would have a serious conversation with this girl but not while he was angry. He was too furious to discuss anything with her right now. *I will not stand for any more silliness.* He would see to that. Though, first, he needed to resolve the current infuriating situation. Neither of them would be safe nor happy while there was a third person lurking in the background.

The more he thought about Mollie's call with George, the more furious he became. He was raging! And he cursed aloud.

Marie Therese, who was still blabbering on about her recipe, stopped talking and froze. Then she scurried along out of the room, thinking she had annoyed her young master with her ramblings.

He cursed even louder when he realised that he had offended his old housekeeper.

Mollie blanched as the scene unfolded before her. She opened her mouth in an attempt to say something, but one look at him, and she shut it again.

It all got to be too much for him. Her lies and secrets engulfed him. He couldn't breathe! He stood abruptly, so much so that the chair rattled behind him.

"I am going for a spin," he snapped.

"The boat? Now? But we haven't finished lunch yet," she murmured.

"I am done with lunch."

"Then, I'll come with you," Mollie ventured. She was about to get up.

"No. Stay!" he bellowed sharply, glaring at her.

At his words, she jerked back into her seat and looked up at him for a second. "I am not your bloody dog!" she exclaimed.

"Umm," he murmured, closing his eyes and clenching his fists, trying to keep his fury under control.

But no. Not the time to make him angrier, she thought. She picked up her fork and toyed with the food on her plate.

"Finish your lunch." His voice was outwardly calm again, but his head was in turmoil.

"What about my swimming lesson this afternoon?" she said after him, agitating her fork in the air.

"Not now," he yelled. He needed time away from her, time to think alone.

Mollie's sweet and demure behaviour. *Was it an act?* Did Molly feel that way every time he touched her, or was it a pretence? Was she a great actress? For his benefit? To keep him sweet on her? In his mind, Zac questioned everything about her now. While spinning the boat furiously on the choppy sea waters, these thoughts were driving him mad.

Mollie's call with George had plunged him into a somber and dangerous mood, bringing all their problems back to the fore. Though he loved her, he didn't trust her.

He demanded answers about George and her ex-lover. *Were they one and the same?* He needed to know the man's name, her ex-boyfriend's name. He must have it!

She was a peril to herself and a hazard to him. *My wife should come with warning lights.* How had he allowed a slip of girl to play him like a schoolboy? He was angry with himself, and with her.

Heavenly, sexy, and oh, so bloody dangerous, but he couldn't help wanting her. He would not give her up; he couldn't. She was his weakness, his major weakness. Mixed emotions exploded in his soul. Tenderness and love intermingled with fury and exasperation, all building inside him. Worst of all, he didn't realise the green-eyed monster had raised his ugly head. He dismissed it as ludicrous. But it had, raw jealousy overflowing!

All his life, women had fallen for him. He'd never been jealous of a woman before but… suddenly, jealousy seemed to cave in on him.

Jealous of George, and even more of her ex-boyfriend, whoever the man was. Images of Mollie in her lover's arms were now mixing in his head. He was tormenting himself with these images. A faceless man kissing her, touching his wife, alternating with images of Mollie and George together, intimately. He was going insane.

The more these thoughts intruded on his mind, the faster he pushed the craft. The more dangerous he was on the sea that day. His blood boiled with frustration at her lies and secrets, and now with jealousy. He would never admit to being jealous. *No, no, no!* He wouldn't even admit it to himself. These thoughts tortured him.

SHE WATCHED him from her bedroom's balcony as he took the boat to sea. He spun it around and off at a pace on the choppy waters. The sea was rough that day, and the boat looked defenceless against the high waves and the strength of nature.

Her heart tightened.

She took the binoculars, and she saw him on the horizon, steering it at speed, like a man possessed. The boat clashed perilously on the waves as it bounced up and down, and it swayed and rocked hellishly from side to side as if it were a toy. Then he pushed on, in big circles.

She looked on helplessly, while he performed dangerous manoeuvres that made her gasp. It scared the life out of her.

Sweet Jesus, he's going to kill himself, she thought until she heard a knock on the door.

It was Marie Therese.

"Would you like anything, Mollie?" the old woman asked, noticing more trouble for the young lovers.

"No, thank you. Does he always steer the boat like a madman?" she asked, turning back to stare at him, with sea waves galore hitting it.

"What's wrong with him today?"

"What do you mean?" But she couldn't help a blush.

"Zac steers his boat like the devil only when he is mad about something."

"Does he?" And her face flushed crimson to the root of her hair. Mollie knew he was upset, but she didn't understand the extent of it.

This time, he seemed frenzied. Her call with George had plunged him back into this awful mood, and it was her fault.

"Oh God, Marie. Zac and I make one step forward and then three backwards. What am I to do?"

"Anything I can help you with, ma chère fille?"

"No. Just cook something nice for him tonight; he will need it." They both smiled, but the lady left her with her troubled thoughts.

Chapter 16

Everybody arrived on cue on Friday night and they had a full house. Mollie needed solace. No one other than her mother could do that, given Zac had hardly spoken to her for three days. So, she was glad for the company.

Since George's call, Zac had been unbearable, raving at her. His words were nothing other than to demand the name of her ex-boyfriend. She couldn't tell him that name. It would be too dangerous, so she refused every time, firing him deeper into his bad temper.

Besides her mother, George, Kathryn, Clarissa and her baby came for the weekend too. She was grateful to have them around, to distract her from her sorrow, although her mom and friends knew nothing about Mollie's troubles, of the predicament she plunged herself into. So, she fretted.

Similarly, Zac's friends made their arrival too. And on that score, she would have done anything to be invisible that weekend. Mollie suspected his friends would be less affectionate to her, each one for different reasons. They would make her out as the beast of the situation, a fickle Jezebel.

She hated having "the boys", as he called them, there with a passion. *This will be trouble*, she agonised, *hopeless*.

In the meantime, her husband and his friends had barricaded themselves in his study for the last two hours. At least a small mercy. They stayed away from her. She didn't want to see their accusatory eyes, their reproachful stares, each one for different reasons. On the positive side, it gave her more time to spend with her mother and friends, undisturbed.

What the hell did Zac and his friends have to say to each other, and for so long.

Will he divorce me now? He is so mad at me. That word "divorce" terrified her. She knew Zac would not let her off easy. Not this time! It seemed evident to her that his friends would persuade him to divorce her. That was the reason they were there! *Maybe not all of them. One wouldn't... for his own selfish reasons,* and she wished she was a fly on the wall.

Zac would vilify her. He had shut her out in the last few days. Since her call with George, he had behaved like she didn't exist. She had turned into a loathsome burden to him. And she was suffering.

He's lost his patience with me, and it's noticeable. Exasperated and angry, he couldn't disguise his annoyance any longer. It was visible to her at every occasion.

All the same, he had not missed their lovemaking, though. *Oh, no, that he keeps on cue,* she thought in amazement. Zac had made it clear to her that he had no intention on missing out on sex. 'Part of the contract,' she recalled him saying odiously.

Not that she minded, either. At least, that was still some kind of connection to him. So, she didn't oppose him on this, even though he was so upset with her.

One thing was clear; if she had been absolutely against having sex with him in that situation, she would have told him so, unceremoniously. But having Zac shag her to oblivion was something she willingly exposed herself to. It took her mind off her precarious situation. And still a link to him, feeble, but still a link.

Zac made her feel like his woman. And she liked that despite everything. He shagged her with the conviction that she was his, although he was mad at her. So, she went along with it, and she allowed him his tantrum and with good reason. But it hurt her. She needed back the husband she had grown to love so much, the one she adored, the tender, caring and playful Zac.

His lovemaking was angry, far from the tender love he was capable of, but with a temper.

"If you don't want me anymore, I should go back to my bedroom. Let's have separate bedrooms like we agreed. You are angry with me." At one point, she had protested.

"Don't you dare," he responded in an orotund tone. Then, he had taken her into his arms and kissed her force-fully. She felt his hurt, but there was nothing she could do.

Zac demanded the name of her ex-lover. He wouldn't let go. He dictated to know that name. He commanded, but she refused time and time again. She couldn't tell him. It was for the best, but this cost her. Zac ended up ignoring her.

"THIS MARRIAGE of convenience of yours was doomed from the start. I told you," Alex said, rolling his eyes.

The boys knew everything. That evening, reunited in his study, Zac was debating with them what to do about it. The room was a remarkably light and airy room, with a set of full height glass doors backing onto the gardens.

Zac sat at his antique desk. His high-backed brown leather chair was comfortable, but somehow it seemed on fire, the way he fidgeted on it. He stood and then he sat, and then he stood again, depending on the points he was trying to make. He even leaned on the mahogany panelled book-case on the wall behind his desk.

Alex was perched on a corner of the desk, watched his friend's constant movements. "Flipping heck, Zac! Stop moving; you are giving me a headache," his friend blurted out.

Zac stood still for a moment but soon returned to his jerky actions. His hand combing through his hair, he looked dishevelled.

Finley relaxed on the low-cushioned cream leather sofa on the opposite wall, with his feet on one of the contrasting brown leather armchairs, which he moved close to him for the occasion. Calm and almost horizontal, with a grin on his face, he played with his mobile phone distractedly.

Peter, who had sunk comfortably in the other matching brown armchair, also moved to have a full view of the room and venturing his opinion when required.

"We don't have a clue to the identity of her man. I can't protect you like this. But George is her lover; I am sure of it! Let me speak to her. Let's get it out of her," Finley proposed.

"*Ex*-man, ex-lover. Didn't you hear anything I said? No. I won't let you bully her," Zac snapped. What he had not said to his friends was that he was in love with his wife. His jeal-ousy had burst out, and the visions in his mind of Mollie and a faceless lover or George were driving him insane. So, he stayed away from his wife, avoiding her at all costs, but his thoughts were unhinging him with jealousy. He tried to keep a lid on them.

"Well, if she said she is not with her lover anymore, it must be true. Isn't it? Do you feel she is still scheming? I am inclined to believe her. All the same, she is a danger to you," Alex stated.

"Yes, I believe her too. But she won't give me his name. Why is she protecting him?" Zac retorted.

"Maybe she doesn't want you to turn this into a fight with her ex-lover," Alex ventured.

"Hmm, if I get my hands on him, bloody hell! Or should I say, when?" Zac blurted out, his hands clenched into fists on his desk. He stood, pushing his knuckles down on the desk so forcefully, they whitened at the pressure. Then he sat again.

"Well, perhaps, that's why she won't give you his name," Peter stated.

"You should divorce her. It's the safest thing to do. She is a danger to you physically and financially," his lawyer pointed out.

"She is a good girl. That prick, whoever he is, was a bad influence on her," Zac barked.

In unison, his friends turned their eyes on him as if he was from Mars. For a moment, Zac wondered, *am I the crazy one in this?*

"What do you mean by that?" his lawyer asked as he stood to face him.

"Look, whoever that asshole is, he manipulated her into this. It's not her fault. That man pushed her into this path, and she is too stubborn to turn back. But with luck and coaxing, we can fix this. We can," Zac said, rising again, trying to convince himself more than anyone else. But he sat again, dejected.

"Oh?" Finley narrowed his eyes on him, thinking.

"She is sweet, outspoken, heavenly! Sometimes she does stupid things. Her mother told me a lot of stories. But she is not a bad girl," Zac said with half a grin on his face now. *Am I really championing her?* He couldn't understand his own words, but they came from the heart.

His friends smiled, watching him in love for the first time.

"Well, one thing is true. I have never seen such a case of

puppy love. The way she looks at you. Have you noticed that?" Alex said. "As if you were a God, and I guess you like her adoring eyes on you like that, don't you? But if you want my advice, divorce her."

"Bloody hell!"

"She may be heavenly, but she is very dangerous. She'll bring you nothing but trouble." As his lawyer, Alex was used to debating with Zac. His friend liked a challenge.

"No, hmm… No! I am staying married. I have the Board to think about."

"That's crazy. I assume she is not the only one with loving eyes then."

Zac rolled his eyes, but his friend was right.

Alex had seen that expression on Zac's face too, and he knew his friend had fallen for the girl.

"Peter, you are her tutor, can you persuade her to tell me his name? She trusts you; you are rather impartial," Zac addressed his friend.

"And what will you do after she tells you his name? Duel the man at dawn?" Peter said drily with a laugh. Finley snorted.

Peter, thinking they were going on in circles, tried to stay on the fringes of the discussion. The professor was a man of science; he always stayed out on affairs of the heart. To him, these had no logic.

Zac lifted an elegant brow, ignored his statement, and went on.

"You can convince her." He paused. "I want that name."

"What can I do? If she hasn't told you, I am only her professor," Peter said but then waved a hand with a relenting sigh and added, "okay, fine. I'll have a word with her, but I can't promise anything."

"MOLLIE, IS EVERYTHING OKAY?" her mother asked, an hour after her arrival.

"Yes, of course it is. Why do you ask?"

"Well, it's not every day that one invites guests to their honeymoon," her mother, Mary, said when they had a moment alone. Mary was concerned for Mollie. Besides, the situation seemed rather obvious. Mollie knew her mom sensed that something was amiss.

"Mother, there is plenty of room in this villa for everyone, and I'm glad you're here."

"As glad as I am to see you, darling, this is your honeymoon." Mary put her arms around her daughter's shoulders lovingly, giving her a big hug.

Mollie needed that hug. She stayed in her mother's comforting arms longer than she should have done without raising her suspicions, but it felt so good, so pleasing.

"Everything is fine," Mollie lied with a sweet smile, but on the inside, she wanted to scream.

"Darling, you would tell me if something was wrong, wouldn't you?"

"Of course; everything is fine," she repeated cheerfully, but her smile didn't reach her eyes. Mollie was in pain, and she sent a silent curse to her ex-lover for using her, and to the wretched money.

Chapter 17

I t all started during the trip to Nice.

Clarissa, Mollie's childhood friend, turned up with the rest of the party with her daughter, Mia, in tow. The baby wailed from the moment she set foot on the aircraft. During the flight, Mia had cried for over an hour when he sat next to her.

"Can I try?" he suggested with a smile, without waiting for a reply. Alex took the baby and sat her on his lap. He folded his arms tenderly around her, but the child was still crying.

"Be my guest," Clarissa said, shocked at his request. She was tired and desperate. With an ironic smile, she realised he would not last over thirty seconds with her daughter's bellowing cries.

He stuck with the ten-month-old baby, though. And to her mother's surprise, he soon soothed the child, who fell asleep in his arms.

"Why don't you relax too? I'll see to her until we land," he said.

"Oh, I can't," Clarissa said, looking into his eyes, and it

was then she saw those gorgeous, calm blue eyes, soft and luminous, staring at her. She studied him for a moment and sat back with a warm, contented smile. She could do with a snooze. Her daughter had kept her up since four am that morning. A long day by the time they got to the flight.

He realised her hesitation. "She is asleep; it will be fine. I expect you need some sleep too. I can manage for an hour, trust me. I'll wake you up before we land."

She took him up on his offer. The young woman soon drifted off to sleep, all the way to Nice, unaware that her head nestled on his shoulders.

To her amazement, her daughter continued sleeping while he held her during the car ride from the airport to Antibes, until they reached Zac's house.

What he had not said was he noticed Clarissa when she boarded the aircraft. She looked ruffled. She turned up on the plane carrying the buggy and the bags behind Mollie's mother, who was holding the baby. The flight attendant came to their aid, settling them in.

The baby cried soon after boarding, but Clarissa seemed so tired.

ALEX SAW her pace up and down the corridor with the little girl in her arms, struggling to calm her down, until he felt an overpowering desire to soothe her.

Then while she paced, Mia had suddenly shifted the restraining combs in her mother's loose hair chignon with her tiny hands, and he gasped. Clarissa's dark hair tumbled down about her, long and luscious, to her waist. His first impulse was to touch it, but he dismissed the thought.

What is a beautiful brunette with amazing hair doing with a child at such a young age? She must be the same age as Mollie, Alex thought. She didn't have a ring on her finger. He wondered what her circumstances were. He felt an overwhelming desire to protect her.

He'd first noticed her at Zac's wedding. She was Mollie's maid of honour. She had introduced them. At the wedding, he had not invited her to dance as Clarissa was busy with Mia through the day. At some point, the child slept, and she had been free, although every time he mastered the resolve to invite her to dance, another man had done it first. So, he had given up.

That evening, back on the aircraft to Nice, she'd tied up her beautiful long hair in a messy bun which made her look rather dishevelled. There was a beauty behind all that dishevelled hair, and he wished he could touch it, to see if it felt as silky as it looked.

He wished he could unravel all that long luscious hair on his pillow and soothe her with kisses. *What the fuck! I am tired!* he thought. It had been a long week and his mind was playing games.

He made a mental note to learn more about her, though.

So, the next morning at breakfast, Mia went into Alex's arms again with ease. To Clarissa's dismay, he had picked up the child like a pro. For a seasoned bachelor, he seemed at ease with a baby. By that time, everybody else had left the breakfast table.

"Your daughter is so cute," he said, glancing at her. The little girl was playing with a toy on his lap.

"Yes, adorable. Aren't you, sweetie?" Clarissa directed a sugary smile at Mia and leaned over him to reach her rosy cheek for a kiss.

His face was only a few inches from her long, smooth neck while she kissed her daughter. A breath of her delicate rose scent filled his nose, and he inhaled, closing his eyes. The scent was heady, sumptuous, with a hint of spice. It suited the young woman well, and unlocked sweet memories of his childhood in his mother's garden.

When he opened his eyes, Alex saw her staring at him with her soft and large dark eyes questioningly. He coughed, the spell broken.

"You were saying?" He cleared his throat again.

"Yes, Zac! You know him well, don't you?" she asked.

CLARISSA WASN'T sure why Zac had seemed so uptight with his wife the previous evening. Even that morning, he had snapped at Mollie a few times and had not spoken to her since.

So, Clarissa was raving on her friend's behalf. She had always felt protective towards Mollie. And the worst part of all, she couldn't figure out why she was part of someone else's honeymoon. *All these people in the house, why? It's Mollie's honeymoon, not a group holiday. Not right. What's going on?*

"Yes, I've known him for years. Why? What about Zac?" he asked.

"Then, tell me, why is your friend a bastard?" she asked without beating about the bush. She was not one to mince her words. So, Clarissa blurted her thoughts outright.

It was Alex's turn to stare at her agape, puzzled.

She noticed his fine mouth, with his fleshy lips and even white teeth wide open.

Her words stunned him. "Excuse me?" he said, raising a shapely brow as he thought, *well, well, she has a big mouth...*

"Look at Mollie." She pointed at her friend outside in the garden, looking rather miserable.

"What about her?" He narrowed his eyes on her. Alex didn't like the probing. *Where is the minx going with this?*

"This is her honeymoon, so why are we here? Do you not

realise what happens on a couple's honeymoon?" she asked him flippantly, with her piercing black eyes glaring into his. *I bet he won't respond to that!*

"I can hazard a guess." He cocked his head with an obvious smirk. *Cheeky!*

"And what do you imagine it to be? Oh, what a crush!" she said, this time looking at Mia holding his hand.

"Crush?" He sounded puzzled.

"Yes! Mia has a crush on you." She paused.

Shame her mother doesn't... he thought.

"But back to my question, so?" she demanded.

"Well, I-I..." he stammered, not knowing what to say. She was a bold girl, and it was not an everyday occurrence that a big shot lawyer like himself was lost for words. As luscious as this girl seemed, her big mouth was a revelation. And he began to think how he would remedy that if she were his.

"Well, you don't expect the groom to invite his friends to his honeymoon, do you? That's horrible." She continued relentlessly, tilting her head on one side.

"Her mother and friends are here too. Aren't you here?" he muttered, mimicking that little endearing movement of her charming head with a smile. Their heads mirrored each other's movement, but she turned a scowl on him.

Is he making fun of me? "I bet she had no choice but to invite us. Look at her; she is miserable. What's going on?" Clarissa hissed. *He will ignore me now!*

"Complicated," Alex responded, aware of what she asked. He rubbed a hand behind his neck.

"Is it?" She glared at him and wondered what was so complicated. She studied him, scrutinising him. The more she stared at him, the more she found his blue eyes fascinating, the luminosity in them mesmerising. She noticed the classic set of his high cheekbones, which women would pay good money to have. *Jesus, this man is handsome.* Her skin tingled. *I bet he has broken lots of hearts. Damn, what a thought!*

"Yes, well…" he murmured as he thought, *blast, that mouth must get her into trouble a lot!*

"What?" she asked, recovering from her lascivious musings.

"You should ask Mollie," he said.

"No. I am asking you. She won't tell me," she persisted, a stubborn expression in her eyes. *You hard-nosed lawyer!*

"Sorry. I can't help you."

Typical, he does not like confrontation! So, Clarissa suddenly developed those mingled feelings of want and despondency with him. And, unbeknown to her, the feelings were mutual!

CRAP, the minx was unrelenting. "You need to ask your friend," he said as he returned the baby to her and left the room.

Hell, the woman is stubborn too. But he would have given away ten years of his life to see that long hair about her waist again, preferably while she rolled in his bed.

He could almost feel her eyes following him and knew he had exasperated her.

It was clear Mollie had not told the truth to her friends, but it was not his call to do so. A marriage of convenience was a poor idea as he'd warned Zac all those months ago. Alex had serious concerns. The result, both Mollie and Zac were miserable now. The point was Zac had fallen for his wife even if he objected to her. He was smitten, despite his troubles, and his indignation about it made matters worse.

Ready for the pickings for some time, Zac was in love. And there was nothing he could do about his friend's feelings. *A chaotic and complicated case,* the lawyer thought, though he understood how it would sound to Clarissa, who didn't know the truth.

As he went outside, Alex felt her eyes on him again, even though he couldn't see her.

He turned his head to look back inside and caught Clarissa watching him. But her eyes flicked back to the baby with a blush.

He grinned. Clarissa was bashful, despite her big mouth.

Well, what do you know, I like this fiery brunette!

HE WALKED OVER TO HER. She sulked in a corner, sitting on a wooden bench in the large terrace.

"Hi. How are you today?" Alex asked.

"Awful! Zac is not talking to me." Mollie's face was sullen, looking out to sea.

He wanted to point out his enquiry referred to her health and not to her love life. But he gave her his opinion.

"He was not expecting you to behave—"

"Like what?"

"Well…" He closed his eyes for a moment and sighed. For a fierce court litigator, Alex disliked confrontations in his own personal dealings.

"Are you moralising me? We signed the contract *you* drew up for us! I didn't offer my undying love to him. I never said that! This is an arrangement, a business transaction. Even if it doesn't feel like that anymore. What does it matter whose idea it was?" she spat.

"Zac thinks you cajoled him into marriage, and he does not appreciate that. Who is your boyfriend, Mollie?"

"Cajoled him? As if we could force him to do anything he doesn't wish to do. He married me because he wanted to. And it is ex, ex-boyfriend!" she sulked.

"He feels you betrayed him. Who is your... em... young man, eh?" he asked, ignoring her statement.

"Betrayed him? Why? No. You want to know who my man is? I'll tell you; Zac is my man and my lover. The only one!"

"But—"

"That's it."

"What?"

"I was never in love with my ex-boyfriend. I realise it now. He used me. And now it is worse."

"Worse?"

"Well, I lo—I like my husband, more than I expected to, a lot more!" she admitted, fidgeting with her sleeve.

Alex had noticed the way she stared at his friend; he had seen the love in her eyes, so he understood what Mollie tried to say.

She didn't use big words to describe her feelings for Zac. The lawyer wouldn't believe her under the circumstances. Thus, she loved her husband. But she had lied to him. So, he didn't trust her anymore.

"Then it makes two of you," Alex said with a wink.

"What do you mean?" she asked, hoping.

"Hey, I suspect Zac likes you too. More than you can imagine. But it hurts him. This situation is hurting him, all these secrets. Talk to him."

"Will you help me?" she pleaded.

"Your husband is my friend, but I'll do what I can," he sighed.

Why is Alex being soft with me now, despite everything? What is wrong with him this day?

She didn't know Alex was falling for a gorgeous, outspoken brunette and her baby. And in the lightness of his heart, he had changed his mind about Mollie. He made a promise to her he might not keep.

But Alex felt on unfamiliar grounds for the first time, though his path set.

MOLLIE'S TROUBLES didn't end there. They had just started.

Everybody was aware of her feelings for Zac. Thus, her ex-lover realised it too, and he was not happy. He would not lose her now. Nor the money! Not now that he was so close to fulfilling his plan. He needed her at the centre. It was imperative if he was to succeed.

He would not let her go. The man was manipulative and treacherous. So, he would not allow Mollie to backtrack on this.

Stupid, stupid girl, her ex-boyfriend thought.

It was simple! He would have to remind her of where she stood!

Chapter 18

They finished lunch. The party laughed and joked throughout lunch, but Zac's annoyance was still obvious. He barely looked at her, like she didn't exist.

He'd hardly said a word to Mollie since George's call four days ago. And she was suffering. She missed his company, his naughty schoolboy humour, his tenderness. He had been polite and welcoming to her friends and family, but the warmth he had shown her only a few days ago was gone.

"Please, the truth?" George asked her. Alone in the dining room, he took his chance to find out what she was up to.

At his question, Mollie sighed. She rose and paced, lost in thoughts. He rose with her, but he remained in his spot. He watched her move back and forth, wringing her hands in agitation and waited for her to speak.

"I am sorry I lied to you. I am," she stated, her face gloomy.

"Well," he said, raising his eyebrows, "it doesn't matter

now." He dismissed her apology with a wave of his hand then added, "But please, tell me all. The truth."

"Oh, dear…" she replied, still pacing the room.

"Hey, girl, it's me; come on," George coaxed until she relented. So, she told her friend everything: about her marriage of convenience, about her lies to Zac, about her ex-lover's plan, and all the peripherals that came with it. Her burden shared, her distress in full flow, she was blabbering her misgivings.

"Mollie, stop. Who is your lover?" he asked, with a hand firmly on her elbow to stop her pacing.

"*Ex*-lover, have you not been listening to me?" she cried, but she resumed her frantic pacing up and down the room.

"Well, ex, then. Who is he?" He stopped her again and turned her to face him.

"I can't tell you."

"Why not?" he whispered with a tender smile.

"Please, George, don't ask me that," she said and lowered her eyes.

He sighed, and a nerve twitched in his jaw, but he would not force her. *In her own good time, when she was ready.*

"But Fin thinks I am your lover. What about Zac? He has been eyeing me suspiciously, and he's been odd and cranky with me since I arrived," he blurted.

"Oh, forget them! And who knows what my husband thinks, he is not… well…" She shook her head and looked miserable.

"This ex-man of yours, is he dangerous?" He put a hand on her shoulder to focus her, noting her distress.

"No, I don't believe so," she said. Her ex-lover had never been violent to her, but he had practically bullied her into doing this charade, so she wasn't sure anymore. She sighed.

"How do you know that?" He held her chin and raised her face towards him.

"He has never done me any harm," she ventured.

"No harm? What do you call this mess then?" he asked, this time with annoyance.

"Look, I don't care about the money. I will give it to him. That's all he craves," she said with vehemence instead, avoiding his question.

"Are you sure?" George could see the predicament she was in and the potential dangers. But he could tell Mollie's mind could only focus on Zac. She couldn't think of anything else.

"Yes. He wants the money, but there is another problem now.

"Oh, Jesus!" George cursed then continued. "What problem?"

"My ex wants me back. He called me again."

"Bloody hell! Mollie! What did you do?"

"I have returned none of his messages, but he knows."

"What?"

"That Zac knows the truth," she replied, and she moved, but George stopped her.

"Did you tell him?" he asked, but Mollie nodded her head. "No."

"How does he know?" He frowned.

"Not important now," she retorted.

"Not important?"

"Please, I cannot tell you."

"Mollie, you are so frustrating! Is this why Zac is upset with you?" he asked calmly.

"Does it show?" She glanced up at him.

"Only an idiot could think everything is fine between you two."

"God. What am I to do?"

"But you must be careful. If this man wants you back, he will be trouble."

"I know that!"

"What can I do? Can I help?"

"Nothing, I am afraid." She paused. "I must fix this mess by myself."

"How?"

"Oh, I shall think of something. This is all my fault and —" she said with a wave of her hand.

"I am here for you. You know that," he whispered.

"You are sweet, but this is my mess. I was stupid. I have to deal with it alone," Mollie said and put a hand on George's face, caressing him tenderly. He was a wonderful friend to her.

ZAC PUT his hand in his jeans' pocket to look for his phone.

Damn, where is it? Blast, the dining room. He went back to the room to search for it, but he froze in the doorframe.

Mollie withdrew her hand abruptly from George's face upon seeing him, but it was too late. Her husband had seen the tender moment between his wife and the young man, and he didn't like it, not one bit.

It was then Zac lost his temper completely. His blood came rushing to his head. The green-eyed monster struck him with abominable force. This time, he couldn't stop himself.

"What the fuck are you doing?" Zac roared, cursing like a trooper as he charged for the young man. It all happened so fast.

He pulled George up by his shirt front, and he dragged him until he flung the lad against the wall with all his strength, like a mad bear trying to protect his cub.

The younger man didn't stand a chance against Zac's

force, and George crashed against the wall. The impact stunned him. And Zac's fist smashed into his face.

Mollie screamed. She catapulted herself onto her husband's back, trying to stop him from lashing out again.

"What the hell? Are you insane? Stop!" she yelled at him, trying to pull him back, but he was too strong. He struck George again, which sent him unconscious to the floor.

Finley heard Mollie's screams and the commotion inside the room. He dashed in.

"What the fuck!" he mumbled.

By then, Zac had shaken Mollie off his back, and she was on the floor too. He was about to hit George again.

Finley grabbed Zac's upper arms from behind, holding him back in time. "What the hell are you doing? Stop." his friend bellowed.

Finley's tall frame had a tough time restraining him. The frustration and fury unleashed. Sadly, against poor George.

But with lots of cajoling, Zac calmed down. "Fine, fine," he spat, throwing Finley off him with a scowl. But if nothing else, he stopped his assault on the young man.

The lad was recovering, moaning on the floor.

"Flipping heck, what happened?" Finley said, astonished.

"I was talking to George, and your foolish friend here launched on him for no reason." It was Mollie's furious reply, with a warning aimed at her husband, while rising from the floor and dusting herself off.

"Are you okay?" She flew to George and held one arm while Finley took the other to help him up onto his feet.

"I'm fine," George mumbled, still dazed, holding his face.

"Oh God, you have a bloody nose, and I am sure a black eye will follow," Mollie whimpered, examining the marks on her friend's face, but then she scowled at Zac.

Has he lost his mind? Thus, Mollie's worries and sorrow turned into anger against her husband's stubbornness.

"You are an imbecile," she flared, turning to him. Mollie marched towards Zac with purpose. Close to him, she dug a pointed finger at this chest. "Fool!" she spat at him. "You are a damn idiot! You can't see beyond your nose," she yelled at him, but her husband said nothing.

ZAC STEPPED BACK FROM HER. *Blasted finger,* he thought, while she jabbed at him with it, *if she is not careful…* he was not amused.

His wife's hands on George's face were enough to turn him into a frenzied man. He had always been proud of his self-control, his steady demeanour, but now he was incandescent. And not for the first time, with Mollie around him.

What is she doing to me? She's turned me into this foolish man!

"You are an ass!" she yelled at her husband, pacing forward, she jabbed his chest with her finger again. Instead, he moved her hand out of his way. Then he turned towards the glass doors, his back to her, staring at the garden. Zac couldn't say a word; he was too annoyed to speak.

An ass? Sure, for believing her bloody lies. An idiot? Yes, for hoping we may still have a chance, a future…

"Mollie, I am okay," her friend mumbled to appease her.

Her lips quivered when her indignation subsided.

"Let me take care of that nose. Come on." Finley motioned to the young man to accompany him. "No, I am fine," George repeated.

Finley made a subtle movement of his eyes, and the lad understood.

So, they left the room.

Once alone, Mollie glanced in Zac's direction. He had his back to her. She walked over to him.

"What's this all about, hey? You don't think—" Mollie

whispered, and she reached for his elbow. But Zac shrugged her off.

Is she asking me? Bollocks, I am the one aggrieved here, not her.

"I saw you, tender and loving with him. Do I need to say more? Tell me, is George your boyfriend?" His voice was steady while he raked a hand through his hair, though there was no mistaking the bitterness in his words.

"Oh, for heaven's sake, how many times do I have to tell you? George is my friend. Will you stop being so stubborn?"

Stubborn? Me? "Friend? It didn't look that way to me."

"Why are you being like this? Can you not be polite at least? How many times do I have to apologise? We agreed! But you are acting like a jerk and embarrassing me in front of my mother and friends."

MOLLIE'S EYES WERE SHINY. She was close to breaking down, but she tried to be strong. *I will not give him the satisfaction,* she thought.

But he stood silent, staring at the garden.

"Zac?" Mollie murmured, but he shrugged his shoulders.

"Don't mind me! I am in a foul mood. I wonder why?" he replied ironically with his back to her.

"Please, we must talk," she said, agitated.

"You know what I want to hear. If you won't tell me his name, there is nothing else to say," he spat. "That's all I want."

"That day, when we made love in the pool, you promised..." She paused, lowering her eyes, then went on, "I can't tell you his name; you know that. You vowed you wouldn't ask me anymore; you promised we would start afresh, put all this behind us. Forgive me, remember?

Adamant we should continue our arrangement. But since George's call, you—" she murmured.

"Why are you protecting him, eh? Who is your lover?" he hissed without even turning to her.

"Ex, ex! Ex-lover. Please, stop," she pleaded.

"That's it, then," he said with stubbornness.

"Zac…" she implored.

She waited for him to say something, but he didn't.

"Fine! As you wish. Tell your captain to add me to the passenger's list on that flight tomorrow. I am going home!" she blurted, lingering a few more moments expectantly. But when he didn't say a word, she turned on her heels and left.

Mollie ran out of the room. She flew up the stairs in distress, and halfway up the long, curved staircase, she crossed her friends on their way down.

"What is it?" Clarissa asked.

But Mollie burst into tears and ran ahead to her bedroom. She threw herself on the bed, sobbing, the incident with Zac just now the last straw for her.

Clarissa barged in. Kathryn followed her and closed the door.

Mollie raised her head up for a second. "Oh," she whispered, disappointed to see her friends, hoping it was someone else.

"Darling, why are you crying?" Clarissa asked her tenderly.

"I am going home, back to Oxford. That's it; I have had enough," was Mollie's answer amidst crying sobs.

Her friend flung her arms around her. Kathryn patted Mollie's hair, feeling for her.

"What's he done now?" Clarissa whispered.

"Oh God, I can't," Mollie mumbled, still sobbing.

"Please tell us. What is it?" her friend persisted.

"What's happened? You can tell us," Kathryn echoed.

"No. I can't."

"That's it. Kat, you stay with her. I will be back shortly," Clarissa said determinedly.

"Claris, please don't; it's my fault, not his," Mollie called out after her.

"Now. You watch me," Her friend said as she left the room.

"Wow! She is fierce," Kathryn said, turning to Mollie when the door closed with a bang.

"She has been protecting me since the fifth grade," Mollie replied with a grin.

"Oh, that's sweet." Kathryn smiled.

"I used to do her homework, and she kept the bullies out of my path," Mollie said while hinting at half a smile. Then she cried more.

"WHAT HAVE YOU DONE TO HER?" Clarissa fumed when she saw him in the dining room, still in the same spot.

"What?" he mumbled, distracted.

"She is in the bedroom crying her eyes out. Mollie is going home to Oxford. Why?"

Zac spun to her, with no idea what to say. So, he elected for the easy way out. "Home? I don't know."

"Is that all you can say?" she demanded.

"What do you want me to say?"

"For God's sake, married for just two weeks! Shouldn't you try a little harder?"

"Harder?" he repeated. *The woman doesn't know the half of it!* But he remained silent.

"You are a loser," she croaked.

"Is that so?" he groaned with a furious look at her.

"Mollie loves you," she said.

He scrutinised her as if trying to establish the veracity of her words. "Love? And what do you know about love?" he mumbled, turning back to the glass panes and looking out to the garden.

Clarissa's body stiffened. She straightened up tall and blushed. Tears sparkled in her eyes, but when she spoke, she did so gently, with a tender expression. "I do," she said in a whisper.

"Oh?" He half shifted to her with a smirk on his face.

"Asshole!" she murmured.

"Aha!" He spun back to the garden with a scowl.

But she was not intimidated. She remained silent for a few seconds, while he sulked. Then she said, "When my fiancé died, I-I wanted to die too. I loved him so much! But I had to live for my baby. I was pregnant then."

Clarissa's words were almost inaudible, but he heard them. His face paled. "I'm sorry, I didn't mean to..." Zac turned, staring at her.

She lowered her eyes an instant. "You have each other. It's a crime to throw it all away. Talk to her. I have no idea what's going on. Mollie won't tell me, but you can work out, whatever it is," she replied with conviction.

"Hardly, too much has passed." With a sad grin on his face, he turned back to the garden.

"I would sell my soul for the chance to talk to my fiancé again."

"Too late for us," he taunted with his back to her.

"No. It isn't. But she is leaving you; stop her! You must do something. If she gets on that flight tomorrow, *then* it'll be too late. Your marriage will be over." Exasperated, she tried to calm her words as if talking to a petulant child. *He is pig-headed.*

"It's too late. I hoped we might have a chance, but... I

can't trust her!" he persisted obstinately with his back to her, shaking his head.

"Yes, you can. Mollie is a good person. Sometimes she is silly, does stupid things! We all do! But she is sweet, and she loves you!" Clarissa pleaded.

"No. It's no use."

"Oh, bloody hell! I give up. Have it your own way, you fool. She is leaving you. You deserve to be alone." Clarissa broke into a curse. She'd had enough with his obstinacy, and she left the room and headed back upstairs.

On the landing, Clarissa saw Alex coming out of his bedroom. He was unaware of the upheaval, and a wide, warm smile lit his eyes.

"Tell your friend, tell Zac to... to... to fuck off," she suddenly spat at him, unleashing her frustration.

For a moment, Alex stood there motionless, wordless, confused, and deep in astonishment. *What the hell?* He watched her disappear into Mollie's room, clueless.

"WHAT DID YOU DO?" Mollie asked when her friend returned to the room.

"Zac is a mulish asshole. What happened?" Clarissa's mouth could be a law onto herself.

Mollie smiled despite herself. "Sorry, Claris, I-I can't tell you."

"Oh God! I am not sure who is more stubborn, you or your husband."

"Kat, let's keep packing," Mollie said to avoid more questions.

"Sure. Hey, Claris, why don't you make us a drink while we finish packing? We need one," Kathryn suggested, the ever-conciliatory soul in her trying to restore calm in the room.

"With pleasure, but please tell us what's going on. Maybe we can help. Is it that bad? It's not one of your silly schemes that's out of hand, that got you into a mess, is it?" Clarissa added, kissing her friend's forehead.

"Oh, Claris, please," Mollie said, but her face flashed crimson.

Aha! I thought as much. Clarissa didn't push her anymore. "Okay, darling, that's fine. I'll make the drinks," she said instead. *When ready, she will tell me.* She caressed Mollie's face. Then she mixed a much-needed cocktail for her friends. It had calmed the atmosphere. Mollie stopped crying. The ladies sipped the welcomed drink with delight and "umm," when the door opened.

Zac stood there.

"What do you want? Can't you bloody knock?" Clarissa cracked.

He scanned the room and noticed the luggage on the bed.

"Are those Mollie's clothes?" he growled at Kathryn near the suitcase.

"Yes." Kathryn gulped. Zac could intimidate when he needed to. The girl lowered her eyes and scurried along closer to her friend.

"Ladies, can you please leave us? I need to talk to my wife."

"No. Please stay," Mollie ordered.

"Out," he barked.

Clarissa looked at him, took Kathryn's arm, and led her out. Then she returned to Zac. "If you hurt one hair on Mollie's head, you'll be leaving this room with a fat lip! Understood?" she warned him, but then she winked at Mollie before leaving the room.

Despite his annoyance and his foul mood, there was a hint of a smile on Zac's face.

He went to the balcony and stood staring out without speaking. After two minutes of silence, Mollie spoke first, looking up from packing her suitcase. "What do you want? If you want sex, you can leave now. I am done with you," Mollie growled. But when Zac didn't respond, she lowered her head and went on packing her clothes, aware of his presence.

"Stop what you are doing. I need to talk to you," he said after a long silence. There was a gentle command in his voice which irritated her.

"Oh, yeah? Sod off, you ass," she chided and returned to packing.

He turned to her and his eyebrows shot up. Few people talked to him that way. But in one day, both his wife and her best friend were calling him every name under the sun, and few of them repeatable.

I hope they don't make a habit of this.

"Who is dirtier mouthed, you or Clarissa?" he asked with a half-smile.

She looked up from her packing, and for a second, she saw an inkling of the Zac she loved so much. "Oh, Clarissa! Hands down. Why?" she said with a hint of a smile.

"She instructed Alex to tell me to 'fuck off'. That's after she called me an asshole, a loser, and a fool."

"Yes, that sounds like Clarissa, all right. In this instance, she is correct!" Mollie concluded.

"Mollieee!" His voice was tender this time, extending her name softly but with a warning. He tried to smile, but he seemed worn out.

She felt it. *The hurt I've caused him.* A pang of remorse and guilt shot through her heart. *He still doesn't know the half.*

He was pensive. His eyes clouded with an undecipherable

veil which she couldn't make out. There was pain but something else too.

Divorce, the only viable option! she thought, and as much as she loved him, she couldn't live with him this way. It was too harmful for both of them, too painful!

Divorce would be for the best. Even for her! It was impossible to stay any longer with him, not like this.

I have to go, she thought.

He turned back to the balcony and glanced towards the sea. He seemed mesmerised by the lapping of the waves against the mooring down below, like he had found the pattern to them.

They stood in silence for what felt like an eternity to her.

He finally went to her and wrapped his arms around her.

"Let me go," she whispered, trying to wriggle free, but he stood firm, keeping her tight to him, his closeness giving her a warmth she had missed so much lately.

"Please forgive me. I am all those things Clarissa said. I am sorry." He nuzzled her neck, but she didn't dare look up at him.

"How can I? Forgive you, I mean. I am sorry for lying to you and for this sour mess. For hurting you so much, I am so sorry," she replied with a steady voice. "I know I upset you, and you have every right to be, but you promised. You had forgiven me. You promised to put all this behind us, to start again. Instead, you have been awful to me in these last few days. You have humiliated me. We cannot live together like this, not anymore." She whispered her last sentence and returned to her packing.

"Please, Mollie, let's have another go," he pleaded.

Zac caressed her face, but she wriggled free. She moved away from him.

"I've heard that all before. Let's give it another chance, to the arrangement, to the contract, I mean," she blushed, "remember, after we made love in the pool? That's what you said then. But here we are again; it is no use trying. Deep down, you cannot forgive me; it's as simple as that. You will do it again; you can't help it," she whispered.

"No. I won't. I promise." *Please don't go, he added silently.* He, who could rule the world... he, who had been a callous womaniser most of his life, was begging this slip of a girl to stay in his life. He, who was powerful and had the world at his feet, was pleading with her. A girl who had lied her way into his life, and here he was, imploring her to stay. What had his world come to? But he didn't care.

"I am not sure you can. You want everything your own way, then when you don't get it, you get into a strop. You said you had forgiven me, but you can't bear it. I am leaving tomorrow," she whispered. *He wants that name; he won't let go.*

"Please, don't," he pleaded. *This is crazy, but I need you,* were the thoughts he couldn't express aloud to her.

"You can find another woman to give you the image you need," she said, but a flash of anger went through his eyes.

IMAGE? Is that what she thinks this is? About my image? he thought, vexed.

"Bloody hell, Mollie." He cursed sinfully several times. She winced at him. His curses were so bad, so foul, that an urchin on the streets of Mumbai would have had more propriety. "Sod that. I don't care about my image or the Board, not anymore," he yelled, and he closed the distance between them and touched her face. He put his arms around her.

"No? But you'll ask me for his name again. And when I won't tell you, you'll behave like this, like an asshole!" She spat the last word.

He raised an eyebrow but smiled tenderly at her.

"No. I won't ask again. I promise," he replied firmly.

But she wriggled out of his arms. "You can't help yourself; you demand his name," she said. "You don't mean it. You are only saying that so I will stay."

"I *do* mean it. Please. Stay!"

"You'll forget the whole thing? For the three years of the contract?" she asked, but then she saw another flash of anger hit his eyes.

"I don't care about the contract or about your ex-lover or his name. I want you. You, Mollie! Damn, don't you understand? If you'll have me, for keeps!" The words rushed out of his mouth, half harsh, half pleading. *You, just you! Nothing else fucking matters.*

"OH?" she mumbled, her eyes wide when his words hit home. *Is he saying what I think he is?*

"Please, will you have me?" he repeated, amazed at his own openness and candour coming from the depths of his heart.

"What are y-you saying to me?" she murmured nervously and stepped back to look at him.

"The hell with everything, I need you," he drawled. *You, just you, faults, lies, and all!*

"How do you mean?" she persisted, her face crimson while she bit her bottom lip as if there was no tomorrow.

"Mollie, Christ! Do I need to spell it out? It won't be easy. You're right. I want things my way; the habit is engrained. And you, well, you are… you! Heavenly, clever, troublesome! So bloody stubborn! But I want you, the more for it. I will try hard to cherish you and to love you, like you should be, like you deserve." He came closer to her and took her into his arms again. He squeezed her close to him, and she looked up at him with tears in her eyes.

"You know what you are asking, don't you?" she urged with a smile.

"I do."

"I always get into trouble."

"Are you telling me?" He laughed.

"And it is no use warning you?"

"Nope." He shook his head, "But we will work hard to keep you out of trouble, together. Promise me to behave. Stay out of trouble, I mean," he said, caressing her face.

"Yes. You won't regret it?" It astonished her. He needed her despite everything. *He wants me! Me! Dear Lord.* Her heart did a somersault.

"No. I won't. Look, I am a selfish beast. I have been all my life, but I need you." And in that moment, he knew he would even trade his place on the Board for her. The thought shocked him, but it was true.

"You do?" *Oh God, this handsome man, my splendid husband, wants me… me, silly Mollie, a troublemaker par excellence, oh sweet Jesus, thank you!*

"But no more lies. Agreed?" he dared.

"Agreed!" She smiled warily.

"Good!" He kissed her nose, resting his forehead on hers.

"What about the marriage contract?" she asked.

"Fuck the contract. You are my adorable wife, and that's how it will stay, now and forever. That's all I need." He kissed her lips with reverence. Then, passion ignited his senses, and he took her mouth fervently.

She returned the same heated emotion. It consumed them. Then, with a warmth unknown until that day, he made love to her, a honeyed love that caused their world to rock into ecstasy. That afternoon, their lovemaking was full of sentiment. Even when in the fever of passion, and it became wild, fierce, and burning, there was a connection between them that was strong and unmistakable. Their pleasure heightened by the renewed devotion to each other.

It was like he had opened the gates of heaven; she was in Paradise sampling all the celestial pleasures to be had.

Zac liked control in the bedroom, but for a while that afternoon, he surrendered to her, abandoned himself to her.

"You are heavenly," he whispered, nibbling at her earlobe.

She hesitated for a moment, but she caressed his body with her open hands, trailing them with kisses. Then she went for his lips. She smothered his face in kisses.

He was relishing each kiss, and he wished for more. *Bloody hell, the sweet creature!* Deep down, he realised that now. Incredible as it was to him, that day, he understood. It was a revelation! That's what he had always wanted, a heavenly wife to love and cherish, and for her to need him until the end of time. This adorable girl, Mollie, was that wife.

Her loving kisses, and her tongue teasing his lips sexily, tantalising him, soon made him hard again. Zac couldn't have enough of her, and he took command. He placed himself on top of her, and she parted her legs for him. He plunged into her hard, in one swift motion. She gave a loud sigh.

He entered her with the conviction of a man who knows she is his woman, the only woman for him. He plunged into her, deep, long and hard thrusts, again and again. She felt every inch of him inside her.

"Oh, Zac," she moaned.

The melody of his name on her sugary lips in the throes of passion, with lust in her eyes, made him proud. He had her, with a consuming desire and hunger that made them forget the world around them. Nothing existed outside of the two of them.

She reached her peak in his arms.

Bloody hell, I love this woman! he thought, moments before the world twirled around him in an almighty orgasm.

Their passionate and explosive lovemaking continued for the afternoon, until they were sedated and exhausted.

"Promise me you'll stay out of trouble. No more silly schemes," he said afterwards. Her head lying on his chest, he was caressing her hair, pulling a handful of strands through his fingers. He pulled each strand in his hands, gently letting them down again. She shivered with delight at his simple touch.

"I'll try my hardest." She placed small kisses all over his chest, inch by inch, tenderly.

"Christ! I adore you!" he said then kissed her mouth fiercely.

"Do you think your friends will understand?" she asked apprehensively when they came up for air.

Zac kissed her forehead and stroked her hair back. "Fin won't let go," he said with a smirk, "but I'll handle him. The other two are fine." He laughed, but she was not so sure.

"What do we do?" she asked.

"Do? Nothing," he said.

"We've been in bed for hours. Will this not give them a clue?"

"Don't you worry about them. Leave them to me. If I am fine, they'll be fine," Zac said, and he regretted having guests during his honeymoon. He would have happily stayed in bed with his bride on top or under him or in whichever other position for the rest of his life, but alas, it was time to return to their guests. So, reluctantly, they did.

Chapter 19

That evening, dinner was a scrumptious affair. Marie Therese had excelled with a mouth-watering appetiser. The "eggs en cocotte" with spinach puree and prosciutto fingers turned out so tasty, it stunned them into silence. Only "ums" and "ahhs" were heard while they devoured the delectable dish. A succulent leg of lamb with pumpkin gratin followed as the main course. With this, the butternut squash with the caramelised onion galette disappeared in a bat of an eyelid. A whiff of the delectable aromas spread around the house. To finish it all, the apple and pear tart tatin, with champagne ice cream that was out of this world, sent their taste buds into overdrive.

To top it all, everyone noticed the change between Mollie and Zac. The couple couldn't suppress the revived passion that engulfed them.

Sitting next to her at the table, Zac did not stop caressing her. He brushed Mollie's face with his fingertips; he brought her wrist to his lips and even leaned over twice to kiss her cheek. This delighted her mother, who, at seeing her daughter smile again, couldn't squash flows of happiness.

Zac's amorous attentions pleased Mollie a lot, even if she tried to act aloof.

His friends seemed to have forgotten the dangers lurking in the background as they were upbeat too. Everyone wallowed in the joyous atmosphere.

Even the baby was in a lively mood. Mia was giggling, feeding out of Alex's hands.

Zac also apologised to George for hitting him, and they had shaken hands. Intensifying the light-hearted spirit, it restored harmony to the house.

From the garden, the warm-scented breeze floated through the room, as the relaxed atmosphere and the tasty food gave rise to a lovely evening for the whole party.

Well… all but one!

After dinner, the party moved out into the extensive gardens for a stroll. It was a beautiful, starry night, the surrounding sea in darkness, but the moon casting a beam of light over its mass of water, making it shine with a silvery glitter here and there. The white ripples of water dimly illuminated by the stream of moonlight and the gentle rustle of its waves filled the air with calmness, while the fragrant scents from the garden mingled in the soft breeze.

They all strolled to the waterfront loggia. Then they scattered, some to the pool, others to the terraced gardens and towards the Moorish pavilion.

Mollie roamed through the gardens, and while alone for a moment, a hand grabbed her upper arm and pulled her firmly into the secluded Moorish pavilion, away from the main party.

It was then Mollie's new world collided with her past.

"You!" she gasped, not altogether surprised. She had been expecting it, dreading it. Now that he was upon her, he terrified her. She had tried to avoid him the whole weekend. But she knew what was coming.

He took her hands to his lips, but she wriggled them out abruptly.

"Now, now…" he taunted with a smirk.

"What do you want?" Mollie asked him sharply.

"Well, that's not the way to greet an old friend, is it Mrs. Sorensen?"

"Please, Zac will wonder where I am," she replied in alarm, trying to tone down her sharpness, but with a crack in her voice. Thus, her body tensed, and the hair at the back of her neck stood on alert. Her breathing shallow with dread.

"What's going on?" he urged, raising his eyebrows. At his full height, he loomed mightily over her.

"I don't understand what you mean," Mollie answered anxiously.

"Are you playing happy families with him?"

"Happy families?" she echoed, though she knew what he meant.

"The fool has fallen in love with you, hasn't he?" he said with menace in his tone.

"I can't help that," she bellowed, "you tossed me to him." She stared at him defiantly, but he either ignored her comment or pretended not to hear it.

"Why have you not answered any of my messages?" he asked instead, with a calm voice. Even in the dim light, his dark, cold eyes were uncompromising, revealing his feelings. He was furious.

"I couldn't. Zac knows everything; you realise that! He screened my messages," she replied to keep him at bay.

"Or you wouldn't?"

"Please, we agreed the rules at the outset. Wait these three years for me," she mumbled.

She had no intention of going back to him. Not now, not in three years. Never! What she didn't say to her ex-lover was, her emotions had changed, and she was deeply in love with her husband instead.

It was not the right moment to tell him about her feelings for Zac, though she assumed him to be well aware of that too. She tried to manage the situation, though it had long been outside her control.

"Rules? No. Those were your rules, Mollie, not mine." Her ex-lover laughed. He touched her arm with his fingertips, but she withdrew from his touch and shivered with disgust.

"Please, Zac will see us. Stay away from me," she begged.

"I can't. The two of you, like love birds at dinner, nauseating, really! Have you fallen for him?" he hissed.

"No. Of course, not. But everyone must believe in this…" she lied.

He studied her with suspicion and raised her face to him. She had tears in her eyes, but she needed to be convincing to protect Zac from her ex-lover.

"You wouldn't be lying to me, would you now?" But he knew.

"No, I'm not. You can have the money. All of it. I don't mind," she blurted out. *As long as you leave Zac and me alone,* she thought. She cared for nothing else.

"Can I now?" he taunted her with a smirk.

"I don't care about the money," she mumbled.

He snorted, whispering almost to himself, while he caressed her face, "Oh, Mollie, for someone so clever, you are really disingenuous!"

She withdrew further away from him. "Please, stay away," she said. Mollie turned, about to walk out of the Moorish dome when he grabbed her arm and pushed her hard against the mirrored wall of the pavilion. She gave out a shriek.

He spread his elbows on either side of her and pressed

his body against hers, trapping her in. The impact stunned her for a few moments.

There were mirrors around them in the pavilion, and for a second, she saw their reflections multiplied many times over. She felt like she was in a nightmare from which she would soon wake up. But it wasn't. It was all too real! She felt faint.

He taunted her with a smirk, licking her neck with his tongue.

Mollie winced. She tried to push him back, but he was too strong, and he didn't budge.

"Are you trying to cross me?" he crooned while he pinned her to the wall, his face an inch from hers. He smelled her hair and brushed his lips on hers.

"Please. Stop." She winced.

"Have you fallen for Zac?" His voice was steady, and he paused for a moment, but the demand was unmistakable. "You did! You silly girl!" he spat with venom.

"I have thousands of pounds in my account. You can take it all," she blurted the words out to avoid his question, but her ex-lover didn't buy it.

His proximity made her ill. How had she fallen for him? How had she ever contemplated love for this vile man? How could he be Zac's friend for so long and do this to him, be so callous, so treacherous?

Then, with flashing thoughts suddenly racing through her mind at the speed of light, clarity dawned on her. She realised this was not just about money. This was about Zac! She gasped, shivered, and braced herself for what was coming next. Why had it taken her so long to realise it? She had let her ex-lover manipulate her into this mess. *How blind I was...*

"Thousands? When I can have all of this?" he tormented her with a brittle laugh, waving his hand towards the house.

"But this belongs to his grandmother; it's not even Zac's. It isn't mine to give you," she mumbled.

"I'm not talking about this house, but all of it. All of what he has to offer you," he said, ignoring her objections.

"But this is crazy. You read the prenup; it's tight," she tried to deflect.

"But if you were to have a child..." He cocked his head to one side. He caressed her face with one hand and placed the other with an open palm on her belly.

"Wh-what?" she stammered. He had stunned her. One day, she might have children, sure! She was young and in love with her husband, although the thought had not crossed her mind yet. Mollie trembled. His demands were outlandish —fantasies! But there was more.

"A widow with a child; imagine what you could get from his family," he sneered.

Her blood ran cold. She gasped. She felt as if she would pass out... this was what he had been striving for all along, the vile man!

"You can take the money. All of it, I promise. It's yours, but please leave Zac alone," she implored him when she regained control of herself.

He laughed at her "You silly, silly girl!" he said with a crisp laugh, but his eyes were menacing. He scared her.

"Listen to me—" she murmured, but he interrupted her.

"You have fallen for him! You fool, all that cleverness, psst, for nothing," he smirked.

"Please, this is madness. You cannot be serious. You can't hurt Zac; you wouldn't."

"But my love, you are naïve. Why would I want a little money, when I could have more, much more? Let's say, if Zac had an accident and left a beautiful sweet widow with a child..." he crooned. She gasped at her ex-lover's devilish plan.

"But he is your friend! How can you even think that way? You said you wanted money; this is not what we agreed!" she pleaded, but he didn't hear her, and he continued on his path.

"Then, if you were to get remarried to his loyal friend, Zac's family would love you all the more for it. That's where I come in," he taunted.

"Please. I beg you," she said frantically, but he went on, undaunted.

"His family would deny nothing to his young widow and baby. They've always liked me. His grandmother adores me. So, I would remind them of him, and with his baby, and me as your new husband, the sky would be our limits. The child will be the heir to a fortune!"

"This is insane." She tried to push her ex-lover back with her open hands on his chest forcefully, but he was too strong. He pressed his body tighter against hers.

"Think, Mollie. And don't get any ideas, or he will pay the consequences sooner than you expect."

"No!" she shouted at him with determination. "Go to hell. I won't do it. This has gone far enough! You must stop now," she retorted, her chin up, struggling to be brave. But she was terrified! She tried to move, but he restrained her in place.

She couldn't allow him to harm Zac, couldn't tolerate this madness any longer. She would not do it. She tried to run and forced him back with both hands. "No, no!" she spat.

But this time, he grasped her arm and shoved her brutally against the mirrored wall.

She hit the wall and winced. She touched her head; it hurt, and a trickle of blood dribbled down her neck. But there was no time to dwell on this.

He wiped it for her, smiling.

"I'll tell Zac this was *your* plan if you don't," he taunted.

"But that's not true. You know that. I didn't want to do it," she murmured.

"I'll confess, with contrition, that you cajoled me. *You* seduced *me* into it. Who will he believe, eh? A woman he considers a liar, or his devoted friend? I'll tell him you are a scheming bitch who pushed me to do this for money," he smirked.

"It isn't true! You wouldn't."

"Want to bet?" He smiled. "He will choose me. You lose him the moment he learns I am your lover, anyway."

"You are not my lover! Go to hell!" she said with fervour.

Then, Mollie saw red! She punched his face—a tight fist right on his chin, with all the strength she possessed.

He lurched back two steps, surprised, not expecting it, and rubbed his chin with his hand. His cold stare was menacing, but he didn't retaliate. "Stupid girl!" he spat, though, "I should have seen it coming." He cursed.

"Please, he is your friend," she pleaded, changing tactics. Making him angrier would serve no purpose, but he ignored her.

"I grant you; he is in love with you, but he does not trust you. Not really. No one trusts you! He'll never believe you over me." He chuckled, still rubbing his chin. "Bloody hell, Mollie! You have a good punch! It hurts like hell."

"This is absurd," she whispered. *It's a nightmare.*

"Enough with these games!" he hissed this time, getting hold of her upper arms and shaking her roughly. She screamed, and he put his hand over her mouth to muffle the sound.

"Shush. Quiet! They'll hear us," he said.

But her legs were shaking. She felt dizzy and thought she might pass out.

"Umm…" she mumbled, with his hand still on her mouth.

"I don't want to hear any more excuses. Just do it, or I will kill him before his time. Understood?" he blurted out in a chilling tone.

Her face turned pale, the energy leaving her body. An icy sweat ran over her. Her belly was churning, and she felt sick. He took his hand off her mouth. She watched him, fear gripping her.

"You never loved me, did you?" she murmured suddenly.

"What?"

"Did you?" she said, a sob escaping her, knowing too well how badly he had used her for his own purposes. He had exploited her and pushed her into this situation by his treacherous cunning.

"My love. You are gorgeous. Your naiveté is endearing," he whispered, caressing her face. "Zac and I have always had the same taste in women. That's why you were ideal, vital to my plan," he finished icily and caressed the length of her body.

She wanted to scream, but the air left her lungs. Her limbs were weak, her breathing laboured.

"You planned this? All along?" She could barely get the words out, but she would rather die than hurt Zac.

"Well…" Her ex-lover smiled, a cold and calculating smile. It chilled her.

"Did you?" she whispered.

"I waited years for the ideal moment, for the right girl. Then you came along, and you were perfect. You are! I knew he would fall for you, and as they say, the rest is history."

"But he is your friend," she pleaded with no strength in her voice. She thought she would collapse.

"Friend? He took her from me, then he tossed her away.

Like he will do with you when he tires of you. That's why he needs to pay for what he's done!" he cried out, a veil of anger across his face, contorting his mellow features. His hands went to her throat. His stance was rigid and threatening. He lost control and squeezed her neck. He pressed his hands around her neck tighter and tighter. She put her hands on his, trying to loosen his hold on her neck. Mollie tried to wriggle out, but to no avail. She realised she would die. He was strangling her.

"Y-you are h-hurting me. Please, I can't breathe. Please..." she choked the words out.

Her ex-lover behaved as if in a trance, but she punched his face again, hard, with her fist. He grimaced, blinking several times. He relaxed his grip on her and he dropped his hands by his sides.

Mollie collapsed on her knees. She bent over, her head down, coughing. She gasped for air, trying to win back control of her breathing.

"See what you force me to do. You must not challenge me," he sighed as he helped her up.

"Who was she?" she asked after some time, when she'd recovered.

"She? Never mind. Just do as you are told."

"I beg you..." she trailed off, her words faint, anguish in her eyes.

"A child, Mollie, that's what you have to produce for me. His baby, no excuses. I am serious! And in case you have any ideas, a teaser will come your way later, my love, should you assume you can cross me again."

There was no doubt as to the menace he fired at her. "What d-do you m-mean?" she stammered.

"Wait and see." He winked, "A child! If the time you spent in bed with him this afternoon is anything to go by, it won't be long before you become an expectant mother.

Three months, Mollie. You must get pregnant. That's all you have to do. A baby, and no games!"

Mollie was about to implore, but noises outside told them they were no longer alone. She felt feverish, faint, her face as pale as a sheet, her legs hardly sustaining her.

"Mollie? What are you doing here? Zac is looking for you," George said when he saw her outside the pavilion.

She stared at him, terror still in her eyes, then turned towards the pavilion. Her ex-lover was no longer there. The blasted man was gone. She turned to George.

"I-I—"

"Are you okay? You're shaking; what is it?" her friend asked with concern when he noticed her pale face.

"I d-don't f-feel well," she stuttered. George took her by the elbow and led her towards the house. When she stumbled, he steadied her. She clutched his arm with both hands, and they moved on towards the rest of the party.

Her nightmare had only just begun.

"YOU'RE NOT WELL YET. You must be careful."

"I'll be fine in a minute," she reassured him, though her husband would not hear of it.

"No, the evening is over for you. Go upstairs and lie down. You need a good night's sleep. You'll feel better in the morning. I'll take care of our friends." Upon seeing her in that state, he issued the orders.

"I-I…" Mollie protested.

"No. Please, rest! Off you go." He put his arms around her shoulders and kissed her forehead. Then he led her up to her bedroom. He helped her undress, caressed her face, and encouraged her to get into bed.

After what had happened, Mollie welcomed some time alone. She needed to think.

"Don't worry, Mollie. I'll take care of everything," he assured her.

If only that were true, she reflected in irony.

Zac closed the door behind himself. He remained there for a few seconds. He fretted about his bride. She looked pale and feverish, her hands and skin cold and clammy.

She had not fully recovered from her sunstroke and fever yet, when he had put her through a lot of stress. He considered how badly he had treated her in the last few days—awful, even for him. First, he'd humiliated her, demanding the name of her ex-lover, his motives, calling her a liar and treating her like a jerk. Second, by welcoming friends over as part of their honeymoon, he had embarrassed her.

So, Clarissa had wanted his blood. It must have distressed his wife more than she'd let on.

Third, the hours of lovemaking to satisfy his lust, though she had been a delightful, eager, and willing participant to the activities, it had absorbed her strength while still unwell.

Clarissa was right. He had behaved like an asshole, a brute. No wonder the poor girl looked so ill. Pain hit his heart. He wished to run to her, take her into his arms and beg forgiveness.

But he promised himself, he would look after her from now on, the way she deserved, no more pressure on her. Zac would give her time to recuperate, to relax. Despite her lying, he forgave her—completely! He was so in love with his bride, he would have condoned anything she did. He wanted Mollie, and nothing else mattered regardless of the pitfalls. And no doubt there were many! He was not a fool. This girl would not be easy.

He was in uncharted territory. But he could not bear it if she was not in his life. *What has she done to me? I am under her spell…* His only desire was to protect her, to love her, and to make her happy.

AN HOUR LATER, Mollie was still awake in her bed, turmoil in her mind. A scarf covered the marks Peter had left on her neck when he'd tried to strangle her. She had to hide them; she had been lucky Zac hadn't noticed them earlier, in the dim light.

The trembling subsided. Though the experience with her ex-lover… it had been a nightmare.! *The man is insane!*

On the surface, a guest in Zac's house, one of his best friends, but in reality, her ex-boyfriend had revealed himself for what he was. *A treacherous bastard! How could he do that?* The evil scumbag was now blackmailing her too. *A child? A widow? Oh, my God! Is the man out of his mind?*

Should she believe his threats? Though, that evening she had witnessed a new side to him—a much darker side, one that terrified her, a violent one.

She tried to convince herself that her ex-lover was bluffing, to force her to do what he wanted. But it troubled her. She didn't know what to think, although, she sensed impending danger. She felt it in her bones!

The girl couldn't rest. Not when she had dreadful thoughts racing through her mind. Not when her ex-boyfriend intended something despicable. *He wants to kill Zac.* The thought terrified her, making her feverish.

The moment her husband had told her his friends would come for the weekend, Mollie knew the unpleasant effects of her actions would come to roost. She had avoided her ex-lover like the plague the whole weekend, avoiding being near him or being left alone with him anywhere in the house.

But it was inevitable, her fate inexorable! Now they were

in danger. Never in her wildest nightmares, though, could she have foretold a lethal outcome to the plan.

Time to come clean with Zac; she must! Come what may! *Even if the relationship is doomed.* She couldn't allow the bastard to hurt her husband. *She must tell him everything.*

She had tears in her eyes; she was grieving. Lost in her gloomy thoughts, she heard a scream. She sprang out the bed, confused! She thought she had imagined it, but soon, more shouts struck her. A commotion reached her from downstairs.

Out of the room in a sprint, through the long corridor, she rushed down the tall, curving staircase. She stopped midway down and froze. It was chaotic. As she looked down, everybody was talking at once around something on the floor.

Then the scene hit home, and she screamed. Kathryn lay at the bottom of the stairs in a pool of blood, amidst the confusion, until Finley took charge.

"Quiet! Stand back! Give her space," he shouted.

They all quietened down and stepped back.

Mollie stared, paralysed.

"Darling, Fin is with her," her mother told her when she ran up to her but kept her from moving further.

"Let me go," Mollie cried out, suddenly recovering from the shock, but her husband reached her to restrain her.

"Let Fin deal with her, please, love. He knows what to do," Zac said, but she struggled to wriggle free.

"No, let me go to her."

"Please, the army trained him to handle emergencies like this. Let him help her. The ambulance will be here soon," he tried to appease her.

"Oh, my God, how bad is she?" she asked with tears in her eyes.

"She'll be fine." He tried to put her mind at rest, but Kathryn's injuries worried him.

"Will she?"

Zac nodded. "The ambulance should arrive any minute now," he repeated, staring at the scene below.

"What happened?"

"She must have missed a step and stumbled down the stairs. I don't know." He wrapped his arms around his wife, their eyes fixed on the action below.

Finley, stooped over the still unconscious Kathryn's body, dished out orders. George and Marie Therese complied with them. Then, kneeling by her side, he tried to stop the bleeding. Everyone else stayed back to give them space.

As she watched the frenzied activity below unfolding, for a second, their eyes met, and her ex-boyfriend looked at her with a subtle grin on his lips. Mollie's face emptied of the little colour left. She understood!

The evil man had done it!

Her limbs gave way. The air left her lungs. She would have passed out, but Zac held her up.

"This is my fault," Mollie mumbled. Overcome by panic, emotion, and grief, she sobbed.

"I'll give her a sedative. It'll calm her down, make her sleep," Mary said.

Mollie's heart was aching for her friend. She was aware of her own guilt in this too, and it could become much worse. The vile beast had done this to Kathryn. The regret at indirectly hurting her friend had shattered her heart. Mollie realised, finally, the perils were too real. She had no more doubt now that her ex-boyfriend could kill Zac, and he wanted nothing more than to comply with his threat!

It horrified her.

Chapter 20

"Who is with Kat? How is she?" she asked the moment she opened her eyes the next day. She stroked her temples.

"She is a little battered but fine. George and Fin went to the hospital with her last night; they are still there. Your husband followed later on, but he is back now," Mary told her as she sat at Mollie's bedside.

The sedative had sent her to into a deep sleep for hours. But the moment she'd awakened, all of her worries had returned with a bang.

"What time is it?" she asked. She was still groggy from sleep, but she had to clear her head fast.

She wouldn't let him do it. Her ex-lover could hang himself for all she cared. She didn't know what she would do, but she would not allow him to hurt anyone else.

That monstrous bastard had done it, Mollie was sure of it. She didn't know how, but there was not a doubt. Her ex-boyfriend had sent Kathryn tumbling down the stairs. It was his way of warning her. He wanted to mould her to his will, and she was scared.

"Six am," her mother answered.

It's a miracle Kathryn is not dead. Mollie got up, but then her mother gently pulled her down to sit on the edge of the bed next to her, her face pale. She looked at her with concern and put a comforting arm around her shoulders.

"Please go back to sleep. You need to rest."

"I must see her," she stressed. They turned to the door as Zac came in.

"I need to go to the hospital." She ran to him.

"Perhaps later. Are you better?" He pulled her to him and kissed her forehead.

"Yes. Please, let's go now." She wriggled free and went to the wardrobe to get some clothes.

"Hey, hey, stop. Kathryn is resting; she is asleep. You can see her when she wakes up. I promise. She is in good hands." Zac's arms circled her, steadying her, somehow calming her.

But his wife's mind was in turmoil. "Please," she pleaded.

"Darling, why don't you go back to sleep?" Zac said, but he sensed his bride's agitation.

"No, I am fine." Mollie was stubborn, but he manoeuvred her back to bed.

"Mary, you get some rest; you must be exhausted. I'll stay with her," Zac said.

"Don't you need some sleep too?" Mary ventured.

"I'll be fine," he responded, shrugging his shoulders.

It delighted Mary that this affectionate man was looking after her daughter now. "Relax, darling. It's too early. George and Fin are taking good care of her. I will see you later." Her mother kissed her temple and left the room.

"You promise? Later?" she asked him the moment her mother closed the door, but she lay down on the bed, with her mass of red hair on the pillow.

"Later, I promise. Once Kat wakes up," Zac said, sitting on the edge of the bed, holding her hand.

Mollie was desperate to be with Kathryn. She felt responsible for what had happened to her friend. *I need to warn George too…*

She thought of her ex-lover's ultimatum. But as long as she was not pregnant, Zac would be safe. Time was on her side, but she dreaded what could happen next. She realised the vile creature would carry out his threats.

She must do something but was uncertain on what to do. The treacherous bastard had revealed himself a dangerous man. He had shown his true colours.

I don't know him. Evil! He could have killed Kathryn. Mollie, you are a blind, foolish girl…

In all this mess, for his own selfish reasons, her ex-lover had thrown Mollie and Zac together, her silver lining! But no one would harm him if she could help it.

I would rather die than see him suffer again. The sudden realisation made her heart thump faster. She glanced at her husband, and he repaid her with his sexy smile, caressing her hair back on the pillow. *I love this man!* She squeezed his hand, and he caressed her face.

But for how long would he love her? *Once he knows who my ex-lover is, he will hate me forever!* Mollie had no choice; she would have to come clean. Game over! It had turned too dangerous, and she couldn't hide her ex-lover's identity for much longer. *But perhaps not just yet. Maybe! No. no. I must tell him. Steal one more day of happiness!* Yes, then she would tell Zac. Even if that meant losing him, but at least he would be safe. If there was another way… but there wasn't, whatever the consequences.

I am doomed, anyway, she thought, *it will be the end of us.*

She shuddered. "Can you hold me? Please?" she asked her husband, and his grin widened. He wrapped his arms around her until the soothing feeling relaxed her into sleep.

LATER THAT MORNING, Zac drove her to the hospital. Despite the beauty of the scenery, the car drive was somber. Not even the turquoise sea water, with its lulling waves, and the bright sunshine caressing her skin could uplift her spirit.

With turmoil in her heart, her head was throbbing with anguished thoughts. All this charm around her, and her ex-lover brought nothing but darkness to her soul and sorrow to her life. She sighed.

"Are you all right?" Zac asked as he drove, retrieving her from her troubled reflections.

"Yes. I am okay. I'm worried about Kat, that's all," she mumbled.

"She'll be fine," he said.

"Are you sure?"

"Yes, positive."

She smiled, not convinced.

"Why did you say it was your fault?"

"What?" She spun to him.

"Last night, when Kathryn fell. You said it was all your fault. Why would you say that?" he asked, focused on the road ahead.

"Did I?" She turned towards the window. She dared not look at him.

"Yes." He side-glanced at her for a moment.

"I don't remember. I felt distraught," she lied. She didn't like it one bit, but she had no choice.

Mollie had already promised no more lies, and here she was, lying to him again. She cursed silently several times, curses as dark as hell for her stupidity.

Zac studied her. He was dubious. He knew by now, there was always more to Mollie than met the eye, but he said nothing.

"KAT, DARLING." She ran to her friend and put her arms around her, squeezing her hard.

"Hey, don't squash me; it hurts!" Kathryn blurted.

"Oh dear, I am sorry. How are you?"

"I am okay. A hell of a headache, but I'm fine." Her friend smiled, stretching in her hospital bed.

"Oh, Jesus. You have stitches on your forehead," Mollie said, aghast.

"I'll survive." The girl dabbed her forehead.

"Five stitches, and it will leave a scar," George interjected gloomily from the other side of the bed.

Mollie turned to him, and then she lowered her eyes.

"The scar will heal," Kathryn replied.

"How are you feeling this morning?" Zac asked her. He took Kathryn's chin in his hands to study the stitches.

"Much better, thank you. It looks worse than it is, a few cuts and bruises, but I am fine. The doctor is keeping me under observation, wants to make sure I am not concussed. I am okay, really."

"I'll talk to him. Where is Fin?" Zac asked.

"He is getting us coffees," George answered with a shrug.

"Okay, I'll talk to the doctor. I won't be long." Zac went in search of the physician.

"What happened, Kat?" Mollie asked when Zac left the room. Seeing her friend talking and moving had restored her mood and she heaved a sigh of relief.

"I don't know. One minute, I was on top of the stairs, the next, I was tumbling down."

"Anyone behind you at the time?"

"What?" Kathryn looked up at her and touched her forehead.

"Yes. On the landing, when you were about to go down the stairs, was anybody behind you?" Mollie insisted.

"What do you mean? As in… someone pushed me down the stairs?" the girl asked, shocked. She turned to George, bewildered, and then back to Mollie. Kathryn shifted in her bed. She couldn't contain her astonishment. But she couldn't recall what happened. Her memory was hazy.

"Yes. Was there?" Mollie insisted when she didn't answer.

"No! Of course not," her friend blasted out.

"Are you sure?" she persisted.

"Mollie, what are you saying? Why would anyone in the house push me down the stairs? That's ridiculous."

"I don't mean on purpose!" Mollie tried to backtrack.

George's scowl deepened.

Finley returned with a tray of plastic cups.

They sipped their coffees and had a few laughs about the whole incident, but Mollie was uncomfortable.

George looked at her pensively.

At the perfect moment, Mollie signalled to George, who excused himself and went outside the room.

"I wonder where Zac is?" Mollie said to Kathryn a moment later. "I'll go look for him." She excused herself and left the room too.

George was outside, in the corridor. She went to him, grabbed his arm, and pulled him away. They wandered until they found an empty room. They got inside, and Mollie closed the door.

"What is it, Mollie?" George asked, watching her with a frown.

"Well, I-I—"

He interrupted her, "Do you think someone pushed Kat down the stairs?"

"Yes," she whispered.

"Incredible!"

"True."

"Who? Why?" he asked, still dumbfounded.

"It's true. Someone pushed her," Mollie said adamantly.

"But why? Who?"

"I-I—" She hesitated.

Mollie, for heaven's sake!" he said, exasperated, a huge breath leaving his lungs.

She murmured her ex-lover's name, barely a whisper.

George's eyes went wide. "What?"

"You heard me," she mumbled.

"I don't believe you."

"It's true."

"You are kidding me. Why would he do that?"

"He's done it. I am sure," Mollie said, searching his eyes for a reaction, but then she lowered her eyes.

"Look at me. Why would he push Kathryn down the stairs?" His tone was impatient. She tugged at her sleeve and glanced at him askance, "Mollie…" he repeated, irritation growing in his voice.

She had no choice but to tell him. "He was my boyfriend." And this time, she told him the whole story, leaving nothing out—her ex-lover's full plan, his menaces, threats, and even the intimidation in the pavilion.

George was astonished, her story unbelievable.

"What am I going to do?" she said in anguish.

"But that's crazy. Are we talking about the same person?" he asked, not believing Zac's friend was behind this.

"He wants to destroy my husband. He wants his money, all of it! He wants me. He wants Zac's life," she blurted out in despair.

George whistled and sat on a chair. His jaw clenched. He looked at Mollie and shook his head. "Is he still your lover?" he asked, dumbfounded.

"No. Of course not! How can you even ask that!? Was.

My. Lover. *Was!* Now, he is a treacherous, manipulative, evil bastard of an ex-lover. But it is all true, I assure you. Every word. When you saw me outside the pavilion yesterday, I was not sick! He had scared me out of my wits."

"But that's absurd. They have known each other for years. They are friends, the best of friends. He is a guest in his house, for heaven's sake!"

"George, he wants to kill my husband. I am telling you; I swear. I cannot let him do that. He pushed Kat down the stairs to prove to me he is serious. It was a warning to me! He had a plan all along, and I am the stupid girl who fell for it," she said frantically.

"Mollie, you need to tell Zac. He has a right to know," he stressed.

"The bastard will tell him it was my idea. All my doing! That it was I who manipulated him, that I want his money!"

"Zac will believe you."

"No, it's his word against mine. Zac may be fond of me, but he doesn't trust me."

"Zac loves you. He will."

"Not when he finds out who my ex-lover is. The damn bastard will lie to save his own neck; he'll say I cajoled him into doing this with me."

"He is a dangerous man. You and Zac are both in danger. Well, bloody hell. He pushed Kat down the stairs. Jesus! Everybody is in danger."

"Promise me you'll say nothing until I have time to think."

"Oh, I don't know. This is dangerous, risky, too crazy."

"Please, George. One more day is all I ask. Zac will hate me once I tell him the truth. Promise me, one more day, please?" she pleaded with him.

"Okay. One more day, that's all. Then, you must tell Zac

everything. Understood?" he stressed in no uncertain terms. Against his better judgement, George agreed.

They had left Finley and Kathryn alone in the room.

FINLEY HARMAN WAS a tough and burly man who took everything in his stride. He was an expert soldier who had hardly flinched at being shot at by the Taliban in Afghanistan when he was in the army, threading through minefields in many hell-raising army missions.

So, to him, by comparison, everything else was a walk in the park. He was composed and self-possessed at all times with whatever life threw at him. But, as much as he was all those things, he didn't have the savoir-faire that his friends had with women. So, there was an awkward silence until Zac returned to the room, and they both breathed a sigh of relief.

"The doctor will see you in half an hour, and if everything is fine, he says you can go home today," Zac said.

"Great. I'm glad. I feel so foolish coming to the south of France and ending up in a hospital bed," Kat said with a nervous laugh. She side glanced at Finley, who had fixed his eyes on her forehead with the stitches.

Kathryn blushed and played with a strand of her long hair.

"Where is my wife?" Zac asked.

"Somewhere outside," Kathryn mumbled.

"I'll go and fetch them," Finley ventured, and he left the room with a sigh of relief.

ALONE IN THE hospital room with Kat, Zac moved to take the chair next to her bed, closer to the window.

"I am sorry I wrecked your weekend with the fall. I apologise—" Kathryn mumbled, but he interrupted her, raising his hand.

"No, please! I am relieved you are fine. You could have been seriously hurt," he said.

"Well, I am sorry, all the same. Everyone is here, instead of enjoying themselves, and it's all my fault. I spoiled everyone's weekend."

"Look, Kat. If anyone ruined anything, it was my terrible temper. Mollie and I were not... well..." He paused, waving his hand, not realising quite what to say. "...but we are fine now, my wife and I, I mean. So, it was not you. A weird weekend, long before your fall, trust me," Zac said openly with a smile.

"Well, you were in a filthy mood, I must admit," she replied with a chuckle and a blush, shifting her position in her bed.

"Yes, I was."

"Dear Mollie cried buckets, you know. She really cares for you," she ventured.

"And I care for her," he came back with a grin, amazed at his own candour talking about his wife.

"Mollie is a lovely girl, the best of friends. And I am glad she is happy with you. But I have to say, I never saw it coming." Kathryn chuckled.

"That we reconciled?" Zac asked, turning his full attention to her.

"No. Not that. I knew you would!" she snorted in an unladylike manner.

"Oh? What then?"

"What I mean is I never imagined Mollie would end up with you," she said with a blush.

He smiled, glancing out of the window, and back to her. "Well, yes, I guess it was a little sudden, a whirlwind romance," Zac said with a genuine smile. The thought of his marriage of convenience, the arrangement it had all begun with, seemed to him now light years away, in the remoteness of his past. He loved his wife, so he would not go there. He turned to face the window again.

"Oh, I know. But I never imagined it would be you, but him, instead."

Him? He whipped his head to her when the word registered, not sure he had heard her correctly.

She continued talking. "Well, I'm glad she is with you. You are much nicer, even if sometimes a little intimidating." She grinned.

"Intimidating? Me? No! But back up a step. Him? Who do you mean?" he asked, glad his voice sounded calm, but his brain was racing ahead.

"Well, for months, Mollie did nothing but talk about him. So, I believed she would end up with him, you see. But I'm glad she is with you. There is something about him that scares me a bit, you know. I can't put my finger on it."

"Excuse me?" His voice was composed. *Him? What the hell, Mollie's lover?*

"Well, it wouldn't do. Mollie went on and on about him. It was about a year ago—"

"Kat?" he called out, his frown deepening. He shifted in his chair, but Kathryn blabbered, unstoppable in her tale. The crash on the stairs and the headache had made her less conscious of what she was saying. So, she kept on babbling about it.

"She was so infatuated with him. I even thought she was in love with him at one point. Suddenly, nothing more. Not another word about him. Then, you came along. Mollie married you instead," Kathryn said triumphantly.

"Kat, who are you talking about?"

"I told her, not good for her. I understand he is your

friend and all that," she added, pausing for a moment, and a chill ran through his spine, "but he wouldn't have been good for her. So, I am glad she married you instead." She smiled, but she continued prattling on much in the same manner.

He winced at her words. "Christ, who?" he stressed and stood up, his exasperation getting the better of him.

"I had completely forgotten that until this weekend," she said, frowning. It was then she realised she had blabbered, when she saw him standing tall, shoulders square and fists clenched at his side. The realisation hit her. She knew it would be trouble.

She looked up at Zac's face. He was ashen, and a flicker of anger flashed through his eyes. *Oh, sweet Jesus,* she thought, finally aware of what she had just said. *Doesn't he know?*

Thus, the girl became anxious. *Oh my God, he doesn't! Oh, bloody hell! What have I done?* She gulped.

"Kat, please?" His voice remained calm, but he couldn't avoid the icy twinge. His eyes flashed, piercing into hers now, his patience at an end.

She winced at him.

"Well, I…" Kathryn had navigated into deep waters, but it was too late now.

Zac would not let it go.

The fall made Kathryn blabber more than she would in normal circumstances. Though, she was known for her big mouth, renowned for always putting her foot in it. Today, she brought the whole term to another level. She heaved a desperate sigh. *Oh, damn!*

"Kat. Who. Is. He?" he asked, beyond exasperated, exhausting his favours.

"Zac… you should ask Mollie," she murmured, trying to get out of it, but his eyes narrowed on her. They were a thin slit, dark with anger.

She lost.

"You tell me. Now, Kat. *Now!*" he bellowed.

She squirmed. "Professor Blake. Peter!" she blurted in a rush. "Oh, please don't tell Mollie I told you," Kathryn pleaded.

The others returned to the room then.

"Please," Kathryn shouted from her bed when Zac marched off and went for the door, almost colliding with his friend upon entering the room.

"What's the matter?" Mollie asked, but her husband walked on without a word.

Zac couldn't hear anything or see anyone; he had only one thought in mind, Peter!

She tried to grab his hand, but he shrugged it off, and left the room.

At that moment, every particle in his body had one purpose, to find Peter. He was blinded by the purpose. He had to find his treacherous friend.

"Zac?" she called out after him, but he kept on walking.

"Where the hell are you going?" Finley ran after him, grabbing his arm, but his friend shook him off.

"Stay with my wife," he commanded with a thunderous look in his eyes and kept on walking.

"What's up with him?" Finley stared at Kathryn when he returned to the room. She avoided his eyes.

"Why is my husband so upset?" Mollie asked her friend, her voice strained. She was perspiring. An awful feeling crept up inside her belly.

"Well, I may have said something that u-upset h-him," Kathryn stammered.

"What?" Mollie asked, but her friend shook her head and lowered her head.

The tall man lifted her head, so he could stare squarely in her eyes and said, "Kat, it's okay. You are not in trouble. But we need to know what you said." His words were soft but firm while holding her chin.

"Well, I-I didn't mean—"

"Kat!" Finley's tone was harsh now, while his hand dropped by his side. The sound of a firm command was unmistakable.

"I told him about Peter," she blurted out.

Mollie gasped, and her hand covered her mouth while the colour drained from her face. George eyes widened, and he cursed several times under his breath.

Finley took one look at them and understood. "Kat, are you talking about Professor Blake?" Finley asked.

"Yes," she whispered and nodded furiously, her eyes downcast.

"Oh my God!" Mollie cried out.

"I'm sorry. I thought he knew. I told him it was only an infatuation, long before you met him anyway—" Kat was still blabbering.

"Oh, God. What have you done?" George cried out.

"Mollie, is Peter your lover?" Finley asked, glaring at her.

"Lover? What lover? What do you mean?" Kathryn shouted in agitation, her eyes darting wildly around the room at her friends.

"Kat, shut up," Finley commanded, his voice raised and sharp.

"Sorry," she mumbled, but she felt the crack in her voice raise, and so did he, when he turned for a second to look at her. Kathryn's eyes welled up, and the blood rushed to her face. She was trying her hardest to suppress herself from crying.

Finley noted the girl's distress, but he had no time to deal with it. That would have to wait.

"Is he? Is Peter your lover?" He raised his voice again, this time at Mollie.

"He *was* my lover, *ex*-lover," Mollie bellowed, but then she burst into tears and added, "Oh, God! Peter wants to kill Zac; they will kill each other. Fin, do something, please." She was pleading with him.

"George, you stay here. Don't move from here. Do you understand? Stay with Kat," Finley commanded. "If Peter comes here, call security! Press the alarm button next to her bed."

The young man nodded.

"Mollie, let's go. We need to find your husband before he finds Peter," Finley ordered. He grabbed her arm and marched her unceremoniously out of the room.

As they were leaving, Finley heard Kathryn burst out into tears. He paused for a nanosecond, but then he continued on his way.

At that point, George was free to tell her about the storm that was brewing.

Chapter 21

*Z*ac drove from the hospital to the villa like the devil chased after him. He stormed into the large marble foyer when he arrived at the house, cursing and ranting. After climbing up the staircase, two steps in one go, he wrenched Peter's bedroom door open with such force that it crashed against the wall and bounced back. He stopped it with his hand to avoid being hit, but the man was not there. Out in a dash, he retraced his steps down the stairs to the kitchen.

"Where is Peter?" Zac barked at the housekeeper who had her back to him.

Marie Therese was busy. She was taking a tray out of the oven with a batch of buttery soft Madeleines. But the loud growl behind her startled her out of her skin. She screamed and dropped the tray. The biscuits showered on the floor with a crash of the tray.

"Oh, mon Dieu! You made me jump," Marie Therese cried, turning to him.

The woman sighed at the mess on the floor, scattered with her delicious biscuits. She was about to open her mouth to scold him, but when she looked at Zac's thunderous face, she changed her mind. She closed her mouth abruptly. Whatever was troubling him, it was not good.

"Where is Peter?" he repeated with fury in his eyes and no apology. She caught the flash of anger contorting his face.

"Monsieur Peter?" Marie Therese inquired timidly when she looked at a vein twitching in his forehead.

"Yes, Peter. Where the hell is he?" he growled at her again.

She winced. "I don't know," she mumbled.

"What is it?" Alex asked when he came in, having heard the crash in the kitchen. He took in the mess on the floor.

"Where is that bastard?"

"What?"

"Yes, the treacherous bastard," Zac shouted, "where is he?"

"Who?" Alex asked, detecting his friend's furious countenance.

"Peter!"

"Zac, calm down. I don't understand."

"I'll kill him. I'll break every fucking bone in his body." He paused and then said, "Where the hell is he? Because he will not live beyond today," Zac repeated, getting hold of Alex's shirt front in his fist.

"What's going on?" Clarissa and Mary came in then with the baby.

"Ladies, please leave the kitchen," Alex said and took his friend's hands off him.

Zac turned on his heel and paced up and down frantically, trying to control himself while the ladies were there.

"What's going on?" Clarissa repeated.

"Claris, get Mary and the baby out. Please," Alex said.

"But—"

"For fuck's sake! Clarissa! Out. Now. Do as you are told,"

Alex bellowed. She had not seen this side of him before. She'd only experienced the sweet man who adored her daughter. But something told her that to retreat was the best option. Curious and obstinate as she was though, she remained there, motionless. The scene, unfolding in front of her, mesmerised her.

It was Mary, with eyes as big as moons, who picked up the scene and moved into action. Holding the baby with one arm, she took Clarissa by the elbow with the other. With a nod of her head to the housekeeper to follow her, Mary walked them out the kitchen.

"Go upstairs and stay there," Alex yelled after them.

"What's going on? Relax," he said when they were alone.

"Where is Peter?"

"He's left. What's gotten into you?"

"Left? Where?" Zac growled, an inch from his friend's face.

"To see Kathryn in the hospital. What's he done? Why are you so angry?" he asked, though he had an inclination.

"The two-faced, deceitful, bastard!" Zac said, staring at his friend.

Alex understood. "No! It can't be. I don't believe it!" His mouth was wide open in astonishment, but one look at Zac's stony eyes told him a different story.

MOLLIE CAME CLEAN. She had no option. So, during the drive from the hospital to the house, she told Finley every-thing through crying sobs. She left nothing out.

He listened with a blank face. *Is she talking about my friend?* The thought tormented him. But she was. A friend had betrayed Zac. Peter, no less. Finley worried what Zac would do if he got to Peter first.

They arrived at the house and got to the foyer, when they noticed the ladies climbing up the stairs.

"Mollie, what's going on? Alex ordered us to go upstairs. Why is your husband so mad?" her mother asked as she stopped midway up the stairs.

"Ladies, please, do as you are told. Go to your bedrooms. You too, Mollie. I will deal with this." Finley paused. "And stay there until I tell you." He delivered his orders like an army captain.

"No. The hell I am! Mom, Clarissa, you go, please," Mollie said.

"Mollie, I have no time for this. Please go," Finley insisted.

"No. I am staying." Now that everything was in the open, she would face the music, whatever that brought to her.

The ladies were alarmed, but they obeyed and went up to their rooms.

Mollie followed Finley into the kitchen.

He sighed, annoyed.

When Zac saw her enter, the expression on his face said it all. He glared at her with such loathing that she would have sworn she heard her heart shatter in a million tiny fragments, her pain violent.

She lowered her eyes and welled up. But she couldn't allow tears to cloud the moment. "Zac," Mollie whispered, but the revulsion on his face was too much. He strutted towards her. His eyes blazed, revealing his anger. Fury bellowed from his every pore.

She gasped and backed up a few steps until her back stood at the door's post. His long strides reached her in a second. He clutched her upper arms. "Peter! Peter?" His eyes flamed with a blend of disgust, confusion, and hatred. But at no time, did she see any love there.

She raised her chin up a notch.

Zac had promised! He'd said he would not ask her again, that what was done, was done. He had promised his undying love to her and that he didn't care about the past. He'd promised to look to the future. But that was not the case, though, under the circumstances, she couldn't blame him. The shock was too great for him.

But a promise was a promise!

"I—" Tears shone in her eyes.

"I don't want to hear a word from you. Understood? Get the hell upstairs with your mother. Out of my sight," Zac said, nudging her out.

Mollie almost lost her balance. "No. I am staying with you; I will not let him harm you," Mollie mumbled, this time with more confidence.

"Psst. A little late for that, don't you think?" he taunted sarcastically. Then he shut her out. He ignored her.

"Zac, please! You promised. That's why I couldn't tell you," she pleaded, but he ran out of the door in a flash.

"I am going after him," Zac said.

"No, you are not," Finley shouted, running to him. "I already called my contacts with the police, and they can deal with him. He wants to kill you." Finley gripped Zac's arm to stop him.

Zac froze at his words. "Kill me? Why?" Zac whipped around, staring at his friend. His face drained of colour. Then he glanced at Mollie, who dropped her eyes. She couldn't bear the pain in his eyes.

Finley pulled him back into the kitchen and gestured to a chair. Zac sat. Then Finley told him of the details of Peter's plan, starting with his treachery, blackmail, greed, and ultimately, the intention to kill him, the wish to appropriate Zac's life for himself. Peter wanted it all, and he wanted Zac dead!

Zac heard every word in confusion but said nothing. His

handsome face changed into an expressionless mask, seeking to hide his pain, but to no use. It was too visible; it was so strong. Zac looked at Mollie. Pain mixed with shock and anger; a multitude of emotions fleeted through his face. But soon, his stony facade came back on.

"I am sorry. I thought he just wanted the money you would pay me," Mollie murmured in her defence.

"I said, not a sound from you," her husband cried out in anguish, pointing a finger at her. But she went on, "I swear, please, believe me. I didn't know about his real intentions." His glare shut her up.

She had stunned him.

Finley finished the story. The more Zac learned about Peter's treacherous plan, the more his rage grew. The naked truth hit him like a thousand stones. There was grief, outrage, and abhorrence in mingled emotions. His friend and his woman had deceived him.

"Is this your plan?" Zac said in an unbroken voice, devoid of emotion, his tone steady while he watched her. She had crushed him. He sat at the table, lifeless.

"No. Not my plan. It was Peter's plan. I didn't know of his real intentions until too late."

He snorted, but it was a sarcastic laugh full of pain.

But she persevered. "I thought it was all about money. He lied to me, too. I swear, please, Zac?" she said, moving closer to him but not daring to approach him.

He swept a hand over his face in frustration. "Didn't you?"

"I didn't know until yesterday. Please believe me; it's true," she pleaded with him, kneeling by the side of his chair and touching his arm. But he pushed her away.

She fell.

"That's enough," Alex yelled at him and helped Mollie up.

Her tears were streaming down.

"Alex, can you keep him here? I am going to the hospital; I need to make sure the police are ready to pick up Peter for questioning when he gets there. I've texted my contacts in the French police already. They'll be discreet. My men are coming to guard the house," Finley said.

"I'll come with you," Zac stood up abruptly.

"No. You won't," Finley said.

"Watch me!"

"No, I don't—" But before Finley could finish his sentence, Zac was already out of the house.

"PROFESSOR!" Kathryn shrieked in alarm. She went pale the moment he stopped in the doorway of her hospital room. The panic in her voice was clear, the lack of colour on her face betraying her fear.

George stood up and started dialling. Peter glanced at him, then at Kathryn. He knew. His game was up!

"You treacherous scum," George yelled, while he dialled furiously.

Before he realised what was happening, Peter walked over to him and punched him hard and square in the face twice. George's head hit the wall. The professor grabbed the phone from his hand and pocketed it while the young man fell unconscious to the floor.

Kat screamed; Peter turned to her. She tried to get off the bed, but he reached for her hair with one hand, while he struck her with the other, hitting her with force.

Kathryn gave out a piercing cry, but he tightened the hold on her hair and pulled her up to him.

She whimpered.

"Now, you foul creature, tell me exactly what's going on."

"I-I..." she mumbled with panic in her eyes. She thought she had rivulets of sweat coming down from her forehead, but when she tasted them in her mouth, she realised it was blood.

He grabbed her hair firmly as he clasped her face. She attempted to scream, but no sound came out.

"Now, tell me. I have no time to waste."

"Zac knows about y-you and Mollie, about your p-plan," she stammered in a rush of breath, horror in her eyes.

He tightened her hair in his hands even rougher. She shrieked again.

"How? Who told him?"

"Aargh." She was feeling faint. "I-I..."

"How?"

"I said something to Zac. I didn't mean to; I am sorry," she sobbed.

"You stupid bitch."

She cried out at the impact when he hit her again. She fell backwards in the bed, stunned, her consciousness gone for a few seconds. Three of her stitches had reopened when Peter first struck her, but a couple more opened on his second blow, and she was bleeding profusely, the blood streaming down her face. But just before he struck her again, Kathryn had pressed the panic button near her bed.

THE ALARMS SOUNDED, booming loudly across the hospital, the noise deafening.

Peter stopped. *Think man, fast!* No alternative but to run.

He would have smothered Kathryn's silly face into death. But alas, he had no time, the likelihood Finley and Zac were on his tail, if not the police.

He couldn't go back to the house or go home to Oxford, either.

That trollop wrecked my plan, shattered my life.

Kathryn, of all people, had unravelled it all.

The wench ruined everything for me, and with all probability, now I've lost it all. After years of careful planning, he'd failed!

All because of Kathryn! *She will pay for this.*

So, Peter left the room and ran as he knew there was not much time before Finley used his connections to get to him.

Mollie? he wondered.

THEY ARRIVED AT THE HOSPITAL, but there was chaos, with the alarms at full blast. The shrill noise was deafening. Hospital security was everywhere, and the French police arrived too. People were running around like madness had been unleashed.

Finley ran to Kat's room, with Zac hot on his heels. For a tall-framed man, he looked agile and fast, and it didn't take him long to reach her room. There was pandemonium there, too. Doctors, security staff, and nurses were everywhere in the room; even a gendarme stood there. Finley saw Kathryn covered in blood, and he blanched. George was sitting next to her with ice on his face, but no sign of Peter.

A security guard and the gendarme stopped them.

"It's okay; they are with us," George cried to the gendarme with a grimace; even talking hurt him.

After a while, they restored order, and only Finley's contact in the police remained in the room to contain the problem.

"Are you okay?" Finley took Kathryn's hand and kissed it.

His usual grave nature around the girl was gone, too concerned for his usual austerity to get in the way.

"I am fine. I'm so sorry. This is all my fault," she said in tears but let her hand wallow in his.

The ex-soldier could be too serious and forbidding, almost harsh in front of a woman he liked. But not that day... And he liked Kathryn a lot.

Upset when she fell down the stairs the night before, Finley's training had taken over. He had commanded everyone into action to stop her bleeding until the ambulance came.

Once at the hospital, and first aid had been administered to her, he held her hand through the stitches, encouraging her with soothing words.

Then, when all was said and done, he watched over her until she fell asleep under a sedative.

He stayed with her the entire night. Not that he needed much sleep at the best of times, anyway. So, on that occasion, he didn't flinch an eyelid.

He watched over her.

So that morning, after Peter's aggression, Finley had the overwhelming desire to protect Kathryn, to sooth her.

"Shush, it isn't. Trust me," he said and kissed her hand again.

After the initial shock at Peter's plan, Zac had recovered his composure somewhat. He was still furious and hurt but able to function. In the circumstances, he had no option.

He was now talking to the senior detective and then over the phone with Alex. He asked him to be on guard, in case Peter should return to the house. Even with a troubled heart, he feared for Mollie, with Peter on the loose. They didn't think he would; it was just a precaution.

Finley's men camped at the villa too.

"We need to get Kat home. We can't police two places. The nurse will take care of her at home," Zac said.

His friend nodded.

"Can you do that?" he asked her.

"Yes. They have stitched me up again. I have bruises all over, but I will survive. George's face hurts too." She grinned at her friend.

George hinted at a smile too. But his lips, too, were swollen, and he had a new black eye on top of his old one, now huge.

Finley ran a tender hand over Kathryn's jaw, but she blinked in pain. Even a slight touch hurt her. He became furious, staring at the sweet girl in that state. He couldn't believe Peter had done this to her. To harm a girl and to take advantage of Mollie in that manner, it was outrageous. He shook his head. It was grotesque but true.

"Settled, then! I'll make the arrangements to get you guys home," he said instead.

So, they agreed. Finley would travel in the ambulance with Kathryn, while George and Zac rode in the car with his security escort, all the way to the house.

Under the circumstances, owning his own security firm had come in handy, now protecting him.

Chapter 22

"Listen! She didn't know of his plan. She misread him," George said while Zac was driving them home.

"What?"

"When I found Mollie outside the pavilion last night, she was in a daze. Peter had threatened her. He told her of his real plan yesterday. She thought he only wanted the money, but he's crazy."

"She should have told me all of it!" Zac bellowed.

"Look, don't be like that. She would have told you; she just wanted one more day with you. She felt that once you discovered it was Peter, well…"

"You bet."

"Mollie loves you!" George persisted. "She would let no one hurt you."

"Well, no. I suppose she has the prerogative," Zac said bitterly then added, "love, my foot!" He laughed, but it was a sad, ironic laugh.

"She does; she loves you. Peter deceived her. He took

advantage of her infatuation, to manipulate her, of her innocence."

"George, please. Stop! I don't want to hear this right now." Zac rubbed his temple, too upset to think straight. He didn't want to talk about Mollie. He didn't want a reminder of her treachery and her duplicitousness with his friend.

"Peter lied; that's all there is to it. He used her to get to you."

"Enough! Please…"

George hurt to say these things, given he also harboured feelings for Mollie in his own way. But Mollie's happiness was important to him. Even if it meant that happiness didn't include him.

"Mollie adores you. Please don't be too hard on her," he persisted, but Zac would not listen to him.

———

"I ALWAYS KNEW you had no common sense. You've always been too naïve, despite your cleverness. Now, you've proven me to be correct. Absolutely! I should smack you. I really should," Mary bellowed.

Mollie had come up with the truth for her mother and friend. She'd kept nothing back.

Mary was standing by her bed, arms akimbo and shaking her head in disbelief and shock.

They were huddled up in Mollie's bedroom. Clarissa perched on the edge of the bed, baby on her lap, caressing her friend's hair.

"Mother, please, it's hard enough as it is, without you adding to it," Mollie blurted out, face down through crying sobs, lying across the bed. She had not stopped crying since Zac had left the house.

"Oh, my God! You are a silly girl," Clarissa pointed out.

"No wonder you didn't want to tell me. What a mess! I would have busted that scumbag's ass!"

"But, darling, how could you go along with such foolishness? For money? Have you lost all decency? Hardly surprising, your husband is about to explode. Poor man!" Her mother continued. "What the hell is wrong with you? Can't you ever stop getting into trouble?" She walked to the balcony, staring out to sea, her anguish reflected on her face.

"When will you grow out of these foolish plans of yours?" Clarissa asked, not expecting an answer, shaking her head disapprovingly.

"Oh, please, it was never my plan," Mollie pleaded through crying sobs.

"Remember when you were ten years old, you tried to save the gerbils from the pet shop, bringing them to my B&B? Within a day, I had mice everywhere. All my guests were screaming their heads off. But this? This dangerous plan? It tops it all," her mother hissed with dismay from the floor-to-ceiling glass doors.

Clarissa laughed despite herself, remembering the gerbil debacle, but one look from Mary, and she smoothed her features into a serious scowl again.

"Mother, please. He used me. I didn't know of his real intentions." Mollie raised her head to her.

"What about when you were eleven, and you tried to rescue the little puppy from the lake? Oh, yes, you rescued the puppy all right, but you almost drowned three children in the process with your plan. Remember?" Clarissa smirked, but again, she had another stern glance from Mary who silenced her.

Mollie's mother was a petite, wiry woman, with a mass of red hair which age had mellowed into a dark copper colour, but when she was angry, her wiriness made her look twice her size.

"How could you? Did you think this would work? A marriage of convenience? For money? With a treacherous man as a lover? Unbelievable!" Mary was livid, her copper fringe shaking with the rest of her head.

"Oh, Mother." She flushed.

"Of all your stupid plans, this must take the biscuit!"

"It wasn't my plan. I didn't want to do it. Besides, I tried to do a good deed, by helping Zac with his problem with the Board. With his image, the Board is happier now. That must count for something," Mollie defended herself, but to no avail.

Mary would not hear of it. "But you did! Have I not taught you anything? Oh, Mollie, what a disaster." The woman was upset and anguished at the mess her daughter had created. She crossed her arms on her chest, placed her eyes on Mollie with a scowl, and then looked back out to the sea with disappointment written all over her face.

"Oh, darling, how could you be so silly, trusting a man such as Peter, really?" Mary walked towards the bed and took Mia from Clarissa. She paced up and down with the baby in her arms. But her disapproving stare told her more than words.

Even the baby uttered a harsh sound which seemed to tell Mollie off.

"You should have told me; I could have stopped you," her friend said, and Mary echoed her agreement.

When Kathryn and George returned from hospital later and joined them in Mollie's room, Mary's chastisement of her daughter increased twofold at seeing her friends full of cuts and bruises.

"Look at them! My God, someone could have died! Oh, what am I going to do with you?" Mary cried out in anguish, staring at the young people in that poor state.

The reprimands made Mollie cry even more. Feeling

gutted with remorse, she wanted to run away and hide, but alas, the worst had happened. *Nothing can be worse than this!* she sadly mused, and it was high time to face the music.

Thus, was the tone and mood of the conversation that day. After some time, there was a long silence, Mollie's sobs the only audible sound for a while.

But her mother returned to her and sat on the edge of the bed. After a long pause, Mary caressed Mollie's hair. "Come on darling, stop crying now. You are still infuriating me, but that's done. Now, think how you'll make it up to him. You need to make amends," her mother whispered.

"Make it up to him? Amends? Have you seen how he looked at me?" Mollie cried out.

"Sure, but it will pass," Mary reassured her.

"Pass? He hates me, Mother. Zac can't stand the sight of me. He loathes me," Mollie blurted while raising her head to look at her mother.

"Well, you hurt him. What did you expect? But you can't just give up, can you?" Clarissa murmured.

"Peter wanted Zac's life. He was prepared to kill him for it. You didn't know that," Kathryn added.

"I didn't. I swear," she stressed.

"I believe you, darling. I do. Shush, shush," Mary whispered to her daughter. For all the silliness in her daughter, she knew she couldn't hurt a fly.

ZAC BARRICADED himself in his study for the rest for the day. The only ones allowed in were Alex and Finley.

They gave him details of what the detectives were doing to trace Peter's whereabouts. They searched his room for clues but found nothing. However, his passport was still there.

When lunch came, Zac faced nobody, taking his food in

his study, not that he was hungry, anyway. He hadn't eaten a thing. Not even the tantalising aroma of spiced lamb that drifted from the tray enticed him. The same happened at dinner, a tray in his study but unable to eat.

His friends wanted to stay with him, but he refused.

The fact that a twelve-year, long-standing friendship had been ruthlessly and devilishly destroyed was upsetting enough for him. But his wife's involvement in Peter's perfidious plan made him come up in a sweat! He couldn't bear the thought. So, he avoided Mollie like the plague.

Chapter 23

Erin had driven the whole day non-stop, from where she lived in Banbury, to France. She reached her destination at four am the next day.

Port Vendres was a small village on the Côte Vermeille in the southwest of France, in the Pyrenees Orientales, a charming French fishing port near the Spanish border, characteristic of the area. It was one of the few deep-water ports in this part of the Mediterranean coast. It took freighters, cruise ships, and fishing boats—perfect for her purpose.

She parked her rented car in the small parking bay facing the cheap B&B.

For a moment, she leaned her forehead on the steering wheel and sighed. Then, raising her head, she flashed the headlights on.

PETER HAD AN ADVANTAGE.

He knew the South of France well, like the back of his hand, which was fortunate in his predicament. Though, like always when in trouble, he called his sister, Erin. And as expected, she was ready to help.

Peter was her twin brother. Like most twins, they were close and shared a strong bond. Many times during his teenage years, when he had been in trouble, she'd felt it before it had even materialised. She wasn't sure what it was, but she'd sensed it.

That day, the same feeling churned inside her, that inexplicable anguish, and she realised Peter was in trouble.

Since childhood, Erin Blake was the sensible one, the prudent sibling, the twin sister who invariably rescued him from trouble. Even though she was the youngest by several minutes, she had become used to it. As usual, she was ready to help him through this one too.

Peter was a faculty member at Oxford University with a Doctorate in Physics. He had gotten the Chair of the Faculty, the previous year. One of the youngest professors to win it, destined to glory in academia, Peter had an impeccable pedigree.

But all that glitters is not gold and all that, she thought. She knew better. She had acknowledged the fact, he would come undone at some point, and she guessed this might be it, if he wasn't careful.

She had no clue of what had happened, though she could hazard a guess. If he couldn't return to the house, it could mean only one thing. He'd messed up big time! What had her mischievous brother done this time? What had his temper and his scheming nature drawn him into?

HE WAS WAITING FOR HER. He recognised the 'flash the lights' signal through the window. *She's here!* He went down the stairs of the small B&B where he was hiding, before she reached the front door.

"Peter," she said with an icy undercurrent, when he opened the door for her.

"Shush. People will hear you," he whispered, and then he led her up to his tiny room.

"What have you done this time?" Erin asked once they were in the privacy of his room. She sat at the edge of the bed, dejected and tired after the long drive.

"That bitch told him everything."

"Mollie?" She glanced up at him.

"No. That friend of hers, Kathryn. My girl is innocent."

"I don't know the details, but I told you then, this was crazy."

"She was doing well until yesterday."

"Oh, dear Lord, Peter. Were you expecting a woman to bed Zac and not fall in love with him? It would have failed, even if it wasn't for the trouble yesterday. Even if she is not in love with him, the money alone would do it." Erin shook her head.

"No. It's not like that. Mollie is not like that. She doesn't care about money. Kat ruined it all." He paced up and down.

"Never mind Kat, did you really think she would pull this off?" She crossed her arms on her chest and heaved a heavy sigh.

"Yes, she would have if that bitch had not interfered." He felt like a caged animal, pacing the room.

"We must move fast now and get you out of here."

"I want her back," he stated with an icy tone.

"What?" She looked up at him with her mouth agape.

"I want Mollie back," he said calmly.

"Don't tell me that!" She stood up, exasperated. She was tired, having been up all night, and she didn't need nonsense from her brother. He was not the romantic sort. What was he on?

"She is sweet, and I—" he whispered, but his sister stopped him.

"So, what happened? Tell me, from the beginning!" Erin said, raising a hand to divert the discussion from the girl.

So, he told her everything, leaving nothing out.

"Dear God, that's assault, aggravated assault! Who knows what they may charge you with if they catch you?" she said when she heard her brother had struck Kathryn and George in the hospital several times. "What about Mollie; was she there?"

"No, but I was mad at her last night; she was refusing to cooperate."

"What do you mean?" Erin asked in alarm.

"She may have marks on her neck."

"Marks?"

"Yes."

"What did you do?"

"I-I—"

"Did you harm her?"

"No. No. You weren't there. She wouldn't listen. Sometimes that girl can be stubborn."

"Oh, Peter."

"Seeing her playing the loving wife with him…"

"You are an idiot. There is blackmail, aggravated assault, God knows what else, do you want me to go on?"

"Shut up."

"No. You tune in! This is not a small thing. You crossed one of the richest men in England. Zac has the money and the power to come after you until he finds you. Don't you understand that?"

"Yes, yes, I know." He breathed in a long sigh, ridiculing her point.

"This is not a game. I told you then, and I am telling you now."

"Fine, fine. What are we going to do?" he asked, exasperated, dismissing her point with a wave of his hand.

She rolled her eyes at him; he didn't realise the trouble he was in.

"We? You! You must leave France! That's why I asked you to meet me here, but first we need to work on your appearance, like the photo in your new passport. I brought you some clothes too."

"New passport?"

"I always thought someday you might call for one. And I was not wrong. Slight change of name, too. Cost me a small fortune, Professor!" she said and smiled. "And we must leave this country, pronto," she added. She was pleased at her own extraordinary foresight. But her head whirled with her brother's mess.

"Leave France? No," he said.

"Excuse me?" she asked, bewildered.

"I am not going anywhere," Peter mumbled with a perfunctory smile on his lips, his eyes cold and impassive as he looked out the window.

Erin turned him to face her. "What do you mean? We must leave the country!"

"I am not going without Mollie," he said, his face blank, "I want that silly girl back. Only then, am I leaving." He had waited to action his plan for a long time. But even if his plan failed, he was not turning away from his woman.

Erin convinced her twin to take a rest for a few hours.

He relented and went to sleep.

WHEN HE WAS LIKE THIS, there was no reasoning with him, nothing she could do. There was no convincing him, but she needed to take him out of Port Vendres and out of France.

It would be easy to get him into Spain, either by sea through the various cruise ships or by land, with Port Vendres' proximity to the Spanish border, the reason she had chosen that village. Once in Spain, she would think her next move.

Her twin's only chance of survival was to convince him to leave the country. If set on carrying out his threat, he was doomed. Erin knew she must act fast, before it was too late.

Lost in thought, she knew her brother was obstinate.

Ever since her twin had lost Kristen, years ago, he'd thought of nothing but revenge! Peter wanted Zac to pay for it.

Erin could sympathise with her brother's sentiments. She'd tried to warn him that Kristen was merely a money grabbing woman, a social climber. She had used her brother. He was a platform for Kristen to get her hands on Zac, but she had failed.

Her brother blamed Zac for losing her, even if that was not the case.

Erin sighed. She looked at her brother. Peter slept, and her mind returned from her musings. It was imperative to protect him. That was her primary concern, and she would do it.

Then she would deal with Kathryn and Zac and his whore some other time.

She looked at Peter again, and then she caressed his face. That rich and spoiled bastard had ruined her brother, her brilliant brother.

When the time came, Zac would pay for it.

Zac has a lot to answer for, Erin mused.

Chapter 24

"Darling, you can't just sit here and let things go," Mary tried to console her.

Mollie had lost the will to live.

Zac behaved with complete contempt for her, and she felt disconsolate. Guilty for causing him so much pain, she also missed him terribly. She missed his caresses, his kisses, his schoolboy humour, her playful Zac. And he was nowhere to be seen.

Instead, he hated her with a vengeance. Nothing could make it better.

"Mary is right. Yes, you are a damn fool, you must own up to that, but you were never part of his crazy plan, not the killing part. Zac can't possibly think that. You never meant to harm anyone. I cannot believe anyone would think such a thing of you." Clarissa caressed a strand of her hair back from her face while she poured out a loud sigh.

Mollie was heavy-hearted. She had always known this day would come. But now that it was upon her, she felt miserable.

Zac had lost a friend. Someone he had learned to

count on as a brother, had revealed himself deceitful—a common criminal! So, he was hurting. He felt crushed. Worse, he believed she had taken part in Peter's obnoxious plan.

Mollie blew her nose in her handkerchief, but a sob escaped her.

"See? Look what that bastard did to me. You can still see the marks. The cuts, the bruises on my face and arms. Look at George's face." Kathryn pointed to their injuries to emphasise Clarissa's point.

"Oh, I am so sorry, it's all my fault," Mollie whispered with melancholy.

"No, it isn't. You didn't do this to us. It was Peter, not you," George bellowed.

"Your husband cannot ignore these vile acts. Peter is evil; that's all there is to it. But you were not part of them," her mother said.

"Zac blames me for all of this. He does!" Mollie blurted out.

"No, you were silly and unwise to trust Peter, but you thought you were in love with him. Love does silly things to people; it clouds their judgement. So, that scumbag convinced you it was okay. A great deed all around. He manipulated you. You didn't know of his wicked, murderous plan. He deceived you too," Clarissa said, caressing her friend's hair.

"I really believed I was doing a good deed, helping Zac to rebuild his image. And I have. The last few months have helped him a lot. But it's all for nothing now. He hates me," she replied with a sigh.

Three days had passed since Peter's treachery had emerged. They were in the massive sitting room, as another evening was drawing to a close in a tense atmosphere.

Kathryn lay on the big white sofa, her stitches visibly sore and purple. Her face was a black and purple mask, her head resting on a cushion on Mary's lap, still throbbing.

George's face had a black eye and a cut above his cheekbone.

Mollie smiled at her friends. They tried to raise her spirits but just glancing at them was a reminder of the consequences of her disastrous actions, regardless of how much her mother and friends tried to console her.

She slumped into the big armchair with Mia on her lap, caressing the baby's cheeks. She dug herself into the chair as if she wanted to disappear into it. The baby gave her a great comfort, as if her purity of soul could somehow rub off on her, giving her a hint of the sanctity a babe possessed. Seeking absolution from her bad deeds, but alas, there was no absolution for her!

How was she supposed to know it would turn out so badly? *I'm stupid and naïve,* she concluded, *clever for books, yes, but nothing else! I am useless!*

She had lost her husband. Forever! So, she grieved.

But with Peter still at large, there was danger too. He had not been found yet, and this worried her.

Clarissa and George perched on her chair armrests, on either side of her. They worried about Mollie's melancholy. It had been over three days, and she was still feeling wretched. It was not like her. The Mollie they knew would have picked herself up, dusted herself off, and tried again. But she was crestfallen.

"Well, look at Mollie's neck. That's enough to send him to prison. The detectives took photos of all our injuries, you know. If they catch him, he is in deep. And he was such a brilliant professor. What a waste of a life. What a misuse of a talent," George said, shaking his head.

"Come to think of it, he always scared me." Kathryn shivered.

"God, imagine the field day the press will have with Zac when they find out. It'll destroy his image forever. It was working well with the Board. He'll never succeed his father now, all because of me," Mollie mumbled, rubbing her temple, closing her eyes, and resting her head inconsolably on the back of the big armchair.

"Don't worry; Fin is taking care of this with his connections. I heard him say he was doing *damage limitation*. He is using men from your husband's security firm, men he can trust. The senior detectives are family friends. Zac knows many people, so the police in France will be discreet. No press!" George told them.

Thank God for small mercies, Mollie sighed with relief. Otherwise, she would not have been able to forgive herself.

"You need to talk to Zac. You *cannot* just give up on him. He is your husband," her mother said.

"He doesn't want to see me. I went to his study yesterday, and the same today, but he won't even let me in, won't even open the door! He is not speaking to me."

"He is angry, and I guess it will upset him for a while. You must give him time. But you can't ignore the situation. You must talk to Zac soon. Otherwise, the more time that goes by, the harder it will be to clear the air," Mary told her.

"Clear the air? He won't talk to me, has not spoken to me for days. He hates me!" Mollie sulked.

"No, he doesn't. He loves you, but it upsets him," her mother replied.

Mollie got up from her chair. She wandered up and down the room, with the baby in her arms, looking lost. She was patting the baby's back relentlessly. Clarissa took her daughter from her arms and smiled at her. George walked up to her, put his arms around her, and brought her back to the chair.

"Come on, Mollie. It will be fine. You'll see; give him time," he said.

Thank heaven for friends!

"YOU SAID SO YOURSELF. She is not a bad girl. Misguided by someone she thought she loved, that's all. She knows Peter used her. She loves you now. Don't throw everything away," Alex protested, trying to help his friend see the obvious, but he was stubborn.

"Psst." Zac rolled his eyes.

"Give her a chance. I know you love her too."

"How can I? She will remind me of Peter's treachery forever. We were friends! How can I forget that?" Deep down, the thought that Mollie had something to do with Peter's brutal plan devastated Zac.

"Peter is crazy. Think of him this way, to make any sense of it." As a lawyer, he was pragmatic. He was trying to ease what was hurting his friend.

"Assuming I could, the years of friendship... I don't understand, why? For money? If he needed money, I would have given it to him," Zac said. He was sitting at his desk, as they were in his study.

Alex, perched on a corner of the desk with his arms folded across his chest, sighed.

Zac's head in his hands, he rubbed his forehead.

"I don't know. Peter is mad. That's all I can say. You saw what he did to Kat. Not the behaviour of a sane person, is it? Did you see her? Kathryn's face?"

"Bloody hell!" Zac said, curses as vile as Peter's deeds leaving his mouth.

He got up from his chair, stepped to the sideboard, and poured himself a brandy. He half-filled the glass. Contemplating it, he filled it almost to the brim. He turned to his friend, wagging the bottle at him. Alex nodded, so he poured another glass and gave it to him.

Zac brought the glass to his lips. He took a hefty gulp; the spirit burned a warm trail as it went down. A brief relief, and Zac sighed. He returned to his chair and took another gulp of the amber liquid.

"Did you notice Mollie's neck? The bastard!"

"No. Why? I haven't seen her for days." Zac raised his head to look at him.

"You mean, you don't want to see her. The marks on her neck are purple."

"What marks?"

"Peter tried to strangle her that night, in the pavilion, when she refused to do what he wanted. She even punched him, but he almost killed her. Still, she refused. Mollie said, to prove his intentions, later, he pushed Kat down the stairs as a warning to her. She's been out of her mind with worry for you since then. She would have told you herself, but Kathryn beat her to it."

"Christ!" He stood up, raking a hand through his hair. He paced up and down in anguish. He took the glass and finished his drink in one gulp.

At that moment, unsure whether he hated her for what she had done, or whether he hated himself for his weakness for her, despite all the mess, he worried about her. Zac still craved Mollie, and he loathed himself for it.

"Is she all right?" he asked, wanting to run to her and soothe her. But the thought made him angry again.

What had this woman done to him! What hold did she have over him? She'd bewitched him; she would drive him mad. Then he reminded himself he was in love with her. Despite everything that had happened, he still adored her. He pined for her.

"Yes, she is fine," Alex said with a grin, but his friend soon changed the conversation.

"Where is Fin?" he asked instead, trying to keep his mind off Mollie.

"He is making some calls to sort this mess out, damage limitation."

"Good," he replied, but the lawyer would not allow him to wallow in his hurt.

"Talk to her. She is heartbroken. She is a nice young woman, foolish and misguided. The girl made a mistake; she knows that. She admits to it. But she loves you."

"How do you know that?"

"I use conversation, my friend… conversation, a lot to be said for it," Alex said, "it makes things clearer. You should try it sometime, instead of moping around and feeling sorry for yourself."

"Smart ass."

"You are sulking and hurting, and that's understandable. But you forget that Peter was our friend too. He betrayed all of us, not just you. I am hurt, but I'm not blaming Mollie for his madness."

"Alex, you are doing my head in. What makes you Mollie's champion suddenly?"

"I talked to her. I believe her. Don't let her go. The girl was messed up by a vulgar, venal man. That's all! Her eyes are bloodshot; she has been crying, you know."

"Stop, please. You are a sucker for a woman's tears. I won't have it." And with that, Zac cursed. Then he opened the glass doors into the garden and stepped out.

"Hey, I am not finished with you!" Alex yelled after him, but he ignored him.

Zac walked away until he reached the edge of the swimming pool.

He stopped there and shed his clothes. Leaving his boxers

on, he launched himself with his arms outstretched, head-first, into the pool. He hit the water and went in deep. He re-emerged and swam, hard and fast, as if he was in a race, his hairline cresting the surface. The more he swam, the more he gathered pace, the rapid movement of his arms and legs propelling him energetically through the length as if he had a record to break. He swam wholeheartedly.

His honeymoon with Mollie had been a turmoil of highs and lows, no doubt, but he was in pain, and it felt almost physical. It was as if someone had battered his heart and tossed it out to the wolves. So, the pool became his refuge once more.

Despite the evening chill, as always, his swim served his purpose well. An hour into it, the tension lessened with each stroke, his mind clearing with every length of his body.

There he was, flogging himself up and down the vast pool for the umpteenth time, when he saw her silhouette flickering through the water in the glowing moonlight. She was standing at the edge of the pool, as if she were an angel of light, a fairy lighting up a dark woodland.

He raised his head above the water.

She stood there looking at him, poised and elegant in her short and sparkling dusk rose halter-neck dress. The shimmering paillettes on her dress reflected the silver moonlight, casting delicate shadows on her face. Her red hair was up in a low chignon, with some tendrils covering her neck invitingly.

The vision of a divinity, a goddess, he sighed. *No, ah, ah! Don't give in; have some pride, man!*

Mollie smiled at him. When he didn't return it, she cast her eyes down but not before she noticed a fleeting shadow in his gaze. Was that desire she saw? Or hate?

She had not mastered the courage to go to him for noth-ing, so she persevered. Now that she was there, she needed to explain, perhaps even attempt to win him back before throwing in the towel.

"Feeling better?" she asked, beaming the smile he loved so much, but it didn't work.

"What?" he repeated harshly, his voice raw, reprimanding her.

She bit her lower lip. "Yes, well, are you relaxing with the swim?" she persisted, but a slight colour crept up her neck.

"What do you care?" His tone was bitter, showing his disapproval.

She lowered her eyes again and flushed crimson. She was faltering.

His garrulous scowl had not left his face. She looked down and played with a leaf on the ground with her foot.

He noted her jerky movements, but he was impassive.

"I—" she ventured, briefly glancing at him, but he didn't allow her to speak.

"Do you think all you have to do is smile at me, and everything is fine?" he asked sharply, the chastisement of his belligerent tone clear. A glower still reflected on his face.

He wanted to punish her, and it was working. She wanted to run away and glanced behind her. She was not a coward, though.

"I am worried about you." She continued, undeterred.

"Now?" he bellowed. "You worry about me? *Now?* Well, that's a first!" he replied savagely, glaring at her in astonishment.

"Please, I just want to talk," she said. She couldn't bear his anger.

"Late for that, don't you think?" he responded. *She thinks she can wrap me around her little finger.*

"I am so sorry; I really am. I didn't know of his plan. I didn't," she pleaded.

His face a mask of fury, he growled, "I don't care for your apology. It's all poppycock."

"Zac, I-I, please, let me explain—" She was about to say something else, but he interrupted her.

"Haven't you said enough? Done enough?"

"I am sorry. I truly am. I met Peter before I met you! I didn't realise what he was. What he was after. I was stupid! He lied to me too. But I love you. You promised me. We agreed that we would only look to the future, not the past. You said you would give us a chance; you promised. That's why I couldn't tell you his name. Please listen to me; we can put this behind us—" she rushed out in one breath, pleading with him.

But he would not have it. "Listen to you? You take me for a fool!" he spat.

"Let's leave emotion out of it for a moment. Shall we?"

"What?" He laughed, but it was a hurtful laugh.

"Please,"

"No, enough is enough!" he bellowed.

"Ooh…" she wailed.

"You don't let up, do you?" he said, but this time it was as if he was resigned to it, closing his eyes.

"We need to talk. You promised you wouldn't—" she pleaded, but he shook his head.

"Enough!" he kept saying.

"Well, if you'll behave like your usual… ooh, God! Well…" She shrugged.

"My usual what?" he said defensively. *She is not pretending I am in the wrong, is she?*

"Oh, I give up. You bloody fool!" she spat and threw up her arms in the air in surrender, exasperation getting the better of her. Then she turned on her heels and ran back to the house.

Suddenly, his blood rushed to his head. "I have not

dismissed you yet!" he shouted as his eyes flushed with rage. *The bloody minx from hell,* "I said, not so fast. Stop!" He kept yelling after her, but she continued running towards the house.

He pulled himself out of the water and onto the ground. "Mollie, wait!" He grabbed a towel from a chair and ran after her, "Stop. I am not finished with you." He was dripping wet as he raced into the house. When he reached the bottom of the staircase, he almost lost his balance on the wet marble floor, but he saw her halfway up the stairs already.

He left a trail of water everywhere, to Marie Therese's dismay, as she came out of the kitchen. But he ignored his housekeeper's protests and followed his wife up the stairs, his long strides, catching two stairs in one go.

MOLLIE RAN to her bedroom and was about to close the door behind herself rapidly, but he caught up with her. She tried to resist him behind the door, but he pushed it open. He was too strong. He got into the room. He slammed the door shut, which ricocheted in its frame.

She gulped and stepped back.

He glared at her.

She retreated a few more steps back. "You are furious. We can't talk when you are like this," she said, trying to stay calm, but his eyes were spitting fire at her.

He rested his body against the door for a moment, and he smacked the towel on his own thigh with force, in exasperation. It left a mark on his skin, then he let it drop to the floor.

Zac was raging. He closed his eyes in frustration. He sighed, opening them again to glare at her. "I told you to wait," he said, the words rasping out of his throat. "You don't listen too well, do you?"

"If you've come to y-yell at me, d-don't bother. Please leave," she said, trying to look in control, though she couldn't hide the tiny tremors in her voice. For a moment, she stared back, lifting her chin up in defiance, but she gulped. And then she realised—he was standing there almost naked but for his wet boxers clinging onto him, his hair wet and sexy, his beautiful chiselled body gleaming with droplets of water.

Ahh, a marvellous sight… but by God, he is fuming mad.

She didn't know whether to lust after him or fear his temper.

Right then, she could have sworn billowing, angry steam was squirting out of his pores. Even furious and menacing as he was, he looked so damn gorgeous. And she licked her bottom lip with her tongue, her baby blue eyes growing wide, taking him in.

HE CAUGHT the slow movement of her pink tongue over her lips. For the first time in his life, he had a moment of hesitation. He didn't know what to do. Part of him wished to take her in his arms, pin her down on the bed, and ravish her until all her intimate parts swelled and ached with passionate lovemaking. The other part of him wanted her face down on his knees while he thrashed her mischievous little ass until she couldn't sit. He wanted to smack her perfect bottom until she came to her senses, leaving absurd and dangerous plans behind her.

The urge to spank her prevailed!

He ran a hand over his face and exhaled. Then he walked mightily towards her. She stepped back, but in two long strides, he grabbed her upper arm.

"Let me go," she blurted out, trying to wriggle out of his clutch. She forced her arm free and darted for the door.

"Oh no, you don't!" he said and reached for her again. She tried to open the door, but towering over her, with the palm of his hand, he shut it again with a bang. Then he grabbed her wrist tightly and turned the key in the lock.

"What are you doing?" she demanded. "Let me go." She let out a loud squeal.

Still gripping her by the wrist, he tugged her towards the bed.

"I said, let me go. Do you hear me?" she snapped. With her other hand, she slapped his hand, the one holding her wrist harshly, repeatedly. She was trying to pull it free, but to no avail.

He sat on the edge of the bed and pulled her down in one slick movement, across his knees. She ended up lying face down on his lap.

"What are you doing? Let me go, I said. You caveman!" she shouted. But she was over her husband's knees.

OH, no, he is not! she thought, bewildered. Her inner voice, the loving one, told her, *girl, you've been nothing but trouble to him.* The modern girl, the scientist in her, said, *nonsense, this cannot happen!*

"Be it a lesson to you, Mollie. You will learn something useful, and no need for a book," he hissed.

"Stop. Don't you dare. You Neanderthal," she yelled, trying to get back onto her feet, though her efforts to liberate herself from his clutches were rather flimsy.

Am I willing him or dreading this? She wasn't sure, yet she couldn't resist her curiosity. Her doubts made her wriggle more. There was no logic to them.

HE HELD her down firmly on his lap and lifted her short dress up to her waist. *Trust Mollie still to wear cotton underwear,* he thought. A half smile appeared on his lips, the tension in his shoulders dropping. He pulled her panties midway down her thighs.

She was wriggling and complaining, "I said let me go. Don't you dare! Do you hear me?" She was shouting at him now.

The sight of her naked bottom gave him an instant hard-on, and he knew she felt it too, lying on his lap.

"Ouch. It bloody hurts. Are you insane?" she cried out when the first smack hit her backside. She was not expecting it to sting that much.

"My dear girl, a little spanking is overdue." Then he smacked her other buttock hard, with his open hand.

"Aargh, you boorish yob, stop!" she boomed.

"This is for lying to me and for getting involved in this nonsense plan with that bastard," he said, pausing for a moment. "And for behaving like a stupid woman. Poor Kat is black and blue! Someone could have died. You silly girl!" Zac yelled, and he spanked her buttocks one more time.

She protested strongly. She cursed. She directed her vile profanities at him in no uncertain terms.

At her raucous curses, he raised an elegant brow, but a slow grin spread on his face.

She put her hands on her backside, trying to protect her bottom, and they wrestled until he grabbed both of her wrists in one hand, holding them out of the way behind her back, and he went on, "From now on, no more crazy plans. Agreed? Answer me." And he whacked her buttock again.

"Yes, yes, please stop."

THE WEIRD SENSATION WAS THAT, despite the spanking, she had the belief it was releasing her from months of guilt and remorse. Atoning her bad deeds. Yes, no doubt four smacks on her bottom stung, her sore arse, red and raw, like the fires from hell. But she felt cleansed by the action. With that liberating thought, a most peculiar feeling came over her. There, on her husband's knees, this unfamiliar sensation flared as if a torch had ignited a fire within her. A thrill ran through her body! She liked it!

As he whacked her buttocks again, a warmth spread between her legs. She was soaked. A dribble came out from her pussy.

Holy cow, I am wet, she realised.

"Are you done with scheming plans?"

"Yes, please. Stop," she cried with the dichotomy of liking and hating it.

Her bottom was sore, but the stinging was bearable, making her now wanton and lustful. Before she could get too comfortable, he gave her one last hard smack.

Pain and then delight mingled together. She gasped at the sensation. The mixture of pleasure and the sting on her backside made her hot. Her pussy let out another drip on her inner thigh. *Flipping heck!*

No one had spanked her before, but this was a new-discovered sensuous delight.

Her eyes welled up with the stinging, and a few tears streamed down her face too. *Oh... this is heaven and hell; it bloody hurts but oh so delicious and insane.*

At one point, a rocket of pure pleasure shot through her. She moaned.

His breathing became laboured too. "You promise?" he asked between gasps of air.

"Yes, please, stop. I promise!" she pleaded.

"Good. We are done, then."

With one swift action, he pulled her up, and sat her up on his knees. "No more craziness! Understood?" he boomed, glaring deep into her baby blue eyes.

"Yes," she mumbled.

"Don't try any more foolish stuff or I swear... Anything else I need to hear? If so, now is your chance to say it all, eh?" he bellowed.

She shook her head and whispered, "No. Nothing."

"Are you sure? Nothing else is there?" he asked again.

She nodded her head again. "No."

"Good. I swear to God, Mollie, next time I will not stop this easily. Understood?"

"Yes," she whimpered, looking at him, but somehow, she felt good.

He sat there watching her, silent for a while.

"Bloody hell! You make me so mad!" he said finally, but his eyes softened on her. He peeked at her fire red ass and stroked her buttocks, first one, then the other cheek, until the redness subsided, while his eyes were firmly on her face. His body relaxed, and his eyes warmed. Then, he wiped a tear still hanging from her eye.

"Are you okay?" he whispered, the tension gone from his shoulders. His beautiful features relaxed, in full lust once again.

"Yes." She nodded.

"I am sorry. I don't know what came over me. I don't know where I am with you!" he said, caressing her face with one hand. He rested his forehead on hers and sighed.

"I am sorry too, for the whole mess. I am," she replied with a tremor in her voice.

He smiled, still rubbing her bottom with his hand. He

kissed the tip of her nose. "You have bewitched me. You have!" he mumbled, and he went on kissing her forehead, her eyelids, and then her mouth. He kissed her like he was kissing her for the first time. Tenderly at first, and then with growing passion every second his mouth was on hers, his lips owning her mouth, his tongue teasing hers, ravishing her fiercely now.

His erection grew even more with his passion and every rub of her ass. He grabbed her panties, still halfway down her knees, and pulled them off. Then he placed two fingers inside her opening.

She gasped and drew her bottom lip between her teeth.

"God, you are soaking wet." He looked into her eyes.

Her face turned crimson.

"I can't believe it. Did you enjoy the spanking?" he asked incredulously with a lopsided smirk, and she nodded. A belly laugh burst out of his mouth.

"Yes, but it hurt like hell too. So, don't get any ideas to do this again. Well... only if I ask you. Understood?" she said with a mischievous grin.

"Fine! I'll do it anytime you want. Christ, what am I going to do with you?" he replied, still laughing, throwing his head back in a wholesome, hearty snort for some time.

His face was a mixture of pride and lust. His anger evaporated for the first time in days, replaced by tenderness, by his love for her, by his desire for her.

She smiled too, and she put her arms around him instead. He withdrew his fingers from her and returned her embrace. They cuddled lovingly for a while, enjoying the warmth of their embrace.

But then, he picked up the hem of her dress and lifted it over her head, thus exposing her bare breasts. He took one of her nipples in his mouth and sucked. He put two fingers inside her again.

She gasped. Now that they were amorous again, she had goose bumps. The spanking had heightened the thrill.

She was sitting on his lap, naked, and so wet, sensing her juices dripping, feeling the desire and the warmth of his smacks still on her buttocks.

He increased the probing inside her. She moaned, wrapping her arms around his neck.

He took his fingers out and sucked them. "God, you taste so good. Try it." His eyes were wide, flushing with fiery lust, offering them to her.

She licked his fingers, tasting herself.

He grabbed her ass.

"Ouch. It still hurts," she said.

"Oh, sweet baby, sorry," he mumbled. He sat her on the edge of the bed, laying her down.

"I'll be tender," he whispered, parting her legs. She smiled, but the desire on his face conveyed it all. He kneeled on the floor and placed his mouth on her clit.

"I can't get enough of you. What have you done to me?" he said through ragged breath, lifting his head from her sex. She was so wet as he rubbed her folds. Then, he sucked until her little button was red and swollen.

"Oh, Zac," she moaned, the pressure building in her.

All the while, she was handing out little sounds of approval. But when his tongue burst inside of her, she screamed with pleasure. His amorous torture made her almost unconscious with ecstasy as her body shattered with repeated bliss, and she left all her troubles behind her once and for all. She would never let him go now.

She opened her eyes and looked at him with so much love in her heart. He stood, smiled, and lay next to her. He kissed her tenderly, then his tongue traced her lips. He kissed her again, deeply, frenzied.

"Oh, Mollie, you are so beautiful," he murmured.

Me, beautiful? No. Not me. You are! she mused.

"You are! The loveliest of mortals!" she sighed.

"Loveliest of mortals?" he questioned and stopped to look at her, perplexed, but a smile spread across his face.

Have I just said this aloud? No! and she bit her bottom lip, having remembered the line from Homer's Iliad, describing Ganymede's' beauty. This line suited her husband's handsome face to perfection. When she blushed, and she didn't respond, he laughed and caressed her cheek. He was lying next to her, his elbow propping him up, with his face in the palm of his hand.

"Loveliest? Hmm… nothing wrong with *loveliest*, I suppose," he mumbled with mirth.

She took a strand of his long strawberry blondish hair and rolled it between her fingers. "Well, I—"

"But given the circumstances, if I had to choose a word or somebody to describe myself, not that I care for one anyway, but I would say Achilles is more appropriate. Don't you?" he smirked, teasing her.

"Achilles?" she asked.

"Yes, Achilles! Strong." And he flexed his biceps, showing his protruding strong muscles. She giggled, but he said, "Handsome," and he raised his eyebrows in quick succession mischievously, motioning to his body. She chuckled. "And powerful," he added and kissed her hard on the mouth. "But with a major weakness," he finished with a wink.

"Oh?" She frowned.

"You, Mollie! You are my major weakness. I can't resist you—my Achilles' heel, you are!" He smiled at her, brushing a strand of her hair back.

A grin spread across her face, from ear to ear, but a sudden frown appeared on her forehead. "Achilles? Well, wasn't he in love with Patroclus? A great love affair. Not proven but—" she mused while she cocked her head to one side, thinking about Homer's mythological hero, but he interrupted her musing.

"Oh, who cares!" He laughed, and he kissed her for a while longer.

He stopped to glance at her. Not only did he love her with a strong passion, but his wife enchanted him. She had captured his heart utterly. *I adore the minx from Hell.* He kissed her again, and again.

Butterflies were causing havoc in her belly. She would never tire of his kisses. Then he went to her breasts, sucking each one. She moaned, wet again.

He grabbed her ass.

"Ouch. It's still sore," she said, panting, massaging her buttocks.

"Oh, I know." He massaged them too. He moved positions and sat on the edge of the bed, moving her with him. He placed her astride of him. "Let me show you Achilles' strength now. That, you cannot deny," he said with a wink, desire in his eyes, and a lascivious dark grin.

She giggled in anticipation.

He kissed her like he owned her; she knew she was his woman now. His tongue found every little undiscovered crevice in her mouth, sucking her lips, making them red and swollen. He then placed his manhood at her entrance and lowered her onto his hard, wet head.

She hissed as he entered her.

"See?" he drawled with a sexy and lustful look in his eyes.

She smiled and tossed her head back. This was the man she wanted forever. The playful Zac. *The charming, loving and sexy Zac, and oh, sweet Jesus! Thank you! He wants me so much.*

He was rock hard. The spanking foreplay had strengthened his pleasure, too, if the size of his manhood was anything to go by.

The fact that there were no more secrets between them

rendered them free to enjoy each other's bodies without reserve. Everything was out in the open, and they both felt liberated. Yes, worries and fears were still lurking, no doubt. But like they had done in the last few weeks, they lived in that moment. And it was the sweetest!

Zac took his time to ensure she got used to his large manhood inside her. They relished each other.

"Oh, Zac," she wailed and wrapped her legs around his waist and her arms around his neck.

He kissed her cheek.

She moaned and simpered.

Meanwhile, he pushed slowly, but increasing the depth with each thrust, until he entered her completely.

No more secrets. It enriched their lovemaking. It set them free, their bodies meshed into one.

She clenched her walls around his manhood, and he liked it.

He thrust, slowly at first, then faster, then he pulled her up and down with his hands on her hips, alternating the rhythm and depth.

"It feels good," she murmured, and he rewarded her with a smile that said *just you wait*, so full of desire.

"I aim to please my beautiful wife," he warned. And he was eager to comply.

His eyes were dark with want, and it left her no doubt he would humour her with more of the same. She whimpered soft moans as he thrust inside her. A few more forceful ones were all it took until the room spun around them, and their universe was shaken and stirred with pleasure until they were fully sated.

Chapter 25

E rin opened her eyes. The light filtered through the blinds. She had dozed off. For a moment, she glanced around. She forgot where she was. Then she remembered. Her breath hitched.

Peter was not in the room. She jumped to her feet and panicked. She peered out of the window to the parking lot. Her car was gone. She rummaged through her purse for her car keys, but they were gone too. Jesus, she hoped he had not returned to Antibes. That would be madness.

She dialled his new mobile number, the one she had given him. "Where the hell are you?" she blasted out when he answered her call.

"Relax. I got rid of my old phone; I couldn't do it in Port Vendres!" he said with an even voice, amused.

"You didn't switch it on?"

"No. Off since I left Antibes. Give me some credit. Fin won't find me so easily." He laughed.

When Peter had first called Erin for help, he'd dialled her number from a street pay phone. This, an old style, pay-as-you-go mobile, which no one could trace to her, was the one they used for emergency calls, in case of trouble.

Through the years, Erin had mastered how to fix Peter's problems, a lesson learned earlier on, in their teenage years. So now, she had bought him a similar mobile. She'd thought of everything, but her impetuous brother might just undermine her work.

"Where are you?"

"Calm down; I am on my way back with breakfast," Peter said while driving to the B&B.

"Do you realise you need to get out of France? And quickly, is this clear to you?" For the last few days, she'd tried to convince her brother to leave the country, but he was stubborn, not wanting to move, not making up his mind.

"We'll talk when I get there." And he rang off.

Erin looked at the phone in her hand and cursed. It annoyed her.

Why was he acting so carelessly? Did he not realise the trouble he was in? This was not one of his teenage tantrums! This was serious. If not careful, he would end in prison for a long time.

He had already lost everything he'd worked so hard to achieve, his physics chair at Oxford gone. Zac would ensure that! And for what? Now in major peril of losing his freedom too, for ever and a day.

She sighed and crashed on the bed. Then it hit her. Her brother was losing his mind.

Erin saw him park the car through the window. He had a brown bag in his hand. She went downstairs to open the door for him.

"Freshly baked croissants," he said with a corner of his mouth in a curl.

She stared at him, bewildered, but she turned back up the stairs. He followed her up.

Once in the room, he picked up a croissant from the packet, and started munching on it. "Two coffees in the bag. Yours, no sugar, has a cross on it," he added, offering the brown bag to her.

She took it from him mechanically, but her jaw dropped. "Peter," she ventured.

"The sun is high, a warm sunny day. Spring is beautiful this year." He beamed at her.

She forced a smile, but he turned towards the window.

She picked up a croissant and the coffee. She was astonished at her twin. Over time, his behaviour had become erratic, but his mind was never nebulous like that day. He munched on his croissant, peering out of the window, as if he didn't have a care in the world.

Yes, she was right. Her brother had lost it. She would need to bring him back, or she would lose him forever.

"Where did you go?" she asked.

"Don't worry. I drove a hundred miles to get rid of my phone, the one the boys know about."

"Where?" Erin repeated. There was concern on her face.

"Carcassonne," he replied with a pause. "So if they discover anything, they'll believe I am heading north," he concluded with a sip of his coffee.

"What do you mean, discover anything?" she asked with a sigh. Still sitting on the edge of the bed, she took an annoyed bite out of her croissant.

He shifted to glance at her and smiled. Then he turned back to the window. "I left her a message."

"Oh, for Heaven's sake!"

"Relax. It is fine. It was from a pay phone,"

"Relax? Are you out of your mind?"

"Erin, stop fussing," he ordered, an edge to his voice.

"I bought two tickets on a ship, for tomorrow. We'll get

on board, get out of here. Do you hear me?" she rushed out, back on her feet.

"I see."

"Yes, into Spain. That's why I asked you to meet me here, in Port Vendres. It's so close to the Spanish border. The moment the ferry crosses the border, we'll leave the ship at the first port in Spain, and they'll lose track of you from there. We have been here for days now; we take that boat tomorrow. It is essential we hurry. We cannot wait any longer. The more we stand by, the risk of being caught is higher, do you understand?" she stressed.

He smiled at her and shrugged his shoulders. "I told you. Not going without her."

"Oh, Peter. Do you realise what you are saying? That's madness." She turned him around. She caressed his face, and he leaned into her hand for a moment.

"Made my decision," he said.

She saw fire in his eyes, a raw emotion burning in them. But she persisted, "I have my theatrical make-up kit to change your appearance. A few touches here and there, you'll be a different man." As a theatre make-up artist, Erin always had her bag of goodies with her. It would come in handy for her brother.

"Do you?" He smiled.

"Peter, go back some other time for her, when they don't expect you. Now they are ready for you. Especially after your message. If you go… it's too dangerous."

"No." A strange light was glowing in his eyes.

She inhaled, exasperated. "Listen to me. If you return to Antibes, they will catch you. Understood?"

"They won't! Not if you help me."

"Ahh," she screamed in frustration and paced up and down.

He sat on the bed instead. "Don't fuss. We sit it out for a

few days, and then I'll move," he whispered with the conviction of one who had a plan. He then moved to her and caressed his sister's hair.

She fretted at his stubbornness. "Oh, darling, do you *want* to go to prison? That's where you are heading if you go back for Mollie."

"I'll take the chance." Poised and tall, his dark eyes had a steely determination in them.

She knew that look well. It meant the calm before the storm, before things went pear-shaped! *Good God!*

"Do you think Zac won't be waiting for you?"

"I said, I'll take that chance." His stubbornness, unrelenting.

She cursed. "But why? You have already lost everything; why do you want to throw your freedom away too, for that silly bitch?"

"Mollie! That's her name," he said with a warning.

"Whatever!"

"I love that crazy girl, and I am not going anywhere without her," he mumbled.

"But, Peter—" she tried to interject.

He would not have it, though. "The funny thing is I always thought we would end up together with the cash, but money or no money, I want her back," he said resolutely.

"What if she won't? Isn't there a chance—"

"Zac will toss her away, like an old shoe. He'll blame her for what happened. He may have already thrown her out. He won't forgive her!"

"If Zac loves her, he will. Love is forgiving."

"Mollie is mine; that's all there is to it." His fist hit the small table hard, shaking the plastic cups on it. Coffee spilled on the tabletop.

"Peter, I cannot help you like this."

"Relax."

"I thought you were only using her to get to the money."

"I was! But I love the wretched creature, and I am not going without her."

"No! Out of the question," she said.

"Enough! I am going back for her. End of discussion!" he said, with no intention of changing his mind.

"And if she doesn't want you? Let's face it—" She tried her last card, but his eyes flashed at her.

"She will," he retorted, "she does!"

Chapter 26

They talked at length about the past and the future. And in-between, they made love.

She accepted Zac's forgiveness eagerly.

They promised to love and trust each other forever. Their lovemaking, amidst discussions on the future, continued until dawn. That night was cathartic! It poured out the affection they craved for one another freely. Their passions unleashed compelling emotions, with a love they had never found before. No more secrets between them. Now that everything was out in the open, including who the other man was, they felt liberated.

They had gone through the upheaval and come out the other end. Their love, so strong, had survived it! Their sentiments poured out willingly, Mollie's actions an innocent by-product of trust in an unscrupulous man.

Zac had no more reservations about her, and he loved her unconditionally, regardless of her faults, and the worries she brought to him.

The trouble with Mollie was, despite everything, he couldn't stop loving her, as he couldn't stop the moon following the sun in the night sky. When with her, it felt as if he were in a cozy room by a warm fire on a cold and stormy night, in the right place, with her.

It was an evening of purging experiences. Stronger, and more in love than ever.

As dawn awakened another day, she fell asleep in his arms.

Zac's mind returned to Peter. He called Finley; Zac wanted the man found. He was uneasy. But so far, they had nothing. He wanted the bastard brought to justice for what he had done to his wife, to Kathryn, and to George. Zac dismissed Peter's death threats against himself. They didn't scare him. But a thought niggled in his mind—Peter's feelings for Mollie. He had read his texts. So, they must find him before he tried anything else.

Zac had loved that man as a brother, and he'd betrayed him, his treachery unforgivable. But uppermost in his mind, he needed to protect his bride.

He struggled to figure out why Peter had acted this way. His wife mentioned a girl Peter alluded to. He recalled Kristen coming onto him, but Zac had refused her. He had never taken his friend's woman. Not his style, not something he did. True, he had been a womaniser. But he had always drawn the line at his friends' girlfriends. He was an honourable man.

It could be all in Peter's mind. He gave up trying to figure out why Peter had done what he did. It made little sense.

Zac had to admit that man was greedy. *He was a duplicitous and a deceitful bastard, no other reason necessary for what he did.*

Despite his tiredness, Zac's sleep was jittery, agitated, and broken that night. He stirred, woken up from a nightmare. He opened his eyes; the light filtered through the silk curtains. He got out of bed and sat on the edge, pensive.

He loved her more than anything in the world. He knew

that, but the situation had taken a toll on him. He cursed under his breath. He turned and gazed at her.

She slept, lying on her front, her naked body on show in all her splendour. There she was, his heavenly, clever, and troublesome young wife. Her red hair spread all over his pillow, the vision tightened his heart. He had forgiven her, and they'd pledged promises to each other.

But he was not that naïve! Who knew what troubles she would bring to him? But his feelings prepared him to withstand the storm. She was a delight to him, a joy. His mouth curved into a smile, looking at her. With her features relaxed into sleep, she looked angelic.

So, Zac had given them a final chance for love and a future "Only time will tell," he whispered.

"Darling, come back to bed. It doesn't feel right without you," she mumbled her quiet words.

"Good morning, love," he said and leaned over to kiss her.

She patted the place next to her in bed. "Please," she pouted with drowsy eyes.

He laughed. "As much as I want you, I need a shower and breakfast. I am famished." He caressed her hair back from her face and kissed the tip of her nose.

"Yep, food sounds good. I am hungry too." She lifted her head and looked at the time on the clock on her nightstand. It was six am.

"Marie may not be up yet. I'll make you pancakes," she said, stretching her arms with a yawn.

"You don't have to, darling."

"Oh, but I want to. I'll jump in the shower first. You can catch up with Fin. No doubt, the man doesn't sleep," she replied, rolling her eyes, turning to look at him.

"I am not sure that he does!" Zac responded with a furrow in his brow, still sitting at the edge of the bed.

Mollie leapt to her feet and went to him. He parted his legs to make room for her. She nestled in, standing between them, putting her hands on his shoulders, and she leaned over until her lips touched his. He circled her waist, and they kissed lazily.

"Okay, shower it is, then," she informed him after more tender kisses, and he released her.

She skipped to the bathroom, humming a song. A lopsided grin appeared on his face, watching her. He adored the saucy girl.

MOLLIE WAS in the kitchen mixing up flour, eggs, and milk. Then, she whisked the ingredients to a smooth batter, a few bits flying here and there over the kitchen counter.

Marie Therese would not take too kindly to me messing up the sparkling clean kitchen, she mused. But she was enjoying making the pancakes for her husband.

The previous night had been her best night ever with him, and she wanted to show her affection to him hastily outside the bedroom. It would be a labour of love for him.

She set a sturdy frying pan over a medium heat and wiped it clean with kitchen paper. Then she waited until it was hot to cook them, while humming the words to an old song, ABBA's *Take a Chance on Me*. Her mother was an ABBA fan, and she had grown up listening to their songs. So, that one struck a chord with her.

"Well, someone seems happy this morning. Should I expect Zac to be this cheerful too?" Finley said with a smirk.

She looked up from her pan and blushed to the root of her hair.

He smiled.

"Would you like some pancakes?" she asked. Though

Finley had been invaluable in helping to manage the whole situation, securely and discreetly, he hadn't accepted Mollie yet. Not like Alex did.

"Oh yeah. I'm starving."

"Didn't you have dinner last night?" she asked him.

"No," he responded dryly, eying her pan with alacrity.

"Neither did I."

"Well, I was busy with the police and our investigators. What's your excuse?" Finley teased her.

She glanced at him and blushed again. This time, her hair matched the colour of her face.

"Hey, are you teasing my bride?" Zac joked, appearing in the doorway. His slender body advanced gracefully, like a panther, into the kitchen. And taking a chair in reverse, he sat straddling it. He leaned forward, posing his elbows on the back. Mollie rewarded him with the sweetest smile, the one he loved so much. Zac's heart tightened.

"Pancakes will be ready in a minute," she chimed.

"Hmm, yummy." He winked at her.

His friend shrugged his shoulders and sneered, *lovers, bah!*

"Do you know how to make them? Or is this your scientific version of pancakes?" Finley asked her, raising an eyebrow while she poured some batter mix into the pan, teasing her, undeterred.

Zac rolled his eyes, but he was glad his friend was warming up to her. It was his way of doing it.

"They are my speciality," she pouted. They both laughed, but a ping on her phone took her attention.

"Zac, watch the pancakes; I have a message on my phone," she said.

"Me?"

"You are asking him to put his hands near a pan? Seriously? I don't think the man knows one end of the cooker from the other. I'll look after them." Finley took over the pan with a grin.

"Okay, you have your fun," Zac murmured.

Mollie picked up her phone from the breakfast bar. She frowned. Then she tuned in to the message, and her face blanched, her eyes flickered.

Zac saw it. "What is it?" he asked, standing up. She dropped the phone on the breakfast table as if it had burned her.

He went over to her and put his arm around her. He grabbed her phone, got to the message, and his nostrils flared. His eyes flashed.

"Is it from him?" his friend asked.

Zac nodded, and she buried her face in his chest.

"Nothing will happen to you. Okay?" her husband whispered, kissing her hair, but it flustered her.

Finley took the phone and listened.

"It's Peter," she said, a crack in her voice.

"I know, love. But he is not coming anywhere near you. Do you hear me?" her husband said firmly.

She nodded but was obviously shaken.

"I'd better find out where this message is coming from. Can I take your mobile? Oh, and my pancakes. I am starving," Finley said, seeking to diffuse the situation somehow.

She nodded, with a faint smile.

He took a plate of pancakes and her phone with him to the study.

Mollie inhaled and exhaled, struggling to calm herself until her breathing evened again. She would not let Peter spoil her peace of mind. "I'll finish the pancakes for you," she said.

"You don't have to; Marie will feed us," Zac offered with an offhand smile. He was livid. Peter had broken the peaceful spell, and he worried what he would do next.

"Oh, no, but I need to. I will not let him win. Watch me. You will have your pancakes. I am not afraid of him!" she said with a mournful grin, her chin up in defiance, after her initial shock.

"DID you find out anything yet? With Mollie's compliments," Zac asked him from the study's doorway, showing up with another plate of pancakes for him.

Finley grabbed the plate, took it to the desk, and splashed maple syrup on them.

"The call came from Carcassonne. Wow, she really knows how to make pancakes. These are delicious," he said, getting a mouthful.

"Carcassonne?"

"Yes, but we don't know where he is yet. The call came from a pay phone in town over three hours ago. He could be anywhere by now, but I urged one of our agents to investigate."

"Have you checked the house? Is it safe?"

"Yes, every door is locked, and I doubled my men outside. I am armed too," Finley said, lifting his jacket, showing the waistband of his trousers with the protruding butt of a handgun. Then he touched his left boot, disclosing the tip of a dagger in it.

Zac nodded. "He cannot disappear from the face of the earth, surely?"

"Relax, we'll find him."

"I can't believe this is Peter. How can he do this?"

"Zac, I never told you this. He once hit a young woman. We were students then. The girl never reported him because she was afraid. He apologised, blaming it on the alcohol and a moment of madness. I gave him the benefit of the doubt.

He was my friend too, the damn fool! He repeated an identical incident a few years later, but his sister got him out of trouble with money. Now I know why I never quite believed his stories both times. I should have followed my instincts. He is dangerous. But there is more... A friend in the Oxford Police sent me a list of two similar incidents, complaints that never went to court. The victims withdrew them, so nothing stuck. They never charged him! The whole thing was hushed up, and it doesn't even come up on the official files," Finley said, handing him a piece of paper from a folder.

"Good God. This is madness. Who the hell was he? Not the Peter we knew!" Zac added with a scowl after reading the paper.

"It is the same man, though. The one who almost killed Kathryn and abused Mollie," Finley said in a matter-of-fact tone.

"He wants Mollie, says he loves her, and he demands her back."

"He won't get to her. I promise you," his friend said, putting a hand on his shoulder.

"It's frustrating, that's all. Did we know this man at all?" Zac hissed, but the question was rhetorical. "Is everything secured in the villa?"

"Yes. I doubled the number of men in the garden and along the perimeter of the house in the street. Even if he tries, he can't get close to the house. I have them discretely placed everywhere," Finley explained.

Chapter 27

They were huddled in the sitting room when Marie Therese came in looking for Zac.

Several days had now passed since Peter's disappearance. No one wanted to leave the young couple with a difficult situation hanging over them. So, their friends had stayed to give them support.

"Fancy a walk in the garden after lunch?" Mollie suggested.

"Oh, darling, that would be nice. It's such a lovely day." Mary smiled.

"What is it?" Zac asked, seeing his housekeeper hovering for a moment.

"A policeman is at the door; he wants to talk to you and your wife. The men outside checked his badge already," the woman informed him.

Her mother looked at her, but the girl shrugged her shoulders.

"Who is he?"

"He is from the Gendarmerie. His name is Dumont," Marie Therese replied.

"In uniform?" Zac asked.

"Yes," the old woman said.

"Fine, show him into the study. I'll talk to him," he said, and he side glanced at his friend.

"Go ahead with Mollie. I will get through his credentials and then join you," Finley stated, "what's he called again?"

"It's Dumont," Marie Therese returned, and he left the room with the housekeeper to examine the officer's badge.

"SORRY TO TROUBLE YOU, Mr. Sorensen. I am working with your senior detectives. As you know, we are working to trace the whereabouts of Professor Blake. I have a few questions for you if I may," the man said in perfect English but with a subtle French accent that rendered him endearing.

"Yes, sure. This is Mrs. Sorensen," Zac replied.

Mollie smiled at the man.

"Won't you sit down, please?" He continued, pointing at one of the leather armchairs. They sat opposite him on the sofa.

"When did you see him last?" the police officer asked. The Frenchman seemed to be middle-aged, and his bulbous nose gave him a jovial expression.

"Our friends, Miss Ellis and Mr. Wilde, had the misfortune to see him last, when he attacked them in the hospital. He disappeared after that, several days ago now. No one has heard from him since. My wife picked up an unpleasant message on her phone, but nothing after that," he said, replaying it on his bride's phone.

The policeman listened to the message and shook his head. "Umm, I see. Mr. Sorensen, before I forget, the glass doors to the garden were not closed."

"Oh?"

"I tried to lock them before you came in, but they are stiff. They don't close well. I suggest you have someone fix them, to secure them shut. You can't be too careful," the officer stated, raising his eyebrows and pointing to the patio doors.

"Yes, thank you. I'll look into it," Zac said and walked over to the glass doors.

"Oh, if I may borrow a pen? Forgive me, but mine has just given up on me," Dumont asked in his lilted English and smiled.

"Sure. Mollie, the pens are on my desk. Get one for the gendarme, please," Zac replied. Then, he moved back the linen curtains so he could have a go at locking the patio doors, while Mollie moved to the desk with her back to them.

Suddenly, she heard a noise, quickly followed by a heavy thud. She turned around and saw the policeman standing by the patio doors with Zac at his feet, unconscious.

"Oh, my God." Mollie ran to her husband. She kneeled next to him and glanced up at the gendarme.

"What happened?" she asked.

"He collapsed. I don't know," the police officer replied, puzzled.

"Sweet Jesus. Zac, can you hear me?" she cried in horror, her eyes never leaving him as he lay sprawled on the floor. She stroked his face, struggling to revive him, caressing his head with her hand and calling his name again, but her fingers felt something wet and sticky at the back of his head.

Blood! Zac was bleeding. Mollie glanced up at the policeman, and it was then she noticed the gun, with a silencer, in his hand with blood on the butt.

"DID YOU SEND DUMONT? I checked his badge; it's genuine. He is from the Gendarmerie," Finley asked his contact over the phone, after explaining a gendarme was asking questions.

"Let me check. What's his badge number?"

Finley gave the information and waited for a reply.

Two minutes later, his contact came back. "We don't have a Dumont in Antibes or in Nice. We didn't send anyone to the house. But there is a gendarme called Dumont in Carcassonne, and that's his number. He was missing for days until we found his body yesterday."

SHE HESITATED FOR A SPLIT SECOND, but then she stood and ran for the door.

But the man turned around and while he tucked the gun into his trousers, with two long strides, he reached for her before she could open the door. Mollie screamed when his hand grabbed her upper arm.

"Let's go, dear," the gendarme dropped the French accent.

"Peter?" she mumbled with wide eyes, recognising his voice. But he pulled her close to him violently.

"Aren't you pleased to see me?" His eyes twinkled with a harsh light.

She gasped. "What have you done to Zac? He needs help," she said in anguish. She struggled to see his face, seeking to recognise his features. Yet, it was Peter's voice, but only the colour of the eyes was his.

"A little make up goes a long way, my dear!" Peter revealed himself, sensing she was trying to recognise him. He pulled off part of the disguise from his face. Erin's make-up bag had done an excellent job at changing his features.

"Please, he is bleeding. Zac needs help," she pleaded with him, but when he didn't respond, she struggled to free herself. She wriggled. She kicked him hard and punched his face with her fist. He stumbled, and she ran for the door again. But he stretched his arm and grabbed her hair with one hand, pulling her back to him. She screamed, but he was too strong. He held her tight by the hair but moved his hand swiftly from her hair over her mouth. Then he placed the other arm tightly around her waist and dragged her towards the patio doors with him.

"If you scream again or move, I will kill him," Peter whispered in her ear, but she didn't respond. "Understood?" he said, this time his voice harsh, and she gave a quick nod. So, he took his hands off her mouth. He grabbed the gun from the waistband of his trousers, and he pointed it at Zac's body lying on the floor. His pupils were huge, his nostrils flaring.

"You are coming with me," Peter groaned. "Answer me." He tightened the grip on the gun's trigger, ready to shoot her husband.

"Yes," she said and nodded. But fear struck her eyes. She glanced down at her husband on the floor and at the gun in Peter's hand, her heart thumping hard.

She was fighting back the tears, but she needed to be strong. She needed to help Zac.

On impulse, she said, "Peter, please."

"Shut up, Mollie. Do as you are told for once. I won't tell you again."

FINLEY RAN TO THE STUDY. As he got to the door, he stopped outside when he heard her scream. He drew out his gun and checked his boot. He listened first, then he opened the door, darting a swift glance around the room. It was then he noticed Zac, unconscious, on the floor.

"If you as much as bat an eyelid, I'll shoot her. No choice, my friend. Now, put your weapon down, and kick it towards me. Lock the door; hurry!" Peter commanded, and he tightened her closer to him.

He pointed his revolver at Mollie's head. With his other hand, he adjusted her body in front of him as a shield. "I said, drop it," he called again, pushing the gun against her skull harshly.

She whimpered.

Finley raised his firearm as if in surrender.

"Okay. Look, I'm dropping it," he said, slowly lowering the weapon to the ground. He kicked it towards them as instructed.

Peter grabbed the gun from the floor and placed it on his trousers' waistband. "Lock the door."

Finley obliged, then faced him again.

"Now, Mollie and I will leave quietly. You will not stop us. Understood?" the professor added with deliberate diction.

Finley nodded.

"Please, Zac…" she begged.

"Shut up, Mollie. Fin, raise your arms where I can see them. Come here; take his feet. Move him out of my way. Hurry!" Peter pointed at Zac's unconscious body on the floor. He wanted him out of his path so he could make his escape through the garden doors.

Finley got hold of Zac's feet and pulled him, trying to assess his friend's injury as he dragged him just a few steps away. He realized then that Mollie was in more imminent danger.

"Stand back. Against the wall. Do it now. With your hands up," Peter said impatiently, waving his revolver.

Finley retreated. "My men are outside. You won't make it. You pushed Kat down the stairs, assaulted her in the hospital. And blackmail, with a murderous plan! You don't want to add kidnapping to your list. Your best chance is to give yourself up," he stated calmly, with his back against the wall.

"You disappoint me, Fin! You always have. The wrong words, at the worst moment. Besides, I didn't push Kat down; the stupid bitch must—" he taunted, and he gripped Mollie's arm, but he didn't finish his sentence.

"Please, Peter, I'll come with you, but let him help Zac. He is injured and has lost a lot of blood!" Mollie pleaded instead, her eyes wide, looking at Finley. She looked down at Zac and frowned.

"Shush, Mollie. I am not telling you again," Peter spat, grabbing her hair and pulling her head back to him.

She gasped and caught her breath, his face an inch from hers.

"There are guards everywhere. You cannot make it. It's suicide." Finley took a step forward to distract him from hurting Mollie.

"Stop right there. I'll shoot her, no more warnings. By God, I'll kill her; make no mistake." The man became agitated, and his fingers were ready to press the trigger.

"Fine, fine, look, I am going back." Finley lifted his arms in surrender and retreated to the wall again, hoping this would calm him down.

"Mollie, open the doors, and then come back to me," Peter instructed, but she didn't move, and he lowered the gun towards her husband. His eyes burned with anger.

"I will finish him," he whispered, with the revolver pointing at Zac on the ground.

"Yes, yes," she mumbled, jerking into action, and she opened the doors. Then she turned her steps back to him.

He grasped her arm with his hand. "Listen carefully," he said, addressing Finley, "Mollie and I are going to the loggia. Then, we will board the boat out of here. Now, ask your goons to stay away from us, or I swear it, I'll kill her. Understood?" He dangled the speed boat keys he had helped himself to from the desk drawer.

Finley nodded. He spoke to his men on the phone and told them to back off. "All clear?"

At his signal, the professor pushed her towards the doors, still holding her arm. They were about to step out, when her husband launched at Peter from the ground and grabbed his legs with strength.

Zac had lost a lot of blood. Hurt and on his knees, he struggled to pull Peter down with him to release the hold he had on his wife.

At his grasp, Peter stumbled. But he kept himself upright, while he hit Zac with the butt of the revolver with force on the head again.

Mollie took her chance, and she wriggled herself free. Fighting him, she tried to reach for the gun. But the man lashed out at her with the back of his hand. She fell backward, while Finley advanced towards them.

"Stop!" Peter shouted at him and pressed the trigger. A shot hit Zac on the arm.

Mollie screamed.

Finley stopped.

She tried to stand.

"Mollie, stay down," Finley yelled. He fixed her on the spot with a look, and she held her breath.

Thus, two seconds of commotion was all it took. Finley drew the dagger from his boot. He hurled his knife at him, but Peter moved, struggling to free himself from Zac, missing him. The knife tumbled on the floor.

Wounded as he was, Zac was still trying to wrestle him

down, but Peter pressed the trigger and fired another bullet on him.

Mollie grabbed the knife instinctively and jumped to her feet. She flung herself at the man with such force to stop him from shooting again, and in the struggle, Mollie stabbed him.

When the knife hit him, the two jagged edges severed Peter's carotid artery and jugular vein; killing him instantly. Blood spurted from his neck. Peter dropped dead on the floor. She screamed in terror at what she had done and at the sight of her husband.

Zac was motionless on the ground in a pool of blood.

EARLIER THAT DAY, Erin had pleaded with her brother not to do it. Not to leave her. Not to go back for Mollie, but Peter didn't listen.

"Please, darling. This is wrong. Let's leave the country. I know a place where you can hide, people who can fake papers for you; you can move far away. They'll never find you. Start over!"

"Mollie belongs to me. He will not have her." A red flash crept upon his face.

She froze. "This isn't about Mollie, is it? This is about Zac. You don't want him to have her. You have always envied Zac, in every way."

"Shut up, Erin. Just do as I say."

She pleaded again. She begged him, but he was not having it. So, she had yielded to his will, and as usual, she helped him with his plan, instead, and with his disguise.

When she finished, he was unrecognisable.

So, Peter had gone back to Antibes, with lethal consequences.

Erin waited for her twin brother to return to Porte Vendres. She sat in that room and remained there for over three days, but he never returned.

Eventually, four weeks later, following a discreet investigation, the police released his body. They returned him to his sister, for burial in England.

Chapter 28

"**M**ollie, here, now!" he called out. "Mollie! Did you hear me? Come here, please," he shouted with more urgency a minute later.

"What's going on?" She joined him in his study but gasped when she looked at the mess. "Oh, dear. I am sorry. Where is she?" She was struggling hard not to laugh.

"I think she is hiding under the damn sofa. Unbelievable! Your dog is as reckless as you are. A hell of a match!" he barked. Mollie chuckled, but he went on, "Not bloody funny! See? The fucking mess! She chewed my report into a shapeless, disgusting gunge. And she took my Mont Blanc pen under there too, no doubt gnawing it to hell. Painful to work with my arm like this as it is, let alone having to do things twice because of your disobedient dog!" Zac chastised her while sitting on his knees on the floor. He tried to peer under the sofa again. He couldn't quite bend fully yet, so he grumbled.

Even though it had been over six months since Peter had shot him, his upper body was still giving him trouble. It was as stiff as a board, suffering from the aftermath.

SOON AFTER THAT DREADFUL NIGHT, the doctor had operated on Zac for the two gunshot wounds. One to his right arm, and the other to his shoulder. He had undergone surgery at the hospital in Nice to remove the bullets. His collarbone and his radius, the forearm bone that runs from the elbow to the wrist and thumb, had shattered when Peter shot two bullets into him.

The doctors had discovered the many fragments of the shattered bones where the bullets hit him. The excruciating pain made Zac pass in and out of consciousness.

The bullet-shaped objects were visible in the X-rays, to Mollie's distress.

During the emergency surgery, the doctor extracted the bullets and inserted a plate and three screws on his collarbone to patch him up. But the radius would never be as new again, even after treatment.

In addition, Zac got six stitches on the back of his head, where Peter had hit him with the butt of the gun, and twelve stitches on his right shoulder after the operation, and almost as many on his forearm. He lost count of the many stitches on his body.

He suffered cuts and bruises on his face and torso for his troubles too. So, the outcome of that infamous night had not been easy for him.

Mollie had stood at his bedside in the hospital. She'd stayed with him throughout, day and night, for three weeks. She would not hear of leaving him. She looked after him.

He was thankful to his sweet wife for it.

But against the doctor's orders, Zac had released himself from the clinic. Soon after, they left Antibes and returned home to Oxford.

There, he had undergone a second operation to his forearm, two months later, at the John Radcliffe Hospital.

This time, doctors implanted a small piece of bone, cut from his good bone in his upper arm, into his right scaphoid bone, a tiny bone in his wrist broken during the fight with Peter too. But the small wrist bone was a tricky one to mend, and hence, it was not healing well, so it had to be replaced. So, the result, he spent months with his shoulder and arm in a cast and sling after the operations.

Over six months after the dreadful night, his arm was still in a plaster, with several muscles of the forearm damaged. He would need lengthy physiotherapy to restore them to a good working order once the cast was off, though his movements would be stiff for a while.

With his right arm in a cast, and Zac being right-handed, his actions and everyday tasks, such as writing and holding things up, were impacted, making him irritable and cranky. It frustrated him to lose his dexterity, in particular for a workaholic such as himself. Everything took twice as long to do. Toughest of all, he couldn't swim, so his grumpiness and bad humour was unavoidable.

He had borne the operations well. He complained very little about the physical pain. He was grateful to be alive and to have Mollie in his life.

Her loving eyes, her soft caresses at his bedside throughout his ordeal, had reassured him.

THROUGH ZAC'S contacts in high places, they left the French police report rather vague as to the facts of that night. They made it sound as if they were casualties of a potential robbery gone wrong. This theory prevailed in the official documents. The inquest, though, with the real facts and events, was carried out quickly, and behind closed doors.

In the courtroom, no one doubted Mollie's actions as self-defence and to save her husband's life; thus, she was exonerated.

But the whole affair was hushed up, so no press backlash would affect him. Though the emotional scars had been high and harder to recover from.

His wife had saved his life! The loving memory of his misfortune.

Unbelievable how a long and, what he'd perceived, a strong friendship had ended, though. How did they get to that point? He would never know.

He still felt sorrowful about Peter, but he couldn't help the outcome. The man had played with fire. He'd shot him twice. He was going to kidnap her; Mollie had no alternative.

Zac revisited the events in his mind often.

Peter could have murdered him straight away when he'd first entered the room, but he hadn't, he mused. He lingered. Two shots on his shoulder and arm from that distance seemed too inconsequential when he could have killed him so easily. How did he miss? Peter waited until the end before pressing the trigger. Somehow, a voice at the back of Zac's mind told him, Peter had bluffed. He never meant to do it. He would never know now.

But he preferred it that way, that Peter never really meant to kill him. Somehow that thought gave him peace.

Through this mess, Mollie was his silver lining. That night, she felt her own actions hard, but they were inevitable. Mollie couldn't let her husband die. She had no choice but to do what she did. It had been unavoidable. The fact she saved her husband's life kept her sane.

Weirdly, she had a lot to thank Peter for. Zac's love for her had been her long-awaited prize. Glad the wretched events were now over and behind them, it was time to end the sorrow and move forward. So, they were hopeful for the future.

It would be difficult, hard; it would take time, but they had to do it.

He would do it for her, and she for him.

MOLLIE crouched on her knees to get to her dog. She had rescued the puppy from a dog's home when they first came back to Oxford. The puppy had become her shadow, always at her side. When Mollie returned to her normal life and to her studies at the University, the dog missed her when she was not at home, thus, getting into awful mischief with the expensive items in the house. But best of all, was her preference to be naughty in Zac's study as the tiny pup was that day.

He was dismayed that a small creature like Peanut generated such destruction. Then Zac half-grinned, thinking the dog suited Mollie well.

"Peanut, come to me, sweetheart," she said in a soothing voice, trying to cajole the dog's attention from under the sofa. "Darling, I expect she is frightened of you, that you will scold her, please stay back. Sometimes, you are too bossy with her," she said.

Zac hissed, "Well, someone needs to control this little beast... who is boss around here?" he retorted.

Mollie snorted, unladylike, and he raised an elegant brow at her, but he stood and paced back, watching her crawling under the sofa and dragging the dog out gently.

"Hey, what have you done, eh? You wicked girl," she said in a pleasant tone, standing up and clasping the tiny tan and silver Yorkshire terrier in her arms. She whispered some more soothing words and scratched Peanut's little head. She removed the pen out of the dog's mouth, which now leaked. She held up the expensive, chewed up pen to him, dripping with ink. Their eyes went wide with horror when they saw drops of ink and Peanut's now blueish drooling dribble sprinkle on his priceless Persian carpet.

"Oops, sorry," she dared but couldn't restrain a snort of laughter.

He cursed and reached for the bin under his desk. Spinning around, he poked it in front of her, his eyebrows knitted in a scowl. She let the pen drop in the bin with an apologetic smile.

He exhaled deeply. "My second pen, and twice as many reports in two months dispatched to the bloody bin," he ventured, but despite himself, he patted the dog's head tenderly with his left hand but murmured some stern words half-heartedly to the dog, who whimpered.

"Hell! You two will be the death of me, I tell you," he replied with a scowl which was half serious and half facetious.

She laughed, with that mellow sound that was so her. And while they stood there, he put his good arm around her waist and drew her to him, while she still held Peanut cocooned in her chest.

She giggled.

Zac brushed his lips on hers. Then, he kissed her languidly for a while, savouring her.

Peanut was making cooing noises in the background, nestled between them.

Zac could have a terrible temper, sometimes acting like a jerk. The girl was in for a ride. He knew it, but he loved her.

She defied the turmoil in her life with determination. She was stronger than she looked, to ride out the storm of the past year and still emerge unscathed, with mountains of love for him, determined to cherish him, despite his temper.

Zac had been correct in his judgement that day when she had first come to see him in his office. His wife had guts. She was feisty, strong enough to withstand anything life threw at her.

Mollie was eager and willing for him. She adored him. And Zac worshipped her.

She made his heart jolt. He kissed her more, then he raised his head to glance at her.

She smiled at him. His heavenly and beautiful wife. *Was she still trouble?* Only time would tell.

He grinned and winked at her.

Her eyes lit up. Mollie beamed from ear to ear, the charming smile that always rocked his world, dazzling him. It made him happy. And he rewarded her with that look, the one that spread flutters in her belly; and her heart warmed, looking at the love of her life.

It was at that point, despite everything, they knew they had won.

The End

Blushing Books

Blushing Books is one of the oldest eBook publishers on the web. We've been running websites that publish spanking and BDSM related romance and erotica since 1999, and we have been selling eBooks since 2003. We hope you'll check out our hundreds of offerings at http://www.blushingbooks.com.

Blushing Books Newsletter

Please join the Blushing Books newsletter
to receive updates & special promotional offers.
You can also join by using your mobile phone:
Just text BLUSHING to 22828.

www.ingramcontent.com/pod-product-compliance
Lightning Source LLC
Chambersburg PA
CBHW020248200626
46816CB00001BA/180